Praise for M. Ullrich

"M. Ullrich's books have a uniqueness that we don't always see in this particular genre. Her stories go a bit outside the box and they do it in the best possible way. *Fake It till You Make It* is no exception."—*The Romantic Reader Blog*

Life in Death "is a well written book, the characters have depth and are complex, they become friends and you cannot help but hope that Marty and Suzanne can find a way back to each other. There aren't many books that I know from one read that I will want to read time and time again, but this is one of them."—*Sapphic Reviews*

"M. Ullrich's *Fake It till You Make It* just clarifies why she is one of my favorite authors. The storyline was tight, the characters brought emotion and made me feel like I was living the story with them, and best of all, I had fun reading every word."—*Les Rêveur*

By the Author

Fortunate Sum

Life in Death

Fake It till You Make It

Time Will Tell

Love at Last Call

The Boss of Her
(with Julie Cannon and Aurora Rey)

Visit us at www.boldstrokesbooks.com

LOVE AT LAST CALL

by

M. Ullrich

2018

ISBN 13: 978-1-63555-197-6

This Trade Paperback Original Is Published By
Bold Strokes Books, Inc.
P.O. Box 249
Valley Falls, NY 12185

First Edition: July 2018

Credits
Editor: Jerry L. Wheeler
Production Design: Stacia Seaman
Cover Design by Tammy Seidick

Acknowledgments

Five full-length novels later, and this is still one of the hardest parts of the process. I have so many people to thank and acknowledge—it truly takes a village to produce a novel worthy of reading. Thank you to Radclyffe and Sandy for your encouragement and for keeping me on this brilliant team. Jerry, I'm so lucky and grateful to have you as my editor. Your patience and guidance are not only a necessity but a gift as well. I've come to depend on your comments for a good laugh or a good lesson. Oftentimes both. A huge thanks goes to Cindy and Stacia for making the last few steps easygoing even in the face of expedited deadlines, and to everyone whose name I've yet to learn. Y'all are a dream team.

The support system and the family I've found within Bold Strokes continues to enrich my career and my life. I'm surrounded by talent that inspires, individuals who enlighten, and goofballs who entertain.

Speaking of goofballs…Kris and Maggie, thank you (a million times) for simply being the sweet friends and magnificent writers you are. You push me and embolden me and accept me for my inappropriateness. GBAR forever!

Heather, my beautiful wife, my lovely everything—thank you for not allowing me to stop doing what I love just because I'm tired. Thank you for continuously reminding me of all the good there is in life. Thank you for loving me and for cooking me the most amazing breakfasts on the weekends. In return, I wrote Berit for you, a character you can crush on. HARD.

And a special thank you to each and every one of my readers. You all make every book a different writing experience. Rach, Kaz, the team at TLR, and every reader who takes the time to review or reach out with feedback: you help the greatness of Lesfic grow. Thank you for putting your time into what we create.

Cheers!

For Heather,
My smooth shot at true love

CHAPTER ONE

Nothing made Berit Matthews feel more electric than pouring the perfect cocktail while a line of beautiful women waited their turn for her services. A little flick of her wrist, a well-timed wink, and the slow rub of a lime wedge along the cool rim of a glass made more patrons swoon than an articulate pickup line. Berit lived for busy nights like these. Her bar was always bustling on Thursday, Friday, and Saturday nights. Berit had opened the Dollhouse nearly five years ago and it became her home, her baby, and the only long-term commitment in her life—a fact Berit was more than okay with. The dim lighting in the lounge area cast faint shadows along the Dollhouse's attractive waitresses as they served guests.

"What are the specials for tonight?" a tall blonde asked, leaning over the bar provocatively.

Berit looked from the woman's cleavage to her smoky eyes. She didn't recognize her as a regular. "It's Friday, so we have three-dollar craft beers and a signature cocktail, the Friday Night Fever."

"What's in that?"

"Gin, vermouth, Dubonnet Rouge, and just a hint of anisette." Berit smiled and pulled out a chilled martini glass but stopped when her customer's face turned sour.

"That sounds disgusting," she said, reaching over and holding Berit's hand to stop her. "I'd love a beer, though. One that doesn't taste too much like beer but will still give me a buzz."

Berit sighed deeply, but her polite smile never wavered. For every three customers who'd appreciate artisan cocktails and local craft beer, one person couldn't care less. Berit pulled a stocky bottle from one of the many refrigerators beneath the bar and popped the top. A thin cloud formed above the lip of the bottle. She placed it on a small napkin embossed with the Dollhouse's logo and pushed it toward the woman.

"Try this," Berit said, leaning forward to be heard clearly over the chatter in the bar and the mix of pop hits and classic rock filling the space. "They added raspberries and a little lemon zest during brewing. I think you'll like it."

"I think you're right." She sipped from the bottle, her move practiced and seductive. "I'm not surprised you know exactly what I'd like."

Berit smirked. "Would you like to start a tab?"

She placed a twenty on the bar and pulled the napkin out from beneath her beer. "Keep the change," she said while scribbling on the napkin with a pen from her designer purse. "Call me sometime. Soon." She held the napkin out for Berit but pulled it back before Berit could grab it. "My name is Annie."

Berit snatched the napkin. "Nice to meet you, Annie."

"Berit, stop flirting and take some orders," a waitress said as she sidled up to the bar behind the partition separating bar guest orders from waitstaff orders. She placed her tray on the glossy wooden bar with a loud smack.

Berit kept her eyes on Annie and smiled. "Let me know if you need another beer, Annie." She added a wink for good measure and sauntered toward the waitress. "Bellamy, what did I tell you about interrupting me while I'm with customers?" Berit liked to sound like a strict boss, but her dazzling smile and playful hazel eyes belied anything firm in her voice. She tucked the napkin into her back pocket and took several orders at once.

"How many does that make for tonight?"

"How many what?" Berit placed two full pint glasses on the bar top and collected a small pile of tips.

"Numbers. How many numbers?" Bellamy said as she waited for Berit's full attention.

"I'm not counting."

Bellamy shot her a disbelieving look.

"Seven, but really only four because a few were from regulars who slide me their number every week."

"Silly them," Bellamy said with a laugh. "I need two Blue Moons, a Yuengling, three Fevers, and a Manhattan, and I swear to God, Berit, if you put them in martini glasses you're cleaning the mess."

"I'll make an exception and use the saucer glasses I usually reserve for champagne, but only for you." Berit went about preparing the drinks, methodically grabbing cherries and orange slices for garnish. She handled multiple liquor bottles at once, counting as she poured a steady stream into two separate shakers. A dash of added flavors went into each cup before she sealed glasses into them and picked them up. Berit stared into the wide eyes of the women on the other side of the bar as she began shaking the cups. She spun them once and then twice on the flat of her palms, smiling when a cute redhead's mouth fell open. A little added flair when shaking up cocktails went a long way for bar patrons. She poured the liquor and garnished the glasses accordingly before pulling back the handle of the beer tap. "Anything else?" she said with a cocky smile. Bellamy leaned farther into the lighting under the bar. Berit loved the way her dark skin glistened beneath the amber lights.

Bellamy waited for Berit to place the drinks securely in the center of her tray. "Plan on calling any of those numbers tonight?" Berit shook her head and Bellamy smiled, her white teeth contrasting with her skin. "What about my number?" She bit her lower lip.

Berit followed the deep V of Bellamy's tank top with her eyes and licked her lips. "Why don't you take those drinks to your table so I can watch you walk away?" Bellamy laughed and lifted the tray. She walked away with the most tempting sway to her full hips.

Berit returned to her work behind the bar. She loaded dirty glasses into a small portable dishwasher and wiped down any vacant spaces. Berit liked the Dollhouse to be clean and orderly at all times. More women lined up to be served, and she took the first of four women's order.

"I'll have two Slippery Nipples," she said so innocently, Berit had to bite her tongue.

Berit flipped her sandy blond curls from her face and looked to the next woman, an attractive baby butch. "And for you?"

"Bud Light in a bottle, please."

"We have some cheap craft beers tonight, if you're interested," Berit encouraged as she started on the shots.

"Just a Bud Light is fine."

"Coming right up."

"I'll take over, Berit." Another bartender, Lou, stepped in with a beer in one hand and a bottle of Baileys in the other. "They need your help in the storage room. We lost a case of Svedka, apparently." Lou brushed the hair from her face with her shoulder.

Berit stepped back and wiped her hands on the towel she always kept tucked into the back of her tight jeans. "Did you check—"

"Where we've kept the cases of vodka for over four years? Yeah, I checked." Lou's attitude was out and proud that night. The butch who'd ordered the Bud smiled, clearly liking her new, feisty bartender better than Berit.

"I was going to suggest the receiving room, but whatever." Berit waved her hands childishly. She stalked off toward the room that housed many, many bottles of liquor and cases of imported and domestic beer. Berit looked around, carefully checking every label on the full shelves to see if someone had stocked them incorrectly.

Berit loved everything about the Dollhouse, even its stockroom. All the different-colored bottles caught the light magically and painted the shelves with hypnotic prisms. She'd started planning for her business nearly ten years ago, and when the doors opened, she'd felt overwhelmed with pride.

She squatted and read each case stuffed below the last shelf on the wall. Lou wasn't lying. She didn't see any Svedka amongst the vodka. Berit made her way out of the stockroom, past the door to her office, and into the small receiving room where they took in deliveries and kept overstock. Each box was marked carefully with receiving dates and the initials of the individual who checked in the delivery. Berit grabbed the clipboard hanging on the far wall and read down the list of that week's deliveries. She ran her finger along the list and landed on the final item: one case of Svedka vodka taken in that afternoon. The initials next to it: BM.

"Shit," she said quietly. Berit hung the clipboard up and rushed to her office. She swung the door open and grimaced at the case of vodka sitting on her cluttered desk. Her lips flapped with a long exhale.

"Mom always said you'd lose your head if it wasn't attached."

Berit jumped at the intrusion. She lifted the box with a grunt and turned around. "Shut up, Lou." Berit stormed past her younger sister and put the box in the storeroom where it belonged, ignoring Lou's laughter.

"I knew I should've checked your office."

"Jeez—"

"Don't you dare say it!"

"Jeez Louise, why don't you just turn into Mom already and get it over with." Berit's smirk of satisfaction fell when the box started to slip from her grip. She stacked it next to the rest of the vodka cases. She flipped her short, wavy hair from her eyes again. "I'd love to stay and fight, but I have a bar full of beautiful women waiting for me." Berit pushed the sleeves of her flannel up, revealing the colorful tattoos on her left arm.

Lou followed Berit out to the bar. Right before they parted, she said, "Wow, I'm surprised your head fit through the doorway."

Berit gave her sister a playful shove and reclaimed her spot behind the thirteen-foot bar.

The rest of the night went the same; women, and a few men, lined up and waited for perfectly crafted drinks. Crowds of people lounged and enjoyed the company around them. Berit knew no other feeling could compare to seeing people delight in her space, the one she had worked so hard to open. Berit would stand back and soak it all in from time to time, when a lull allowed her to watch as people sat and talked contently. Morristown, New Jersey, hadn't been the same since Berit had brought the queer women's scene to them, and if you asked any of the faces in the crowd, they'd agree everyone was better off with the Dollhouse on South Street.

A stout staff member approached Berit toward the end of the night, staring at her seriously as she pointed to a brass bell hanging by the bar. "If you don't ring that damn bell, I will."

Berit looked at her watch. *Almost closing time.* "You do the honors, Dee." Berit stepped aside and flicked the switch for the fluorescent sign reading "Last Call." The last call bell rang through the space.

Within thirty minutes, every tab was paid and Berit sat counting the register as one of her regulars, Rosa, finished her last drink.

"You should stay open until three," she said before taking the final sip of her martini. Rosa never got drunk; she just liked to end some days surrounded by good vibes.

"If the town allowed it, I would." Berit caught Bellamy milling about in her peripheral vision, undoubtedly waiting to get their night started. "But some people in this town barely like me at all, so I won't rock the boat." Berit shot Bellamy an apologetic smile. Their casual entanglement was still very new.

Rosa stood and threw a handful of folded bills on the bar. "What's not to like about you? You got the dimples, the perfectly unstyled hair, and swagger." Rosa looked Berit up and down like she was a life-sized version of her favorite dessert. "You definitely have that swagger."

Berit laughed outright. "Thanks, Rosa. You really know how to make a girl feel special."

"Tell that to my ex," Rosa said with a sad, tired smile. "Good night, Berit. See you next week."

"See you next week, Rosa." Berit watched Rosa as she left. She knew more about Rosa than she did many of her friends. The blessing and the curse of being a bartender. The Dollhouse held nothing more than employees now. "Lou, you ready to close up?" Berit kept her eyes on Bellamy the whole time she spoke. She removed the folded towel from her back pocket and tossed it on the counter.

Bellamy approached Berit slowly, a predatory smirk playing on her full lips. "Your place or mine?"

"Mine," Berit said quickly. "Hugo's been alone all day, and the last time I sent Lou to check on him, she dressed him in a sweater." She smiled at the thought of her loyal Chihuahua.

"Hey, he loved his cardigan. He looked quite *fetching* in it." Lou's mouth fell open in a proud grin. Berit and Bellamy groaned.

"How long have you been waiting to make that joke?" Berit turned off the lights and led the way to the back door. They stepped out into the chilled spring night.

"Too long."

"I figured." Berit chuckled and walked to her yellow Jeep. She stopped and spun around to say, "I can't wait to do this all again tomorrow."

Berit had finished every night with the same sentiment, which had become a superstition of sorts. She felt the short phrase was the key to her success. Bellamy and Lou nodded to her before getting into their cars. Berit hesitated for a moment before getting out and running over to Bellamy's car.

She rolled down the window and looked at Berit in confusion. "What are you—"

Berit cut her off with a long, languid kiss. She reached into the car window and slid her hand into the low neckline of Bellamy's shirt. Berit squeezed Bellamy's breast and toyed with her nipple but pulled back the moment Bellamy started to respond. "I've been wanting to do that all night. Now follow me home."

She climbed into her Jeep and smiled. Berit Matthews had a successful business, a gorgeous woman willing to indulge in attachment-free sex, and the unconditional love of the perfect dog. It was everything she could ever want, and she knew it without a doubt.

Chapter Two

L auren Daly caught every red light on her way home from work Saturday evening. Most law firms were closed on weekends, but Baxter, Smith, Krupa, and Caruso felt differently about business hours. The bigwig lawyers, the old men with their names on the building, worked Monday through Friday. Their assistants and paralegals, however, worked whatever hours their bosses decided. Lauren spent her entire day going over witness statements and double-checking the chronological order of facts for an upcoming trial. Her eyes hurt, she had two paper cuts on one finger, and her feet were killing her from the pumps she was required to wear to meet the office's dress code. She slipped off her high heel and flexed the toes of her right foot while holding down the brake pedal with her left. She could feel the engine stutter and want to die as she waited.

Lauren sputtered her way through the quiet roads of Denville and dreamed of a day where her job would feel rewarding and she'd have a nice, comfortable home to rest her head at the end of a long day. But her stress level didn't decrease when she turned onto her street. The closer she got to her house, the tighter the knot in her stomach grew. Her two-car driveway was already full, and the prime spot on the street was taken, leaving Lauren to park across the street from the small colonial house she paid more than half the bills for and still hated.

She saw more than two people in the small front windows. Lauren cut the engine of her car before it could stall, and she sat back. She didn't know who had company and why they'd invite people over without telling her. But did they ever? Lauren rested her head against the worn cloth seat. She was tired. Her bones nearly ached with exhaustion, but she knew she wouldn't find peace within her home. Everyone would be loud and inconsiderate, as they always were. Moving in with Jorge, her best friend from college, had seemed like a brilliant idea at the time. He was a blossoming engineer, and Lauren had secured a paralegal job at a prestigious law firm right out of school. Together they could afford to rent a two-bedroom home and live comfortably. Until Jorge fell in love.

Lauren watched one of the shadows bounce about behind the thin curtain. Briana was an obnoxious, disrespectful leech. All of which Jorge was blind to. But Lauren couldn't be too mad at Jorge, because their other roommate was her own fault. Rebecca had come to live with them after a mutual friend dumped her and kicked her to the curb. Lauren's natural instinct to fix other people's problems took over, so Rebecca had moved onto their couch, and then into Lauren's bed, and eventually into Lauren's heart. Two out of three went unbroken. Lauren counted the shadows of four people, which meant Rebecca wasn't alone. Lauren sank down into her seat with a sigh.

How did she get here? She felt unhappy and uncomfortable at home, her job with a bunch of chauvinistic old men wasn't taking her anywhere, and her social life was hindered by friends pledging their loyalty to Rebecca. Only one person remained as a confidante to Lauren. She picked up her phone and dialed Amber.

"What's wrong?" Amber said after answering on the first ring.

"Why do you think something's wrong?" Lauren could hear the exhaustion in her own voice. She had to strain to speak at a normal volume.

"You hate talking on the phone."

"Well, I'm too tired to text, so here I am." Lauren sat in silence, leaving Amber waiting for more. "Rebecca's not alone," she said in a whisper.

"Lauren, why is she even still there? You guys broke up for the fourth time three weeks ago. Whether or not you decide to get back together *again*, it's not healthy for you to be living together." Amber muttered a curse under her breath. "You need to kick her out."

"The only reason why she's still here is because unlike Briana, she actually contributes to the bills. Not many, but some. Jorge and I are both buried in student loans, so the extra money helps."

"Where is she sleeping?"

"Excuse me?"

"She's still sleeping in your bed, isn't she?"

Lauren deserved every ounce of judgment she heard in Amber's voice. "Sometimes," she mumbled.

"I'm not entirely sure what you just said, but it didn't sound like a no." Amber's voice sounded far away, and Lauren heard rustling on the other end of the phone. "I'm getting dressed and you need to get ready. We're going out."

Lauren moved to get out of the car, but every part of her body felt heavy. Her hand dropped away from the door handle. "I'm too tired to go out."

"I'll meet you at the Dollhouse in an hour."

"Are your ears clogged? I just said I'm too tired to go out. I'm fried, dead, kaput."

"And you'll rise from the dead to meet me in an hour," Amber said with a deep chuckle. "Look, Lauren, the way I see it is you can either stay home with your ex-girlfriend and her date for the evening, or come out with me and at least scope out other fish in the sea. The right choice seems pretty obvious."

Lauren imagined the interior of the Dollhouse, and a sense of comfort already started to loosen her tense muscles. Something about the wood tones and cheery atmosphere welcomed her like a friendly hug every time she walked through the door. Lauren finally gave in. "I'll go out with you under two conditions."

"Which are?"

"The first round is on you, and you'll pick me up because I'm almost out of gas." Lauren swung her car door open, a new bounce to her step. An evening at the Dollhouse was the perfect way to remember why being single was so great. "I'll see you in forty-five minutes?"

"You have yourself a deal."

Lauren hung up as she approached the front door. The red paint was chipping around the doorknob, just another thing for Lauren to fix in her spare time and on her dime. She tucked a strand of her long chestnut hair behind her ear and opened the door. Loud laughter greeted her like an unwelcome party guest. Every head in the small living room spun to stare at her. Jorge was the only one smiling.

"Tough day at the office?" he said from his spot on the sofa.

"Always is." Lauren didn't look at Jorge when she answered. Her eyes were glued to the stunning blonde sprawled across Rebecca's lap. "I'm going out." She hurried away from the stomach-churning display and closed the door the instant she was in her room. Lauren was bothered by how much Rebecca's happiness affected her. She hadn't been in love with Rebecca since their first breakup, but seeing her with another woman under her own roof hurt, especially another woman who was so much better than Lauren.

A timid knock rang out from the door. "Let me in, Lauren."

Lauren tripped over a pile of Rebecca's clothes on her way to the closet. "I have to get ready, Jorge. I really am going out."

"Just let me in for a minute. I want to talk."

"I'm getting dressed, you'll have to wait."

"I've seen you naked more times than I can count. I think you've actually desensitized me to breasts at this point. Two minutes and I'll even help you pick an outfit."

Lauren smiled slightly. She looked down at her plain white dress shirt and back to her disorganized closet. What did she have to lose? She opened the door and said, "Two minutes. That's all you get."

Jorge sat on the edge of her bed and kept his eyes on the different shirt options Lauren held up. He dismissed the first three button-ups she suggested. "I didn't know Rebecca was having anyone over, and I should've warned you."

"Yes, you should have. What do you think, green or blue?" Lauren held up two flowy tanks, not really caring for either. "Fuck it, I'm wearing a T-shirt."

Jorge scratched at his beard and pushed his thick glasses up his nose. "A T-shirt won't get you any."

"Who says I'm trying to 'get any'? I don't want to be home, and Amber invited me out."

"Why don't you and Amber date already?"

Lauren was slightly put off by the unexpected question. "Because." Lauren pulled off her shirt and threw on the first plain black T-shirt she could find. She grabbed clean skinny jeans and finished the outfit with a pair of black heels that were stylish and comfortable in comparison to her work ones. "What do you think?" She turned to Jorge and held her arms up for appraisal.

He tilted his head and shrugged. "Boring, but not terrible. You may get one number tonight."

"That'll be one more than I usually get." She looked herself over in the mirror. "Why am I taking fashion advice from you?" she said, looking at Jorge in the reflection. "Look at you."

Jorge tugged at his faded T-shirt and wiped his palm on the basketball shorts he wore every day.

"I'm going to meet Amber outside." Lauren grabbed her purse and started for the door.

"Wait," Jorge said. He grabbed her wrist gently and held Lauren's hand. "I'm really sorry about not giving you a heads-up." He apologized every time a detail about Rebecca slipped his mind, a common occurrence lately.

Lauren placed her hand on his shoulder and smirked. "If you were really sorry, you'd get Briana to give us money so I could kick Rebecca out." Jorge closed his eyes and hung his head. "That's what I thought. I'll be back later."

Lauren rushed from her room, keeping her eyes on the front door so she didn't see Rebecca or the model entertaining her for the evening. Any confidence she had was shaky. When she opened the door, the fresh air held the promise of freedom. She took a deep breath and held it for a moment before releasing it slowly. Getting out for the night was a good idea, and sitting with a good friend would be therapeutic. Lauren nodded and tried to shake away her anxieties as she stepped onto the stoop.

"Lauren, wait." Rebecca's shrill voice caught Lauren before she was out the door. Lauren turned slowly and saw Rebecca bouncing toward her. Her inky black curls danced hypnotically.

"What is it, Rebecca?" Lauren stood tall in spite of the desire to shrink into herself.

Rebecca smiled sweetly, the same smile she always wore before sharing something new and exciting with Lauren. "I want you to meet my girlfriend, Savannah. She's a receptionist for a lawyer, too, and I figured you two would hit it off."

Lauren's brow creased. "I'm a paralegal, not a receptionist. They don't even do the same—no," she said, stopping herself and waving her left hand. "You know what? I have someone waiting for me." Lauren looked over Rebecca's shoulder to Savannah and put on a fake polite smile. "Nice to meet you, Savannah. Goodbye, everyone."

"Bye," Briana called out from the couch. She hadn't even acknowledged Lauren until that moment.

Lauren felt her blood start to boil, and she rushed out the door. The chilly air bit at her bare arms. She needed a jacket, but she'd need to go back inside. She briefly weighed her options before hurrying to her car. Amber wouldn't show up for another fifteen minutes, so she made a decision.

Lauren pulled her phone from her purse and typed out a message. *Had to escape. I have enough singles for a couple drops of gas. Meet you at the bar.* She threw her phone on the passenger seat and pulled down her visor to check her appearance in the small, unlit mirror.

Her hair hung listlessly to her shoulders and what little eyeliner she'd hurriedly applied that morning was faint enough to make her look more tired than she was. But her cheeks were rosy thanks to the spike in her blood pressure, which was one positive. Lauren stared at her reflection. She looked tired, and her brown eyes were duller than ever.

Once upon a time Lauren had been confident and proud of who she was, but she had been beaten down as of late. Her spirit now matched her stodgy exterior. But Lauren refused to believe her former, fun self was completely gone. She could have a happier life, and maybe pushing herself to go out tonight would be the start of her self-improvement.

Chapter Three

L auren hummed along as Poison played through the bar. She laughed humorlessly to herself and agreed that every rose did have its thorn. She refused, for the third time that night, to turn around when someone new walked into the Dollhouse. Amber kept insisting she "take a quick look" and "check her out," but Lauren continued to remind her friend she was there to relax and be at peace with herself.

"You sure picked an odd place to soul search," Amber said over the rim of her highball glass. She finished the rest of her whiskey ginger in one long gulp and stared at the remaining cubes in the glass. "I want to know their secret. How do they make these so good?"

The bartender nearest to them laughed. She looked at them and said, "Real ginger ale and quality rye whiskey. Nothing artificial or cheap. Can I get you another?"

"Absolutely." Amber pushed her empty glass aside.

"What about you?" the bartender asked Lauren with a wink.

Lauren looked from the other woman's hazel eyes to her cocky smile and back to Amber's empty glass. "I'll, uh, have another Dolly, I guess," Lauren said as inarticulately as possible. Amber looked from the bartender to her and laughed.

"Coming right up."

Lauren ignored Amber's amused expression. "*Anyway*, I'm not soul searching. I'm just trying to remember who I was before I wound up under a pile of debt, working for old men who require I wear the ugliest heels ever created." Lauren stared off for a moment, watching as their bartender laughed easily with another member of the staff while pouring whiskey. Lauren couldn't recall the last time she felt that relaxed. "I was someone completely different." When she looked back at Amber, her friend had a new softness in her large dark eyes.

"I know you were," Amber said, covering Lauren's hand with her own. "I'll help you remember her, even if that means buying you enough drinks to help you forget who you are today."

Lauren cackled just as their drinks were delivered.

The server wore a brilliant smile. "Here you go. Do you have a tab?"

"Yes, under Amber, thank you." Amber watched, her eyes fixated on the bartender as she walked away. Lauren leaned over to catch a glimpse of the tall, thin woman wiping her hands on the towel hanging from the back pocket of her black skinny jeans. "I love androgyny, don't you?"

"She's okay," Lauren said with a noncommittal shrug. Every single woman at the bar, and probably even the men, would agree the bartender exceeded the simple definition of attractive. But Lauren was feeling particularly stubborn and felt the need to go against the grain. "If you're into that sort of thing."

"Oh, I'm into it, deeply."

Lauren smiled at her friend, so feminine with her long, thick dark hair and naturally tan complexion. Amber was as Italian as New Jersey women got, and did she ever love her women boyish.

"Amber, I think you're drooling." Lauren said and laughed when Amber chucked her chin. "Why don't you leave her your number?"

"Oh, please. Like she doesn't get a dozen numbers stuffed in with her tips every night. And besides, I think you're the one who caught her eye."

Lauren snorted.

"I'm serious. Her attention was on you when she took our

order, and she's been looking over here constantly. She's definitely interested."

Lauren felt a fraction of her limp ego inflate. Amber's kindness and support had been a rock to her over the years. Jorge's earlier question came to mind. She grabbed Amber's hand on the bar top again. "Maybe we should make a go of a relationship. We already have the supportive friendship, we just have to add sex."

Amber chuckled into her drink. Lauren's face remained still. "You can't be serious."

"What if I am? Would it be so terrible?" Lauren felt herself grow offended and defensive, a little dagger of hurt piercing her chest. "I'm not that bad."

"Lauren, listen to me," Amber said, taking Lauren's hand in a stronger hold and bringing it to her chest. "I love you, and I love our friendship. You're funny and sassy and attractive, but we wouldn't work." Lauren tried to argue, but Amber shushed her. "We're looking for the same thing, and it's not each other." Amber placed Lauren's hand back on the bar and pushed it toward her drink. "Now drink and decide what you want to do about the hottie behind the bar."

Lauren hid her sad smile behind her glass. She didn't feel disappointed or mad. Amber was right. In her heart, Lauren felt nothing more than platonic love for her friend, but loneliness and the sight of an ex-girlfriend moving on made crazy ideas seem possible. Crazy ideas like a hot bartender being interested in Lauren. "She can stare all she wants, she's not my type."

Amber's mouth fell open. "Not your type? Honey, she's everyone's type. What part of her aren't you into? Are the dimples too much? Maybe it's her perfect hair, you know, the way it falls into her gorgeous eyes." Amber turned back, blatantly checking out their server. "Her tattoos are so unsexy, and the way she moves with such confidence makes me want to gag."

Lauren shook her head and said, "I'm not saying I don't think she's attractive, but she's a bartender. I'm looking for someone with stability and a grownup job, not someone who flirts for extra money." Amber's pinched features startled Lauren. "What?"

"A lot of what you just said was judgey and made you sound shallow."

Lauren rolled her eyes. "I'm not judging anyone, but you're right. Bartending is a grownup job and should be respected as such, but what's her future? She's probably twenty-five and going with the flow." Lauren watched how the woman in question laughed freely, her smile never dimming. Life hadn't squashed her spirits yet.

❖

Berit grabbed three shot glasses and lined them up perfectly. She shifted the pint glass she had secured in the shaker and started to pour ruby red liquid into the glasses. She filled each to the brim, placing them carefully in front of two waiting women.

"Only two are for us," one of the women said while folding a five dollar bill in half and placing the third shot atop it. "The other is for you."

Berit smiled politely. "Thank you, but my boss doesn't like us drinking on the job. She's pretty strict about it."

"Your boss is a party pooper."

"I know, the staff keeps telling her that. Enjoy the shots." Berit leaned in and added quietly, "I only charged you for the two." She walked toward Lou, stopping along the way to adjust bottles so their labels were facing out. "I just got called a party pooper for not letting the staff drink while they're working."

Lou chuckled. "You are a party pooper, but not for that reason." Lou wiped down a stack of tumblers fresh out of the dishwasher. Water spots drove Berit crazy. "Speaking of staff, what's going on between you and Bellamy?"

"What do you mean?" Berit feigned cluelessness. She knew trying to hide her social life from her sister was pointless, but that didn't mean she shouldn't try.

"You know exactly what I mean. Leaving together, the looks and the exchanges. And don't think for a moment I didn't catch you leaning into her window last night. You're many things, Berit, but subtle isn't one of them."

Berit looked across at the woman in question. Bellamy was wearing tight black pants and another low-cut top. "We're friends with benefits."

"Another friend and more benefits. Just what you need."

"You're starting to sound like Mom, again," Berit said, whipping Lou with her towel.

"I know. I've been dying to tell you to get a haircut, too." Berit laughed heartily and ran her fingers through her floppy waves. "In all seriousness, I understand not wanting to get attached. Relationships are hard and scary, but I want you to meet someone that makes you as happy as this bar makes you."

"It's not that I don't *want* to get attached. I'm completely open to falling head over heels in love with someone. I just haven't met that woman yet."

"And what about sweet, stunning, hilarious Bellamy?"

Berit looked around to check on patrons and make sure no other staff members were nearby. "Can you keep a secret?" Lou gave her an offended look, as if she hadn't kept her every secret since they were five. "Bellamy is crazy about someone, but her crush is going through a tough breakup right now, and Bellamy thinks it's best to wait for the dust to clear."

"Really? Who is it?"

Berit shook her head. She could speculate, but she refused to be the conductor on the Dollhouse's gossip train. "She refuses to tell me," Berit said. She was looking for the waitress in question, but she got distracted by the brunette at the end of the bar. She and the sadness in her dark eyes piqued Berit's curiosity. "Have you ever seen her before?" Berit nodded slightly for Lou to look.

Lou craned her neck. "Which one? There's a crowd of women down there."

"All the way at the end." Berit bit at her thumbnail and stared in the opposite direction, trying to play it cool.

"I've seen her a few times, but only recently."

A new line formed at the bar, pulling Berit away from Lou, but that didn't deter her from learning more. "Is she usually with someone?" she said loudly. Berit started taking orders.

Lou shook her head and stepped in to help. "Only the woman next to her, and sometimes they're in a large group."

"How come I don't recognize her?" Berit stopped pouring a drink at Lou's bellowing laughter.

"No offense, Berit, but you're more likely to remember a drink order than a name or face." Lou patted Berit on the back as she passed behind the bar.

"That's not true. I know my regulars."

"At the bar, yes, but she usually sits at a table. Maybe tonight's your lucky night," Lou said with an elbow to Berit's side. "Maybe she's the woman you've been looking for."

It was Berit's turn to laugh.

"That's highly unlikely." Berit looked back to the sullen woman and noticed her glass was half full. "I'm going to talk to her."

"Atta girl, Berit, go talk to your soul mate."

"Shut up," Berit grumbled. She walked the length of the bar, her confidence building with each step. The two women at the end of the bar looked at Berit the moment she arrived in front of them. "Can I get you another drink?" Berit wore her most charming smile, the one that had landed her more phone numbers than she could count. Both her charm and smile faltered when the woman shot a sour look at her.

"My glass is half empty. Why would I need a refill so soon? You barely gave me time to drink this one."

An unhappy customer was new territory for Berit, and she stood in silent shock. She looked to the other woman for help.

"Lauren, she's just doing her job." Berit perked up at the use of a name. "I'm pretty sure they're required to check on everyone in a timely manner."

Berit's bravado came rushing back. "You are correct, but I also wanted to make sure *Lauren* was having a good time." Berit looked directly into Lauren's dark eyes and waited for a reaction. A smile, maybe a small giggle drawn out by unexpected attention, but Berit didn't expect a negative reaction from Lauren.

She stood and threw her purse on her shoulder. "I'm out of here.

Call me later." Lauren walked right out of the Dollhouse without a backward glance.

Lauren's friend turned back to Berit with a grimace. "I apologize for her. She had a tough week."

"I work at a bar," Berit said with a shrug. "I see it all the time."

"Somehow, I find that very hard to believe. Amber," she said, extending her hand for Berit to shake.

"I'm Berit, and it's very nice to meet you. Can I get you anything else?"

"No. I should get going and follow up with Lauren." Amber stood and placed a fifty dollar bill on the bar.

"I hope I didn't scare her away from the Dollhouse for good."

"There's not a single lesbian in New Jersey that'd willingly stay away from this place. It's amazing."

Berit beamed with pride. "Thank you."

Amber stood and pulled on her light jacket. "Please pass the message along to the owner. She did a great job with this place. Have a good night."

Berit watched Amber leave. She took their glasses from the bar top and went about the quick routine of rinsing and wiping the rim with a soapy sponge before loading them into the dishwasher. Some teased her for being a clean freak, but she had been served too many drinks in dirty glasses to take a chance on being anything less than thorough.

Lou came over soon after. "How'd it go?"

"She left."

"Before you had a chance to talk to her?"

"No. I talked to her, then she got up and left," Berit said, motioning from the barstool to the door. Lou stifled a laugh. "Laugh all you want, but I think you were right."

"About?"

"I think she's my soul mate," Berit said with a wry smile.

Lou's expression fell, and she blew a wayward strand of hair from her face. "The one woman who won't give you the time of day is your soul mate?"

Berit watched Dee as she approached and smiled. She handed Berit a list of orders. After looking over the slip of paper, Berit looked to Lou again. "I really think she may be."

"I love you because you're my sister, but I really hate you sometimes."

Berit chuckled. She grabbed top-shelf whiskey in one hand and sour mix in the other. She thought of what to say the next time Lauren stepped foot in her bar as she tossed a bottle into the air and caught it after two full spins. Berit hoped Lauren was prepared for the full-on Berit Matthews wooing experience.

Chapter Four

Memorial Day weekend was the start of summer, the busiest season for every bar in the area. Berit and her crew had spent most of the week prepping the Dollhouse for what was sure to be a hectic weekend. Berit sat at her small desk and reviewed several orders she was placing. With the recent spike in the popularity of craft rum drinks, Berit wanted to make sure she had an adequate amount on hand. Maybe she'd even come up with a new theme drink during the heart of the season. Lou knocked at the door and leaned against it with her arms folded across her chest.

"The patio is ready to go. We strung the lights, and Matt spent all day yesterday pulling weeds and power-washing the deck. I paid him with a six-pack of that fancy beer he loves but can't afford."

"Most brothers would do it for free," Berit said. She sat back in her cheap office chair and threw her pencil onto her order book.

"No, they wouldn't."

"You're right. I'll bring another six-pack to the next family dinner since I missed him yesterday." Berit stretched her neck and her shoulders. She'd rather be behind the bar, but paperwork had to get done.

"Where were you all day yesterday?"

"I went to a wine tasting in Pennsylvania. A winery in Glen Mills has been reaching out to small businesses in the area. I figured it was worth the drive, and I was right. I ordered a case of their cabernet. The depth of the flavor was amazing." Berit looked pointedly at Lou and added, "Why don't you do any of the paperwork around here?"

"Because I only own a third of the business and you don't trust me enough to do it right. Control freak." Lou turned around and started out the office door. "Your soul mate is here, by the way." Her last words were thrown over her shoulder.

Berit nearly fell out of her chair. "She's here? Where? Table or bar?" She felt dizzy from standing too quickly. "How do I look?" Berit looked down at her outfit of comfortable fitted jeans, a black short-sleeved button up, and her favored black Doc Martens.

Lauren peeked her head back into the office. "She's at a table, and you look fine. But you may want to hurry before Dee gets to her table."

Berit casually rushed from her office into the lounge area of the Dollhouse. She scanned the space for Lauren. Jovial groups of women were on every couch and most of the small, round tables. Berit spotted Lauren at one of the few tables tucked in a corner, but she was alone—much to Berit's delight. Lauren's face still hung with melancholy, but she seemed more approachable this time around. Berit thought she looked as comfortable as ever in a plain blouse and jeans. The simplicity of Lauren's style was wildly attractive. She approached Lauren's table just as she would any other, but admittedly, she felt nervous.

"Hello again, Lauren. What can I get you this evening? Another Dolly?" Berit watched as Lauren's eyes faded from surprised to disinterested, and she worried that Lauren might leave again. Berit was relieved when she sat farther back into the tall bar table chair.

"Are they so short-staffed today that they thought letting you out from behind the bar was a good idea?"

Berit wasn't taken aback this time. "When I saw you, I knew I had to be the one to serve you. I'm surprised you came back after running out of here last week."

"I wasn't about to let one staff member ruin my favorite bar for me." Berit's heart beat in the prideful way it always did when someone said her bar was a favorite. "Even if that staff member won't leave me alone."

"I'm just trying to do my job and make you smile while I'm at it," Berit said, leaning onto Lauren's table. "What'll it be tonight?

I can give you a Climax." At Lauren's unamused and stern glare, Berit said, "Guess not. You look more in the mood for a Dark 'N' Stormy."

Lauren stared at Berit for a moment before ordering. "I'll take your cheapest beer, thanks."

Berit was crestfallen. There's no fun in a cheap beer, no chance of flirty and sexy innuendo. "Are you sure that's all you want?" she said with a frown. Lauren nodded. Berit walked away in a stupor. When she got to the bar, she pulled a beer from the cooler but stopped just before popping the cap. Berit looked again to Lauren, who was counting her money. Berit smiled and pulled a few bottles of liquor from the shelves and mixed a drink. Berit placed a full glass in front of Lauren when she returned to her table.

Lauren looked from the glass to Berit. "This isn't a beer."

"No, but it is on the house."

"Don't try to—"

Berit held up her hand. "I'm not trying anything. Take it as an apology for driving you out of here the other night." Berit inched the drink closer to Lauren. "I can get you the beer if that's what you'd prefer."

Lauren bit her lip and narrowed her eyes. "I'll take the drink."

Berit basked in the small smile Lauren had after her first sip. "I've noticed you're alone tonight."

"And I've noticed you have other tables to wait on."

"They're all covered," Berit said dismissively. "What brought you in so early on a Friday?"

Lauren's sigh didn't sound like one of annoyance, and Berit's hopes of getting her to open up shot sky high. "My choices were here or home, and there's nothing worthwhile at home."

Berit grinned. "Take me home with you later, and I promise to make it worthwhile."

Lauren almost choked on her drink. "That's a bit forward."

"Sorry, again. I should at least introduce myself first. My name is Berit, and it's very nice to get a chance to talk to you, Lauren."

"What kind of name is Berit?" Lauren said with obvious skepticism in her eyes and took another drink.

"A strange one, apparently." Berit studied the way Lauren's throat flexed while she gulped her drink. Her skin looked sinfully soft to the touch.

"Is Berit your real name?"

"Yes."

Lauren placed her drink down with a loud thud. "Tell me this, Berit—why won't you go away?"

"Truthfully, I was struck by how sad you looked the other night. You're much too beautiful to look so sad."

"I'm sure you say that to a lot of women."

"Only the sad ones. Otherwise it'd be weird." Lauren laughed loudly and Berit was struck by the beautiful sight. Lauren's full mouth turned exquisite when smiling. "Listen, Lauren, I'm not going to force my company on you—"

"Could've fooled me."

Berit stifled a smile. "If you find yourself feeling lonely or like you'd enjoy continuing our conversation, come sit at the bar. I'll be there all night."

Lauren tapped her fingertip to her lips as if thinking. "We'll see, but it's unlikely. Especially if another woman approaches to tell me I look sad. That's *such* an irresistible line." Lauren sat back and sipped at her drink.

Berit backed away wordlessly with her hands up in surrender.

Lauren waited for Berit to get back behind the bar before pulling her phone out and messaging an *SOS* to Amber.

I'm getting ready for a date. What's up?

Lauren's eyes went wide. *A date? With who? Oh please, oh please tell me it's the dermatologist.* Amber had been working at a marketing firm specializing in medical marketing for over a year and had been pining after a client of hers for most of that time. Lauren waited impatiently.

We're not talking about me right now. You're the one with the emergency. Amber's message deflated Lauren, but another one came through. *It's not the dermatologist. I'm going out with someone I met at a networking function, and I'll tell you all about it another time.*

"Damn," Lauren said under her breath. She started to type

again, deleting and retyping the message several times before hitting Send. *She's talking to me again.*

She who?

The bartender.

The hot bartender? You're at the Dollhouse without me?

Lauren rolled her eyes. Like Amber wasn't dolling herself up for a more interesting night than watching Lauren wallow. *Her name is Berit, and I came here because I didn't want to go home.* Lauren's phone rang. She laughed when Amber's photo lit up the screen. "You didn't have to call," Lauren said the moment the phone was to her ear.

"You got her name, so conversation must've gone okay."

"That was after she told me I look sad and recommended I take her home with me to make my home life worthwhile." Lauren picked the cherry out of her drink and chewed it slowly. She wore a small, cocky smile. She wasn't a fan of pickup lines, but Berit's words did bolster her ego slightly.

"I hope your SOS is because you're taking her home."

Lauren made a sound of disgust and said, "Definitely not."

"Why not? After Rebecca, you should try to have fun and relax a little."

"I can relax and have fun in a hammock or on the beach while reading a murder mystery, not with some strange woman in bed." Lauren craned her neck to get an unobstructed view of the bar. She watched Berit pour two drinks and hand them to a waitress, who leaned in to whisper something into Berit's ear. "Besides, I doubt a woman like Berit will miss me. I'll be replaced in a heartbeat." Lauren finished the rest of her drink in a long gulp. As delicious as the drink was, Lauren would limit herself to one. She had driven to the Dollhouse, and she also wanted to avoid a drunken depression. "Thanks for calling. Enjoy your date and remember every detail for when you tell me all about it." Lauren could hear Amber's sigh, picturing her friend rolling her eyes at her.

"I will, but, Lauren," Amber said with an odd hesitance in her voice, "this will probably sound weird, but I'm happy you're out tonight."

Lauren heard the unspoken sentiment in Amber's words. Lauren rarely ventured out and never on her own. Hating her home life had turned Lauren from an introvert to someone who stopped at a bar—alone. "I've taken up enough of your time. Have fun, text me later."

Lauren and Amber shared a quick goodbye and Lauren tucked her phone into her purse. She looked at Berit again and caught her staring in her direction. At first, Lauren was sure Berit was looking at another table, but the bartender held up an empty glass and pointed to Lauren. Lauren waved off the offer for another drink. Berit then waved from her to Lauren, offering herself next. Lauren laughed but declined that offer as well. Berit covered her heart with her hands and wore a pout so severe, Lauren could see her bottom lip glistening from across the bar.

Lauren acknowledged the truth: Berit was wildly attractive, seemingly kind, and even a little funny. The perfect woman to many, but just another heartache for a woman like Lauren. Lauren was reliant on mutual dependence and commitment. She loved being in monogamous relationships and preferred to spend most of her downtime curled up in one another watching television or making out. Even if she wanted to change, to become a different version of herself, she wasn't interested in a casual hookup. She watched with rapt attention as Berit tossed a few liquor bottles around effortlessly, her thin arms flexing with every movement. Lauren snapped her mouth shut and swallowed hard.

She stood and nodded resolutely. Berit would serve as a wonderful fantasy and absolutely nothing more.

CHAPTER FIVE

D aly!" Lauren's boss, Samuel Baxter, barked at her for the fifth time in twenty minutes. She didn't always mind working Saturdays, but when Baxter was in the office, she'd rather be on the receiving end of a root canal. "What the hell is this?"

Lauren looked from his alarmingly red face to the three folders in his hand and said, "The evidence log, witness list, and statement files you wanted me to prepare for the Langfeld case."

"No, I asked Sally to prepare that. I told you to hit the road and interview our witnesses again. I need to make sure their statements are rock-solid before we step foot in court Monday morning. How dense are you? Were my instructions too complex for you to comprehend?"

Lauren clenched her jaw.

"If you leave now you should finish up before sundown. And don't expect to be on the clock this entire time. I'm not paying you for more hours because you weren't listening." Mr. Baxter tugged at the collar of his starched shirt and stormed off in the direction of his office.

Lauren released a long breath and walked to her desk calmly. She wasn't sure whether to be proud of herself for learning to handle the abuse or worried. When she had first started at the firm, she'd cried every time someone would raise their voice. Now, if Mr. Baxter's blotchy skin, white hair, and red-rimmed eyes were any indication, she'd realized all the yelling and screaming was bad for your health. She picked up her phone and dialed the office's one other female paralegal. Sally answered on the third ring.

"Hey, Sally, how are the statements coming?"

"I just finished up the last one, and I'm on my way back."

"Mr. Baxter forgot who was doing what again. I just got an earful about having shit for brains," Lauren said as she flipped aimlessly through another file.

Sally sighed heavily into the phone. "I did not go to law school for this."

Lauren always felt for Sally. She'd made it to her final year in law school before she got pregnant. She tried to finish, but her pregnancy turned high-risk and she was forced to sit out for the remainder of the year. Sally's doctor even warned her against minimal participation because heightened stress could hurt the baby. Sally said goodbye to law school then and hadn't looked back since.

"Lauren?"

"Yeah?" Lauren shook herself back to the moment.

"I said I'm about to pull into the parking lot." Their call disconnected abruptly and in under two minutes, Sally came rushing into the office. "It's very warm today. The sun is brutal."

"I'm ready to welcome summer with open arms," Lauren said, spreading her arms as wide as she could. "Did you get everything we needed?"

"Yes, everyone's stories were straight and as solid as they were on day one. I don't think anyone's bullshitting us this time around." Sally pulled a legal pad and files from her leather briefcase. She flipped through a few yellow sheets before ripping two from the pad. She handed them to Lauren and said, "Ready to compare statements and write up some reports? Because I'm ready to get out of here."

Lauren took the pages from Sally with a smile. "Have some big plans for your Saturday night?"

Sally waited to get her computer running before answering. "Stephen and I are going to that wedding I was telling you about. We're spending the night at the hotel."

"So you do have some wild plans," Lauren said, wiggling her eyebrows.

"There will be alcohol and dancing." Sally looked around the empty office and to Mr. Baxter's closed office door before continuing in a loud whisper. "And lots and lots of sex. I fully expect to be walking bowlegged tomorrow."

Lauren adored Sally and Stephen's relationship. They had four kids, the oldest from Sally's first marriage to her college boyfriend, and they had been married for eleven years. Their foundation was solid, and Lauren envied their unwavering connection. "Does Stephen know what he's in for?"

"Oh yes, I've been texting him my most wicked ideas all day." Sally's eyes never left her computer as she typed feverishly. "What about you? Any plans?" The creaking of a door interrupted.

"I don't remember agreeing to pay either of you to be social." Mr. Baxter stood in the middle of the floor, blocking Lauren's view of Sally. "And why are you still here?" he said, looking directly at Lauren.

"We're finishing up with the witness statements. Sally—"

"They've all been interviewed again, and not one statement strayed from the original. Lauren is finishing up to make sure all of our i's are dotted and t's crossed. We thought it'd be best if we both worked on this because we're sure you'd like to get out of here. It's a beautiful day for golf." Sally's voice was steady and Lauren had to stifle a laugh at how well she brown-nosed.

"It is." Mr. Baxter stared at Sally, then turned to Lauren suddenly. "If you don't get your shit together soon and start acting more like Sally, I'll have to find someone more like her to replace you." He stormed off.

Lauren's earlier amusement fell away along with the color from her face.

"Don't listen to him, Lauren."

Lauren shrugged off her coworker's concern. "Of course. I'm just his punching bag of the week, right?" Lauren forced a fake smile and held it until Sally looked away. She could confide in Sally, but did Sally really need that kind of pity party in her life? She wouldn't want Lauren as anything more than an office acquaintance.

Why did it seem like everyone in Lauren's life was just waiting for someone better, prettier, and more talented to come along? Lauren's employer treated her as replaceable as she really was, her ex-girlfriend tried on new relationships and kept coming back to Lauren when they didn't feel right, and even Jorge preferred his deadbeat girlfriend as a roommate. Lauren was growing used to second and third place. She needed a moment, a brief second where she felt like more than nothing special. And dammit, Lauren could only think of one place where that'd happen. She could only hope Berit was working.

❖

"All right, ladies," Berit said, pointing to the bottle of premium vodka she balanced on her elbow. "If I spill even a drop of this, you all get your drink for free."

"And if you don't spill?" a very cute blonde asked. Berit smiled. She was a Saturday Happy Hour regular, but Berit had yet to get her name. "Do we still get something?" Berit only winked.

Berit tossed the bottle into the air and spun once before catching it and flipping it one more time. The bottle landed nozzle down into her mixing cup. The group looked simultaneously impressed and dismayed that not one bit of vodka was lost. "Looks like these won't be on the house, but how does a round of shots sound?"

"Like a bad business move," Berit heard a faintly familiar voice say from farther down the bar, but she kept her attention on the group in front of her.

"Do you all like chocolate cake?" Berit poured more vodka into a new mixing cup. She added hazelnut liquor and mixed it. She poured their drinks and spared a quick glance down the bar. Lauren was smiling at her. Berit finished up with the group, added their drinks to the tab, and collected her tips, trying to rein in her excitement at seeing Lauren again. This was the first time Lauren was seeking her out, a fact that made Berit very happy. She sauntered over to Lauren coolly while she wiped her hands on a dish towel.

"Welcome to Happy Hour at the Dollhouse. All mixed drinks

are half price until nine." Berit leaned forward onto the bar. "How are you?" she said, looking directly into Lauren's stormy eyes. Lauren had looked troubled every time she'd seen her, and Berit wanted to know all about it. A natural trait of a bartender.

"I wasn't sure if you'd be here so early," Lauren said more to her hands than to Berit.

"I'm always here."

Lauren looked up at Berit with a shy smile. "I'm starting to notice that."

"What would you like to drink?"

Lauren knocked on the thick drink menu closest to her and said, "I want to try something new, and I don't feel like looking through this. What do you recommend?"

Berit licked her lips and smirked. "A Kiss on the Lips."

Lauren's eyes went wide. "Berit, I'm—"

"It's a frozen drink," Berit said with a laugh. "Peach and mango, very summery."

Lauren's face twisted into a grimace and she apologized quietly. "I'm not really into frozen fruity drinks. What about something less flashy, like a mojito?"

"I could make you a mojito," Berit said, pulling out a tall glass from behind the bar. "But you're going to have to answer a question for me first."

Lauren looked very, *very* skeptical before nodding.

"Are you a top, bottom, or switch, Lauren?"

Lauren's mouth fell open and she stuttered before saying, "That's none of your business." The rosy tint of her cheeks was incredibly attractive. Berit remained silent as she waited for another answer from Lauren, but when one didn't come, she dropped her playfulness and took on the role of professional bartender.

"We make mojitos three ways here: top, bottom, and switch. A top mojito is a classic lime and mint mojito, a bottom incorporates peach, and a switch mojito is made with raw sugar and golden rum. I like to ask and see if the flavor matches someone's bedroom personality." Berit tore a few mint leaves and put them in the bottom of the glass. She looked back at Lauren, whose eyes were fixed on the green leaves. She added freshly squeezed lime juice and asked, "What'll it be?"

"I'll try one of each, and I'll start with a top."

Berit nodded and started preparing the drink, but stopped when Lauren added to her order.

"Make me a bottom at the same time and give me a shot of your smoothest rum. I don't like mixing alcohol, and I need to start with something strong."

Berit frowned. She grew worried for Lauren but grabbed a shot glass nonetheless. She knew something was eating away at Lauren and had seen more than her share of mind-erasing benders, so Berit decided it was her duty to make sure Lauren was okay for the night. She poured the shot and slid it to Lauren. Lauren contemplated the small glass of rum as Berit muddled the mint and lime juice with a sprinkle of sugar. She finished the mojito and placed it next to the shot.

"You know what works better than a mojito and a shot when something's bothering me?" Lauren looked at her with questioning eyes. "Talking about it."

"Nothing to talk about," Lauren said. She threw back the shot and slammed the glass on the counter, making a loud thud against the wooden surface. She started gulping her mojito immediately after.

Berit looked around and noticed a group waiting to be served. Lou had her hands full with a bachelorette party. "I have to go help them," she said, pointing down the bar. "I'll be back, and you are going to talk to me. Even if I have to take you home with me to get it out of you." Berit felt a little better about leaving Lauren alone once she made her laugh.

Berit returned approximately twelve minutes later and found Lauren halfway through her second mojito, chewing on her straw angrily. Not a drop of mojito remained in the first glass. Berit raised her eyebrows. "Are you ready to talk?" She took Lauren's glass from her.

"I'm ready to try a switch next. Maybe I should trying *being* a switch. I'm already a very active bottom." She started on the next drink, Berit almost dropping the fresh glass. "Being a switch would probably scare women away, too," Lauren said with a snort. "So what's special about gold rum? Berit?"

Berit missed the question because she was still trying to figure out what Lauren meant by very active bottom. "I'm sorry, I was counting my pour. What's your question?"

"What's so special about gold rum?" Lauren's cheeks were flushed, and her shoulders seemed more relaxed. Her rapid drinking was starting to catch up.

"Gold rum is aged in casks made of oak, giving the flavor more depth." Berit muddled and mixed. "These are also known as dirty mojitos."

"Why do I get the feeling everything is dirty with you, Berit?" After a second, Lauren's eyes went wide, and she covered her face with her hands. Berit laughed. "That didn't come out right." Lauren shook her head. "Or maybe it did?"

"I know what you meant. I enjoy clever innuendo as much as the next person, but I do think sex is a great marketing tool for a bar."

Lauren took a long sip of her new drink and grinned. "Speaking of, this is better than sex!"

"Since you're on your way to being drunk, I refuse to believe you. But I will take the compliment." Berit took in the sight of Lauren. Her hair was pulled back haphazardly with a clip and her white button-up shirt was wrinkled. "Now, are you ready to talk to me?"

Lauren rolled her straw between her lips while she considered Berit's question. "I'm replaceable to everyone, and it sucks. I came here after work today because I was tired of being told how I'm not as good as someone else. Or worse, having someone better flaunted in front of me. I came looking for you because your awful pickup lines make me feel better." Berit's smile broadened with pride. "Even though I know you're working for tips and you pay the same attention to every woman here, it still feels nice."

Berit's smile fell. "Lauren, I don't treat every customer the same."

"Don't worry about it," Lauren said, reaching across the bar to place her hand on Berit's bare forearm. "You get paid to mix drinks and listen to people complain about their lives, and you get paid more if you flirt with them…even the women like me." Berit felt her heart drop, but before she could say any more, Lauren spoke again. "I bet your boss feels like they hit the jackpot with you, huh? Look at you—the tattoos and everything. What do you call yourself? Androgynous? Stud? Butch?"

Berit looked down at her black muscle tank and jeans and then back to Lauren. "I call myself Berit."

"Well, whatever. You've probably brought in double the business since you were hired."

Berit was growing uncomfortable with this topic Lauren continued to circle. She leaned forward with her elbows on the bar. "I'm going to let you in on a little secret," Berit said just loudly enough to be heard over the music and chatter in the bar. "I was never hired because I own this place, I don't flirt to make myself more money because all the tips I earn are split between the rest of my staff, and I don't label my look because I don't see myself as anything other than me." She stood back and wiped her hands on her towel. "Would you like another drink?"

Lauren stared blankly before shaking her head. "No, I uh—I think I should get going, actually." She stood unsteadily and took a credit card from her purse and handed it to Berit.

Berit stared at the thin plastic card before sliding it through the reader. *Lauren Daly.* She ripped the receipt and placed it down with a pen for Lauren to sign. Berit took the customer copy and scribbled on the back of it. "I never do this, and I hope you believe me," she said, handing the slip over. "Use it any time, Lauren. I'll be happy to listen. If you need a ride, let me know."

Lauren held up her phone. "I already ordered a ride."

"Promise me you won't drive."

"I won't." Lauren's eyes appeared glassy, and Berit wondered if what she saw was awakening tears or the effects of alcohol. "I promise." Lauren put her phone and receipt in her purse and walked to the door.

Berit blew out a long breath. Lauren Daly was a force she never saw coming, and one she doubted her readiness for. But whatever Berit's next moves were, she hoped they included getting to know Lauren better.

Chapter Six

Lauren lay in bed for a long while the next morning. Her hangover was minimal, and so was her desire to move. She'd picked up and put down her receipt from the night before more times than she could count. On one side was a small charge of five dollars, and on the other side Berit had written her phone number. Each number was clear and legible; Berit's handwriting was mostly sharp with a feminine lilt. Lauren noticed how Berit crossed her sevens, something you didn't often see in America. Lauren shifted beneath her artificial down comforter. She slept in her panties and a camisole, the morning chill nipping at her skin where it was bare. She could get up and pull on sweats, but solving the temperature problem wasn't nearly as important as solving the Berit problem.

Why had Berit given Lauren her number? Lauren had met more than a few female Casanovas who'd taken "no" very lightly and continued to pursue women, but that wasn't the impression Berit gave. When Lauren had taken the receipt from Berit the night before, the moment reminded her how a friend would reach out. Lauren pondered the idea of a friendship with Berit. Maybe such a thing could be possible. Lauren liked the idea of someone new in her life, someone without attachments to her ex, or other friends she'd have to share with. She reached to grab her phone from her nightstand, straining to ensure her back never left her plush mattress, an expensive housewarming gift to herself, but money well spent.

She typed and erased her messaged several times. What if Berit didn't text? Lauren laughed. If Berit didn't text, then a friendship between them would never work. She typed out a simple message that didn't allow for misinterpretation, and she hit Send.

I want to be friends. Lauren read her text, sitting so innocently inside that blue bubble. She wanted to add more, but dancing dots appeared. Lauren was surprised Berit would respond so quickly.

That's nice, but who is this?

Lauren smacked her forehead. *It's Lauren. From the bar.* She considered that answer and decided to add for better clarification. *You gave me your number last night.*

Lauren! I didn't expect to hear from you. See you again at the Dollhouse maybe, but not this way. What a nice surprise.

Lauren appreciated the way Berit messaged in complete sentences. Too many grammar rules had been dropped because of texting. *You broke some sort of unspoken rule and gave me your number. It'd be rude if I didn't reach out.*

I try to keep myself out of any uncomfortable situations.

Get a lot of admirers?

Yeah. I do.

Lauren laughed at Berit's honesty. *What's the craziest thing that's happened to you?* Lauren waited after she sent the question. Talking to Berit had been easy and comfortable so far, which relieved Lauren's anxiety over initiating conversation.

Dancing dots disappeared and reappeared before Berit's response came through five minutes later. *I had a stalker for a while. I had to change my number, file a restraining order, the whole nine yards.* Lauren's eyes widened as she read Berit's message. She had never really considered how many unwanted advances bartenders dealt with. *It all happened while I was at my last job. I was young and naïve and believed all attention was good attention. But that's a story for another day. How are you?*

Lauren smiled at her screen. *What an interesting story to withhold. I'll make sure you tell me sometime.*

Over dinner?

Friendship, Berit, Lauren reminded her.

Friends have dinner together all the time.

True, but I mean it. Friendship only.

Why limit ourselves?

Lauren should've known Berit would be a rapid-fire responder. She always seemed to be ready with a confident answer. Two could play at that game. *Because not everyone wants more with you.*

Ouch.

Lauren felt a flash of guilt. But she needed to lay her intentions on the line if she wanted a real friendship with Berit. *Are you looking for a real relationship? Something long-term and monogamous?* Lauren tossed her phone on her bedside table and stood. She stretched her sleepy limbs and sighed when a few joints popped. Lauren took her time washing her face, brushing her teeth, and rising fully for the day. She could hear the clatter of pans coming from the kitchen. Lauren was in for a cranky Sunday if Briana was making another mess that'd go uncleaned.

Lauren walked back into her room and checked her phone. No response from Berit. Lauren blew out a long breath. She wasn't at all surprised Berit had been scared away. "So much for making a new friend," Lauren mumbled to herself. She walked to her closet in search of workout clothes. The sky was clear and the temperature mild, perfect for a run. She pulled on her shorts, sports bra, and tank quickly before lacing up her running shoes. Lauren was surprised they weren't encased in dust since she hadn't gone for a run in over six months. She left her house with just her phone and keys, but without a second glance at Jorge, Briana, or Rebecca, who was still snoozing on the couch.

Lauren used the railing beside the front steps to stretch a few times before launching from the steps. She started at a casual pace, reacquainting her body with the motions of running. She felt her phone buzz but didn't bother checking it. When her phone buzzed again fifteen minutes later, with the steady vibrations of a call, she checked who was calling. She slowed to a stop and slid her finger along the screen to answer.

"I prefer texting," Lauren said between rapid breaths.

"I did text you, but you didn't answer." Lauren could hear the cocky smirk in Berit's voice.

She pulled the phone from her ear and checked her messages.

Berit did answer her, telling her how she wasn't opposed to a relationship. "We're not going to date, Berit. I'm serious about wanting to be just your friend."

"Why are you breathing like that? I'm sorry if I'm interrupting something, unless I shouldn't be."

"Ha ha. I'm out on a run."

"I should've known you run. You have great legs."

As much as Lauren loved the compliment, she had to put an end to this. "Berit, are you in for friendship or not?"

"I don't understand why—"

"Because!" Lauren said a little louder than necessary. "I'm not what you're looking for. No matter what you've been telling yourself, I'm not your type. I'm not easy or casual, and quite frankly, you may not even like me as a friend." A long silence stretched on after her outburst.

"I think you're right," Berit said curtly. "Let's be friends. Meet me for coffee later, just coffee. And for clarity, I get coffee with my friends and family often. It's my favorite way to catch up."

Lauren stood on the corner slack jawed. "O-okay, yeah, sure. What time? Do you have work?" Lauren started to lightly jog in the direction of her house. "What am I saying? You always have work."

"I do, but it's easy to get away on Sundays. We're only open for short hours, more like an after-dinner shift, but I'm fully staffed. Meet me at Mel's around four? I've been craving a cappuccino."

Lauren looked both ways before crossing at the corner of a busy intersection. "Cappuccino, huh? I pictured you as a milk and sugar gal."

"Which is why I agree we should be friends. There's a lot for you to learn about me. See you at four."

Lauren jogged home with an easy smile on her face. She hadn't had a good cup of coffee in a while, and Mel's had wonderfully indulgent fresh baked cookies. Delicious snacks, coffee, and some good conversation was exactly how Lauren wanted to spend her Sunday afternoon. Even if she'd have to stretch what little money she had left to satisfy her cravings.

❖

Berit buzzed around her apartment, tossing articles of clothing to and fro. Where Berit was organized and tidy at the Dollhouse, she was relaxed at home. She had clean clothes strewn across chairs because she didn't have time to fold them and put them away, and most of her dishes stayed packed in the dishwasher. So quickly finding a perfect outfit for coffee with Lauren proved to be a challenge. Berit was fine with Lauren wanting nothing more than friendship, but what she wasn't okay with was how Lauren assumed so much about her. Normally Berit would get pissed and write a woman off for speaking to her the way Lauren had, but something about her had gotten beneath Berit's skin. She craved the satisfaction of proving Lauren wrong.

Berit picked a simple white T-shirt and dark wash jeans, a worn pair of Chuck Taylors complementing the classic look. Berit mussed her wavy hair to give it a perfectly tousled look, hooked a leash to Hugo's harness, and made her way out the door.

Berit's apartment wasn't far from Mel's and she knew the café had plenty of outside seating to bring her dog along. Hugo loved long afternoon walks when the weather balanced perfectly between hot and cold. "C'mon, little man. Let's go meet a pretty lady for coffee." Hugo looked at Berit and tilted his head before following her down the front steps of the building.

The warm air felt wonderful as it whipped around Berit during her half-mile walk to Mel's. Both the café and the Dollhouse were on the busiest streets of Morristown. People milled about, spending their Sunday in the sun rather than cooped up indoors like they had all winter. Berit's hometown, her favorite city, was coming alive again.

Berit came to a stop in front of Mel's. She knelt to scratch between Hugo's ears and said, "The vet told me you're putting on a little too much weight, but that doesn't mean you can't share a biscotti with me." A shadow cast over her. Berit stared at white running shoes before looking up over her red Wayfarers to catch Lauren smiling down at her.

"I'm pretty sure that's exactly what the vet meant," Lauren said with a giggle. She crouched down to Berit's level. "Who's this?"

Berit smiled down. "This little guy is Hugo. Hugo, meet Lauren." Hugo's tail wagged excitedly as Lauren lavished him with attention. "He likes you, so you passed the first test."

Lauren laughed loudly as Hugo snuck a quick lick of her chin. "I'm being tested?"

"Of course," Berit said as she stood. She motioned for Lauren to take a seat at an open table before securing Hugo's leash to a chair. "You think I become friends with just anyone?"

"I do, you have that kind of personality."

"And what kind of personality is that?"

"A social butterfly. You'll flit around and talk to everyone around you."

Berit was ready to argue, to shoot down another assumption Lauren was so easily making, but their waitress approached. Her smile was warm and friendly.

"Hi, guys. My name is Alyssa, and I'll take your order if you're ready." She placed two glasses of water on the table before pulling a pad and pen from the pocket of her apron.

Lauren was ready to order right away. "I'll have an iced caramel latte with skim milk and an oatmeal cookie, please." Alyssa jotted down the order and looked expectantly to Berit, who sat in thought.

"Alyssa, do you have any of that delicious chocolate chip cake today? I woke up craving it."

"Oh no, sorry. We sold out early," Alyssa said, looking genuinely pained to deliver such terrible news.

Berit sighed. "Dang. I guess I'll take a cappuccino with a sprinkle of cinnamon, two almond biscotti, and a surprise."

"A surprise?" Alyssa and Lauren said simultaneously.

"Yes. Surprise me. Bring me anything." Alyssa looked skeptical before writing the order slowly. She left as gracefully as she had appeared. Berit looked at Lauren, who sat smugly as she sipped her water. "What's that look for?"

"You proved me right. You're a social butterfly that flirts and flits."

Berit rolled her eyes. "Yeah, well, skim milk has no soul."

"What?" Lauren said through a laugh.

"Skim milk, fat-free cheese, sugar-free candy," Berit said, raising a finger for each food, "all soulless."

"Says the beanpole at the table. Some of us are body conscious."

Berit smirked. "I'm very conscious of your body."

Lauren's smile fell, and she sat back. "We didn't even have coffee yet. I thought you were going to take my friendship request seriously."

"I am." Berit removed her sunglasses and set them aside. She leaned forward and looked directly at Lauren when she said, "I would say the same thing to my friends. Contrary to many of your abundant assumptions about me, I'm not always hitting on people. I'm flirtatious, yes, but most of the time I'm just being playful. If you really want to be my friend, you'll have to get used to it." Their order was delivered a moment later, and much to Berit's delight, Alyssa had placed a slice of chocolate chip cake in front of her. She beamed at Alyssa. "You're truly an angel."

Alyssa ducked her head and blushed. "It was really nothing. I remembered they were already working on a batch for tomorrow. Can I get you two anything else?"

"I think we're good, thank you." Berit's grin of pure elation had yet to subside. She watched unabashedly as Alyssa walked away.

"Does every woman fall all over you?" Lauren said.

Berit frowned. "Excuse me?" She broke off a piece of biscotti and gave it to Hugo. His small chewing sounds filled the moment of silence between Berit and Lauren.

Lauren took a long sip of her latte. "Am I the first woman to turn you down?"

Berit's eyebrows rose. Truthfully, Lauren was the first woman to deny her immediately, but how did you say that without sounding gross? Berit bought herself time by removing the saucer from beneath her coffee cup and pouring a little water into it for Hugo. She placed it in front of her dog and sat back up. She blurted the first comeback she could think of. "Maybe."

"I had a feeling." Lauren chewed on the tip of straw, pulling Berit's attention to the slight, uneven shift of her front teeth. Berit was fond of the charm something so small added to Lauren's already captivating face. "Thank you for hanging in there and taking a chance on a friendship with me. The truth is…" Lauren bit her lip and watched as a couple strode by hand in hand. "It's been a long while since I've had a real friend."

Berit felt a tug at her heart. "What about the woman you were with last week?"

"Amber's one of my best friends, but she's also friends with a few of my exes, and the women I *can't* be friends with anymore because they chose my ex." Lauren shrugged. "The lesbian world is small and frustrating." Lauren's pronunciation shifted at the end of her sentence. Another point of interest for Berit to question later.

"I don't mean to be a bubble burster, but you know there's a chance I know one of your exes too, and you mine, right?" Berit took a sip of her cappuccino and closed her eyes while she savored its flavor.

"It's a risk I'm willing to take."

"I do have one other question."

"What's that?"

Berit broke off a piece of cake and brought it to her lips. "Why me?" She popped the cake into her mouth and chewed slowly. Lauren wasn't quick to answer, so Berit elaborated. "Why do you want to be friends with me? Don't get me wrong, I'm happy you reached out, but at first I was willing to bet you were disgusted by me."

Lauren looked shameful. "I was never disgusted by you, you just always saw me on my bad days. Also, I'm usually pretty cold to anyone who approaches me at a bar. Call it survival instinct or just being an old-school romantic."

"Courting, monogamy, long-term love?"

"Yes," Lauren said with exasperation. "And it's all dead in this world. I'm convinced of it."

"No, it's not." Berit loved the idea of falling in love organically, but she couldn't say so, not without getting barked at by Lauren again for hitting on her. She reached down to play with Hugo's ear. "There's plenty of women out there who feel the same way."

"Oh yeah? Then why haven't I met one yet?"

"Look at the pool you're swimming in. You said yourself all your friends know your exes and so on." Berit scratched Hugo's chin and he stared up at her in delight. She lost herself in thought as she stared into Hugo's big amber-brown eyes. *How does Lauren think she'll meet anyone worthwhile that way? She needs help meeting new people and making friends that might possibly turn into more.* A lightbulb went off in Berit's head. She looked at Lauren with a triumphant smile. "That perfect woman is out there for you, and I'm going to help you find her."

Lauren shook her head slowly. "I don't think so."

"You asked for this." Berit folded her hands behind her head and sat back. "You're looking at Berit Matthews: friend and matchmaker." Berit laughed like a mad scientist while Lauren grumbled about regretting every decision she had ever made.

Chapter Seven

L auren should've expected her feel-good weekend to decline into yet another shitty week, considering disappointment was her status quo. But she still surprised herself with how low she could feel and how she approached the day with very little positivity. Lauren's only happiness came from being in a mostly empty office. The lawyers were all in court and Sally was scheduled to accompany Mr. Baxter, leaving her with piles of paperwork to complete and a list of phone calls to make. The downside to menial tasks was how quickly her attention span could wander. Lauren started to think about her home life, the decisions she'd made in the past that led her here—and to Berit.

Coffee with Berit turned out to be surprisingly normal.

They had laughed together, shared mundane stories of their everyday lives, and Lauren directed most of her goodbye to Hugo. The dog had won her heart, and even if she still felt skeptical of Berit's intentions, Lauren would spend as much time as she could with Berit just to be around the energetic Chihuahua. Lauren smiled as she remembered the way Hugo rolled onto his back and presented his belly to her. She recalled Berit's joke about trying the same move with her next time they hung out. Lauren had rolled her eyes.

Lauren's phone buzzed from where it lay facedown on her cluttered desk. She dropped the folder in the corresponding case box and picked up her phone. She had two unread messages: one from Berit and another from Sally. Lauren raised an eyebrow and made a quick decision to read Berit's message first.

Looking forward to chatting about the kind of chicks you dig Friday night. Should I get a few of my employees to model for you? You can pick your type out of a lineup.

Lauren snorted and chose to ignore Berit's message for the time being. She'd have to come up with something snarky, and her brain was too exhausted. She checked Sally's message and her stomach dropped. Berit and her ridiculousness was definitely going to have to wait. She swallowed hard and reread the message.

Heads up. Baxter is fuming, and we're heading back to the office now.

Lauren looked at the clock and calculated the ride and afternoon traffic. She had about twenty-five minutes to mentally prepare for her boss's arrival. She typed out a response. *Thanks for the warning. What is it this time?*

Sally's reply was immediate. *You.*

"Fuck," Lauren said quietly to herself. She'd worked diligently and was obedient as far back as she could remember. She had been keeping her head down and herself out of Mr. Baxter's way since the last time he lectured her. She had absolutely no idea what she could've done, or not done, this time.

After taking a deep breath, Lauren rushed about and made sure everything was where it needed to be. She'd reached the stage of self-preservation that enabled her to clean and organize at an impressively fast pace. She had boxes full, evidence together, and files put away just as the door to the building swung open.

"Sally, call the necessary parties and sort through today's notes. Make sense of them and rewrite everything in a more legible manner," Mr. Baxter barked as he walked in with Sally four steps behind him. "You," he said with a finger pointing at Lauren, "start packing your things. You're done here."

"Whoa. What?" Lauren's mouth hung open as she looked between Sally and Mr. Baxter, who was advancing toward his office at a much faster pace than she thought possible. "Sally, what the hell is going on?"

Sally looked at her with sympathetic eyes. "I think we confused our schedules again."

Mr. Baxter reappeared with an empty cardboard file box. "When I tell you you're to appear in court with me, I expect you to be there."

She slowly realized Mr. Baxter forgot which paralegal he had assigned to court duty that day, again. And he was blaming Lauren, again. "Mr. Baxter, with all due respect, I wasn't scheduled for court today." Lauren walked to find her phone to pull up any schedule she had saved in her phone, but was stopped short when Mr. Baxter continued to yell.

"Pack your things. I want you out of here in the next hour."

Panic flooded Lauren's chest. She needed to work, and she really didn't need a termination on her employment record. "Sally…" Lauren looked to her friend desperately.

"I'm certain I was scheduled for court today, Mr. Baxter," Sally said timidly.

"Get to work on those notes. Unless you want to follow Lauren out the door." Mr. Baxter left after his final threat.

"Lauren, I'm so sorry."

Lauren held up her hand to stop Sally from coming near her. She was barely holding herself together as it was. One ounce of pity would push her over the edge. "I'll be okay," she said without believing the words herself. "I'll talk to him."

After a futile talk, she walked out of the law firm less than twenty minutes later with one box containing what few personal items she had brought into the office. Lauren stared at the darkening sky once she got into her car. She had no idea what would come next. She checked her phone and scrolled through her contacts in search of college friends who could possibly hook her up with a new job, but they were all people she never spoke to anymore. She came upon Jorge's name and her chest tightened. What would she tell him? What if she couldn't get another job quickly? He relied on her income. They relied on each other. The last bit of Lauren's control slipped away from her emotions. Lauren started to cry, feeling hopeless and helpless, and petrified to go home.

❖

Because of Lou, Berit had just dropped and broken a glass for the first time since the Dollhouse had opened. She'd kept to herself since meeting up with Lauren, so when Lou snuck up behind her on a busy Monday night and asked how her coffee date went, Berit lost her grip. She huffed at the small pile of glass and grabbed a small dustpan and brush tucked underneath the bar.

"Wow," Lou said, shaking her head and watching Berit clean up. "Was it that good?"

"Grab me another glass and get back to work." She hadn't meant to sound so curt, but people were lining up for drinks and she didn't want them looking at her foul-up. "I'm making a Cosmo for the woman on the end. The two beside her were next."

"I'll take that as a no." Lou grabbed a towel off the counter, purposely smacking Berit in the side of the head along the way.

Berit watched Lou storm away. "It's only a glass," she told herself as she went about preparing a Cosmopolitan.

"What's the matter, Berit? Leave all your Tom Cruise moves at home tonight?" a young woman Berit recognized as a regular said from across the bar.

Berit shot her a charming smile and said, "The night's still young." She winked and delivered the Cosmo with an apology. Berit double-checked the floor for any stray glass before wandering toward the back. She caught Dee's attention and asked her to cover the bar for fifteen minutes. She needed fresh air.

When Berit stepped out onto the small back patio of the Dollhouse, she felt the promise of a hot summer brush against her skin. The air was slightly humid, and she heard the telltale chirp of insects over the murmuring of her patrons. A lightning bug lit up in the distance. Berit adored summertime, not because it was her busiest season, but because the whole world seemed more alive. *She* felt more alive. She jumped and turned around as hands gripped her shoulders.

"Jesus, Lou, you nearly gave me a heart attack." She gripped her chest with her right hand, her heart beating hard and rapidly.

Lou was clearly proud of herself. "I'm a little sorry. You probably thought I was one of your groupies."

"I do not have groupies, and who's watching the bar?" Berit looked around Lou, but Lou stepped in front of her, blocking her view. "Move," Berit said in her best demanding tone.

"The bar is under control. I wanted a minute to check in with my sis. We can take a break at the same time," Lou said reassuringly. "The place won't fall apart, I promise. Sit and tell me about your coffee date."

Berit followed Lou over to a small table on the corner of the patio where she had a clear view of the bar in case more people came in. "There's not much to tell. We were just two friends having coffee."

Lou stared at her blankly. "She was serious about the friendship thing?"

Berit nodded.

"I think, as your sister, I should poke fun at you, but I didn't think this day would ever come."

"Shut up. We had a great time together, and Hugo really liked her. Maybe meeting a woman and just being her friend will be good for me." Berit cracked her knuckles and lost herself in the satisfying pop. "She's going to stop by Friday night, and we're going to establish her type."

"Her type?"

"Yeah. I'm going to help her find a girlfriend."

Lou laughed.

"What?" Berit said.

"Nothing, that's just an interesting turn of events."

"Well, I know a lot of women, and not all intimately, right?"

"Most, but not all."

Berit glared at her sister. "So I offered to help her find someone," she said with a shrug. "I've been trying to think of a good candidate, but it's hard when you don't know what the other person is into."

Lou's mouth turned into a devilish smirk. "We know what she's obviously not into." She pointed her finger at Berit.

"Really, Lou, feel free to shut up at any time."

"Hey, boss," Dee called from the open patio door, twisting a dish towel nervously in her husky hands. Berit noticed her unease immediately. "You're needed up front."

Berit looked toward the bar and didn't notice a crowd or commotion, so she didn't stand right away. "What's up?"

"Uh, there's a woman here asking for you. She's in pretty bad shape. We tried to calm her down but couldn't."

"Did you get a name? Does she look familiar?"

Dee looked at a loss. She held her hands up and said, "No, maybe?"

"Great," Berit groused. She walked into the bar with her head held high, preparing herself for any scenario. But she couldn't move once she saw a disheveled-looking Lauren at the bar, tearstains on her face. Her heart sank.

She rushed to her and gently took hold of her elbow. She led her to her office without a word, sat her in a chair, and knelt before her. "Lauren, what happened?" Berit felt an odd, protective instinct kick in. She cared for all of her friends fiercely and deeply, but she barely knew Lauren. "Talk to me, please."

Lauren's dark eyes swam beneath heavy tears. She opened her mouth, but no words came out. She shook her head and continued to cry. "It's okay." Berit reached out to place her hand on Lauren's knee but stopped, unsure whether Lauren liked being touched when upset or at all. "Tell me when you're ready."

Lauren sucked in a deep breath and wiped at her face roughly, streaking her eyeliner across her face. Her navy blue blouse was untucked and wrinkled, and her khaki pants had dark spots where her tears had fallen. "I got fired," Lauren squeaked out.

It took Berit a minute to even understand the quiet words. Her eyes went wide. "You got fired? Why? What happened?" Berit winced when Lauren started to cry harder. She backtracked and decided to start with the basics. "Tell me about your job." She reached around Lauren and grabbed a pile of bar napkins from a shelf. They weren't as soft as tissues, but they'd work.

Lauren blew her nose and looked at Berit sadly. "I was a paralegal with a law firm in town. The least popular paralegal in the building, apparently."

"And what happened today?"

"My boss, Mr. Baxter, had a bad habit of forgetting what tasks he assigned to whom. Usually we could easily work around that, but today the other paralegal, Sally, showed up in court with him, and he thought he had told me to appear. I tried to tell him, but all he heard was me blaming him for my unprofessional attitude and fired me."

Berit could think of a few select, colorful names to call this Baxter guy, but she'd save them for later. This time she dared to place her hand on Lauren's. "Did Sally say anything?"

"Kinda. She tried to defend me and explain the mix-up, but Mr. Baxter wouldn't hear it, and he dismissed her. She wasn't there for the rest of the conversation, so she can't be a witness to how he twisted my words." She looked at Berit with worried, wet eyes. "I can't not work, Berit, and no one will hire me on the spot."

"What about unemployment?"

"I doubt I'll qualify because of his side of the story. Even if I fought it and won, I'm looking at weeks, if not months before I see a dime," Lauren said, her voice growing panicked. "I have rent and bills to pay."

Berit could feel the anxiety rolling off Lauren. "Do you have any family that can help?"

Lauren shook her head. "No, it's just me and Mom, and my dad wouldn't be able to send me money for some time."

Berit considered the people she knew and the connections she had made, but not one stood out as an immediate fix. Unless... Berit looked up at Lauren with bright eyes. "I have an idea. It's not perfect, but it'll work."

Lauren looked at her curiously.

"File for unemployment and fight for it," Berit said, "and you can work here while you wait for the verdict. I'll pay you under the table, and you can job search while you're at it, too. I can't pay you as much as you were making as a paralegal, but I'm sure it'll cover your bills." She waited for Lauren to answer, but all she got was a sad stare. "What do you think?"

"I don't know the first thing about bars or serving people."

Berit waved off Lauren's worry. "We're all great teachers."

Lauren chewed on her dry lower lip and looked around for the first time. "Is this your office?"

"Yes. This is my very small office." Berit took Lauren's hand in both of hers. "Let me hire you and help you."

"I don't think us working together is a smart move."

"Why not?" Berit said, trying to mask the disappointment in her voice.

"Because we barely know each other, and it could kill whatever friendship we do have. I could be a terrible employee. I was just fired, for Christ's sake."

Berit held Lauren's hands more tightly. "How well do you think I know any of my employees when I hire them? I have one, maybe two interviews and then make a decision. I know you're responsible, and you very clearly care about being employed. Those are two very important things for a boss," she said. "Please, Lauren, take the job. Even if it's just for a little while." Berit's wide and earnest eyes never strayed from Lauren's.

"I'm a paralegal. I went to school to learn about law."

Berit heard Lauren's sound and solid reasoning, but she also noticed her resolve starting to break down; the tiny upturn of her lips was a dead giveaway. "I'm not offering a career change, just a temporary fix."

Lauren nodded. "Okay," she said with a growing smile.

"If you need to think about it—wait. Did you just accept the job?" Berit felt positively giddy.

"Even with all of my doubts, I think I'd be silly not to. I really like having a roof over my head and being able to buy food." She raised their joined hands. "But this is still just a friend helping a friend, right?"

Berit laughed, happy to see a little of the Lauren she'd come to know return. "Just a friendly gesture, I promise. I actually have a strict no-fraternizing rule here."

"You do?" Lauren's face and voice were heavily laced with shock.

"No, not at all, but I can for you." Berit dropped Lauren's hand and held her own hands up to prove her promise of innocence. She almost yelped when Lauren pulled her into a tight hug. Lauren's hair smelled slightly floral, a bouquet Berit wished she could examine longer, but Lauren pulled away a second later.

"Thank you, Berit, and I'm sorry I just showed up like this. You must think I'm such a mess." Lauren ran her fingers through her hair several times, working out the knots. "I left work and started to head home, but the thought of the bills and of my roommate's deadbeat girlfriend hanging around made me feel worse, so I knew I couldn't go there. My friend Amber didn't pick up, and next on my list was getting drunk and seeing you." Lauren's smile looked small and fragile, as if one more stroke of bad luck would destroy it forever.

Berit licked her lips and stood. She held out a hand for Lauren to take. "I don't recommend getting drunk, but I do have the perfect drink to make you."

Lauren stood slowly with Berit's assistance. She let go of Berit's hand immediately, much to Berit's disappointment. Another moment of contact wouldn't have been so bad.

"Is it strong? Please tell me it's the strongest drink on your menu." Lauren's normally smooth voice had turned hoarse since her breakdown.

Berit led Lauren to an empty seat at the end of the bar closest to the stockroom and her office in case Lauren needed another moment to herself. She held Lauren's upper arms gently as she guided her onto the stool. "This drink is definitely strong. I call it a Long Island Fuck It. It's a Long Island iced tea plus bourbon." Berit started collecting several bottles before returning to Lauren with an empty Collins glass filled halfway with ice. "A little bit of everything," she said as she poured several different liquors onto the ice. "A bit of bourbon, stir it, and top it with a little cola." With a goofy grin, she shot a spritz of cola from the bar's gun.

Lauren laughed lightly. "What? No fancy organic pure sugar cane cola for your Long Island Fuck Its?"

Berit leaned over the bar and got as close to Lauren as she could, whispering, "It tastes just as good. I promise." She pulled back and served the next few women in line. Out of the corner of her eye, she caught Lauren's smile after her first tentative sip.

In between customers, Berit would swing by to check on Lauren, who wasn't in a rush for a second drink. She looked considerably better than when she had come in. Her eyes were still red and puffy, but clear. Berit would make small, terrible jokes every time she stopped by, and Lauren would laugh with ease. Once, when Berit looked back, Lauren had tilted her head and caught the light from overhead. Berit was struck by her beauty. Her lips were swollen from forceful cries and a tiny trace of smudged makeup still clung to her cheeks. No one had ever captured her attention like that.

"Hey, Berit?" Someone pushed at Berit's shoulder. "Berit?"

"Yeah?" Berit turned to find Bellamy staring at her with an empty tray in hand. "Sorry, did you need me?"

Bellamy's full lips split into a salacious grin. "I never *need* you, but wanting you is a different story."

Berit wiped her hands on her towel and tucked it back into her pocket. She used the move as an excuse to check on Lauren once more from afar. "I don't know, Bellamy, I'm pretty sure you told me you needed me the other night." Berit's smile turned smug. "More than once, actually."

Bellamy cleared her throat. "My table is waiting for three shots of Fireball and two Blue Moons."

"Bottle or draft?"

"Draft, one with extra orange."

Berit poured the shots and filled pint glasses with beer.

"Who's your new friend?" Bellamy asked.

The steady stream of Blue Moon stuttered for a fraction of a second. Berit tilted her head casually. "That's Lauren. She's going to come work with us for a bit."

"And she needed a drink right after the interview. Jeez, Berit, that's harsh even for you."

"Ha ha. She got fired and needs the money. So I gave her a job to fix her worries and a drink to drown her sorrows."

Bellamy's expression turned intense, and she stepped close to Berit. "Now you know why I keep ending up in your bed. You're very generous."

Berit blushed and watched Bellamy walk away, holding her tray high above her head and dancing to the latest pop hit that filled the bar. Bellamy never spilled a drop. She had incredible balance, a fact she had actually put on her résumé.

Berit leaned back against the bar. She was trying hard not to concentrate on Lauren, but she couldn't stop looking in that direction. She spotted Lou chatting with Lauren. They were both laughing, which had to be a bad sign. She rushed over. "Lou, Lauren, how's it going?"

"It's going great!" Lou's face was alarmingly bright and cheery.

Lauren was a bit less animated. "I was just telling Lou you offered me a job and how if you had done the same a week ago, I would've never accepted."

"Because her first impression of you was you're a womanizing dick," Lou said. Berit's head fell back, and she let out a long groan.

"I didn't use those exact words." Lauren said. "I just said you struck me as someone who'd offer niceties in exchange for *favors*."

"Sexual favors," Lou added. "This is so good. I'm never going to let you forget this."

"Lauren," Berit said with a straight face and serious tone, "I've never formally introduced you to Lou, my sister."

Lauren's face paled. "Oh, my God. Oh, no. I'm so sorry."

Lou waved her off. "It's nothing I've never heard before."

Berit rolled her eyes.

"Seriously," Lou said. "I haven't laughed that hard in a long while."

Berit watched the confusion on Lauren's face as she looked between them and smiled knowingly. No one would pin them as sisters. Lou was on the darker end of the spectrum, with brown hair and eyes. She had a longer, skinny nose and thinner lips than Berit, and her hair didn't have a fraction of the wave Berit's did.

"Who's older?" Lauren said.

"Berit is," Lou said, flicking her thumb in the direction of Berit.

"Do you have any other siblings?"

Berit laughed. "Oh yeah. We're the two girls, and there's three boys."

"Wow," Lauren said with her mouth slightly agape. "Two out of five are girls, and they're both gay. That's something."

"Oh. I'm not a lesbian."

Berit made a dismissive hand gesture. "Yes, she is, she just hasn't accepted it yet."

"No, I'm not," Lou said directly to Lauren. "*She* just hasn't accepted that yet. Now, if you two will excuse me, I have work to do."

An easy silence fell over Berit and Lauren. The bar was busy, but not busy enough to tear Berit from Lauren's company. She was beginning to really enjoy this new easiness blossoming between them. "What about you?" Berit said. "Any siblings?"

"I have a younger brother, Jack, who's somewhere in the world right now."

"Is he in the military or something?"

Lauren snickered. "No, not Jack. After my parents' divorce, my dad went back to England and Jack said he was going with him. He stayed all of two months before deciding world traveling was his thing and took off. We get postcards or rushed phone calls from time to time, but that's it."

Berit had so many questions. "Did you say *back to* England?"

"Yes. I'm originally from Birmingham."

"I knew I caught a small accent. When did you come here?"

Lauren nodded shyly, and it was adorable. "I was six and Jack was four. He sounds much more American, but his accent will come out from time to time and changes depending on where he's been. Mine has lingered a bit."

"I love it," Berit said dreamily. She stood straight up when she realized what she said. She cleared her throat and stammered through her next question awkwardly. "What did—what caused your family to move here?"

"My dad worked for Boeing, and they offered him a position here. It seemed like a great opportunity and family adventure. My mom loved living here, but my dad missed our life back in Birmingham. That stress eventually drove them apart." Berit's eyes softened, and she reached for Lauren's hand on the bar top. Lauren withdrew. "Wow, what did you say was in these things?" Lauren tapped her empty glass. "I'm talking too much."

Berit definitely wanted to argue. She wanted to know everything about Lauren. With each layer she learned, she knew another lay just beneath. But Lauren had been through enough that day. Berit wanted to be a source of comfort for her. Berit stared into Lauren's dark eyes and felt an electric pull, a connection like a string tying around her heart. Lauren stood, prompting Berit to move as well.

"Do you want to stick around for closing? I can show you around and get you comfortable in the space."

"No," Lauren said with a shocking amount of force. "I should, uh, I'm going to get going. I'm exhausted after today. When do you want me to start?"

Lauren's sudden attitude change confused Berit. Perhaps her family was a sore subject. Berit could definitely understand that. "Would tomorrow work for you? I'd like to get you started as soon as possible so your income isn't affected too dramatically."

"I really can't thank you enough, Berit." Lauren's smile reached her eyes, which was enough to comfort Berit's worry.

"That's what friends are for." Berit wished Lauren a quick good night and hated that the opportunity for a hug had slipped through her fingers. She scratched the back of her head and walked to her office, ready to lose herself to the prep work that accompanied every new hire.

Chapter Eight

"Okay. What are the things you will absolutely *not* do today?" Lauren said to her reflection in the small rectangular mirror on the visor of her car. "You will not insult Berit to Lou or Lou to Berit. You will not spill your entire sob story to Berit every time she blinks those damn hazel eyes at you. And you definitely will not flirt. Especially not with Berit."

Lauren had scared herself the night before. She felt her resolve slip and her chest grew warm when Berit looked at her. A moment of vulnerability had almost shaken her foundation of responsible decisions. Berit was acting true to her word and being an exemplary friend—both a relief and disappointment to Lauren. She'd miss the attention, but now they'd be working together, and a platonic friendship was for the best. Lauren checked her hair one more time before getting out of her car.

Berit had given her vague directions for her first day. She told her to show up at four and that was it. Lauren checked the clock on her phone. She was five minutes early, but other cars were in the parking lot, so she approached the back door to the Dollhouse. The air smelled slightly putrid thanks to a nearby dumpster. Lauren took a deep breath anyway before knocking.

An attractive African American woman opened the door and smiled brightly. Lauren recognized her as a waitress and felt welcomed instantly. "You must be Lauren," she said. She stuck out her hand and Lauren took it right away. "I'm Bellamy. Berit told me you'd be here at four." She held open the door for Lauren and locked it once Lauren was inside.

"It's very nice to meet you, Bellamy. I recognize you from the times I've been here. Don't tell the rest," Lauren said in a low voice. "You're one of my favorite servers."

Bellamy's smile grew larger, something Lauren thought impossible. "And I have a feeling you're my new favorite coworker," Bellamy added with a wink. Her long lashes were hypnotic. Bellamy was the kind of beautiful that made Lauren's brain slow down. Bellamy placed her hand on Lauren's shoulder and led her through the back room of the Dollhouse.

Lauren paused briefly upon stepping into the stockroom. "Wow…" The room was like a museum of modern alcohol.

"Berit takes her alcohol storage very seriously."

"Apparently."

Bellamy ran her fingers along a well-stocked shelf. "This is where we keep everything we unbox after deliveries. I'm sure you noticed a few stacks of boxes when you first walked in." Lauren nodded. "Those are recent deliveries or overstock we'll get to eventually. Everything is organized by category: rum, vodka, et cetera. And then alphabetized within their subcategory. Down on the lower shelves is the beer, since they are usually kept in a case of some sort."

Lauren watched Bellamy move about, switching her attention between Bellamy and thinking of Berit and her meticulous ways. "What goes in those?" Lauren said, pointing to two large refrigerators and what looked like their baby fridge beside them.

"That's where we keep things either frozen or cold, and the little one is a wine cooler. Adorable, isn't it?" Lauren and Bellamy smiled fondly at the inanimate object before moving on. Bellamy pointed down a small hall and said, "The employee break room and bathrooms are down there. Berit is all about us having our own space we don't have to share with strangers, which I appreciate beyond words."

Lauren nodded in agreement. She was amazed by how much thought Berit had put into the layout and design of the bar. "I know

Berit's office," Lauren said with a nod to the closed door. "That's where I had my meltdown." She could now laugh about how embarrassingly broken she was the night before. She had never lost herself like that in front of someone she was just getting to know. Berit made it easy, though. She made Lauren feel more okay than she had in a long time. That made her a great friend.

"Brace yourself." Bellamy stopped just before they stepped through the swinging door separating the employee-only space from the public. "The Dollhouse looks very different during the day. It's almost like watching Santa take off his beard to have a cigarette—the magic disappears."

Lauren shook with laughter at the visual. "I'm ready." Bellamy pushed the door open and waved her through. A resounding round of hoots and hollers erupted in the space. Lauren's eyes went wide and her heart pumped.

"Welcome aboard, Lauren Daly!" Berit shouted, motioning to the few people around her. "Everyone, I'd like to introduce you to Lauren. She'll be working with us for a little while. Lauren, this is Dee," Berit said with her hands on the shoulders of a short butch woman.

"Hi, Dee. Nice to meet you," Lauren said. Dee had the greenest eyes Lauren had ever seen, made more vibrant by her black short hair and more tattoos than the rest of the staff combined. Lauren felt her bashfulness rise when Dee winked at her.

"You already know Bellamy and Lou." Berit made finger guns at the two women in question. "Monica, Cynthia, and Talia will be serving on the floor along with Bellamy tonight." Berit tapped their shoulders as she announced them, and Lauren tried her hardest to keep up and lock the names in her memory. "Dee, Lou, and I will be behind the bar. I'd like for you to shadow Bellamy for half the night and then get behind the bar with us for the rest. How's that sound?"

Lauren's head was spinning. "Uh, yeah, sure. Sounds good."

"I'd like for you to stay until closing, but just let me know if you need to tap out earlier. The first day can be overwhelming." Berit's look was serious and soft, easing Lauren's growing anxiety.

"You're lucky to be starting on a Tuesday," Monica said. Or

maybe it was Cynthia. "I started on a Saturday and I only lasted four hours."

Lauren felt reassured. At least she wouldn't be the first to leave early if need be. "Good to know. Thanks, M—" Lauren stopped when she saw Berit shaking her head. "Cynthia, thank you."

"Nice save," Berit said in a loud whisper. Lauren wanted to smack her forehead, but everyone around her laughed and moved on. Berit clapped loudly. "While they prep the bar and slice garnishes, let's get you dressed."

Lauren looked down at her jeans and T-shirt and back to Berit in confusion. Although Berit's fitted T-shirt looked a little better, the way it clung to her small breasts and toned biceps. Lauren swallowed hard at Berit's unexpected appraisal. She thought of the short shorts Bellamy was wearing and how Monica's toned stomach looked in a crop top. She swallowed again. "What will I be wearing?"

Berit's smirk was the textbook definition of salacious, and it fell away in an instant. "I'm going to hook you up with the uniform." Lauren was about to argue about the obvious lack of uniform she'd seen so far, but Berit beat her to it. "No one is required to wear Dollhouse apparel *except* new employees. It helps you stand out."

"Like a big ol' Student Driver sticker on the bumper of a car on the highway. Got it." Lauren wanted to roll her eyes, but she knew Berit had a reason. She was in training and everyone in the building needed to know it. Berit reached into a tall cabinet standing against the back wall of her office. From where Lauren stood, she could see stacks of shirts, a safe on the floor, and paper supplies. But her eyes wandered to Berit's dimpled lower back, bared by her raised shirt hem, and the way her jeans sagged just slightly on her narrow hips. What was with her?

"Once I kick you from the nest and you're flying on your own, you can wear street clothes."

"I'm not dressing promiscuously," Lauren blurted out.

Berit turned slowly. She stared at Lauren, befuddled. "Okay," she said, drawing out the word.

Lauren stood her ground. "I see how you have your staff dress, and I'm telling you right now, I'm not comfortable with it." Yes, this job was an act of charity, but Lauren wasn't going to compromise herself.

"Take this and sit." Berit threw a black T-shirt at her and motioned to the chair in front of her desk. "We need to have a serious talk—employer to employee."

Lauren sat heavily and her posture remained rigid. She had never seen Berit look so serious.

"I'm not hard on my staff. I expect very little, but the expectations I do have are important to me. I expect everyone to be on time for their shift, give or take five minutes because life doesn't always go as planned. I respect my staff members and expect respect in return. If you need time off, let me know at least a week in advance, preferably more, but I can work with a week. I don't allow anyone to drink while they're on the clock. That rule gets a little tricky when customers are flirting with you and buy an extra drink with you in mind. Just blame the boss, that's what I do." Berit cracked a small smile. "Always card patrons. Unless they are a regular you've seen a dozen times or more, I want you to card them. If they give you a hard time, you can grab me or whoever's working the door that day and we'll take care of it. I've seen what happens to a bar's reputation for one underage slipup. That will not happen here."

Lauren let out a breath of relief. "I understand—"

"I'm not done," Berit said with a hand in the air. "Sex sells, we all know that. I encourage a sexy atmosphere, but I don't do anything to cause discomfort. Some of my employees dress provocatively but appropriately. I've never asked them to. I never even uttered a suggestion. Some do it because the tips are better when a little more skin is on display, and some do it because they're more comfortable and it makes them feel good." Berit leaned forward on her elbows and stared into Lauren's eyes. She looked fierce. "In my bar, women make their own choices."

Lauren felt like a scolded child. "I'm sorry." She lowered her head. "This is all new to me. I'm used to offices and suits. I barely own any casual clothes."

Berit sat back, seemingly more relaxed. "I'll give you a few shirts. Those with a couple pairs of jeans will have you set for a while." Berit looked over Lauren's upper body. Lauren shrank at the attention. "You're going to look good in my shirt." Every sliver of ice fell away from Berit's demeanor, and her unrelenting charm was back in place.

"You already forgot about your special no-fraternizing rule, I see."

"Stating facts is not fraternizing. We're friends, which means I can share my opinions with you. I have shirts in black, burgundy, violet, and navy blue. I'll give you one of each." Berit stacked the shirts on her desk before turning back to Lauren with bright, excited eyes. "Let's get your first day started."

Lauren took a deep breath in an attempt to muster up a little confidence. She could do this job. It wouldn't be a quick adjustment, but she would eventually adapt. She had Berit on her side and a friendly group of women willing to help her succeed. Lauren smiled. "When do we open?"

"We've been open since four."

"But..." Not one soul had entered the bar.

"Never judge a night by its opening. Trust me."

Why did Lauren feel like she had just jinxed something, big-time?

The mood inside the Dollhouse was the complete opposite four hours later. Lauren raced about, trying to help out the best she could. The whole time she heard Berit saying "I told you so" in her head. Customers started to trickle in the moment five o'clock hit, and they hadn't slowed down since. The night wasn't as busy as a Friday or Saturday, but for Lauren's first day, it was busy enough.

Bellamy had been incredibly patient and easy on Lauren. She let her chat with a table or two and carry a few drinks. Learning the lingo from Bellamy helped Lauren grow a little more comfortable with her new role. Working in a bar was more laid back than an office, but no less professional. You had to be kind and engaging with everyone, even the people with personalities as interesting as a dish rag. Bellamy's knowledge of the specials and drink recipes impressed Lauren on several occasions, and it went far beyond simple job responsibilities. Lauren could tell Bellamy genuinely loved her job.

"So how long have you worked here?" Lauren said during a serving lull. Everyone had a drink and seemed to be content for the moment.

"Almost a year," Bellamy said. She took a sip from one of two waters Berit had set on the bar for them.

"You seem to really like it. You're very good at your job."

Bellamy spared her a small chuckle. "I love it here. I'm paid fair, the tips are great, and I'm around wonderful people who make coming to work easy. Especially Berit." Bellamy turned to watch Berit charm a few customers.

Lauren could see the attraction on Bellamy's face, but she wasn't yet on that level with Bellamy to ask her about it. Her new friend Berit, however…

"Hey, Lauren," Berit shouted over the noise filling the bar. She bent her index finger in a come hither motion. "Bellamy's had enough fun. You're mine now."

Lauren looked to Bellamy for help, but she only received a pat on the back for luck. She walked around the bar and came to stand next to Berit, who was looking at her expectantly. "What?"

"Lauren, I'd like you to meet my new friends, Harper and Genevieve." Berit motioned to the couple sitting at the bar. Harper was beautifully dapper, and Genevieve was a gorgeous strawberry-blonde. They were both smiling brilliantly as Lauren took each of their hands in turn to shake. "Harper runs *Outshore Magazine* along with her wife, Genevieve, who happens to love gummy bears." Lauren looked at Genevieve again.

"It's true," she said with a dainty giggle, one Harper obviously found endearing. "I heard about the Dollhouse and a gummy bear martini that's on the menu. I told Harper we had to come down and try it."

"And I'd like to feature a review in *Outshore*." Harper's offer surprised Lauren, but definitely excited Berit. "I'm not sure why I haven't heard of this place until now, but I think it's time for our readers to know about you, too."

"Let's get started," Berit said with bright eyes.

Lauren stayed back as Berit whipped up two different gummy bear martinis, insisting Genevieve try both variations before she decided. Lauren laughed along with Harper as she poked fun at Genevieve's girlish excitement over the beverage. Genevieve loved the drink, but Lauren loved the couple fawning over Berit and the Dollhouse. Watching Berit revel in but be humbled by her success was the highlight of Lauren's first night.

"I've always had a soft spot for businesses like yours," Harper said as she placed a few bills on the bar top. She shot Berit a stern yet soft look when she tried to push the cash away. "There's not enough privately owned and cared-for places like this anymore. Between your drinks and the exposure you'll get in *Outshore*, you're bound to be a great success, Berit." Harper extended her hand and shook Berit's with vigor. Genevieve and Lauren shared a polite smile.

"Thank you," Berit said as softly as the music and the bustle around her would allow. Berit seemed to be at a loss for words for the first time since Lauren had known her.

Harper handed Berit a business card. "I'll make sure you get a copy of the issue you're featured in. Email me and let me know what you think."

Berit took the card. "Will do."

They all exchanged goodbyes, and Berit continued to stare at the card long after Harper and Genevieve were out the door. "I think someone has a crush," Lauren said.

"What?" Berit grabbed empty glasses from the bar and started to rinse them. "On who? Genevieve?"

"Harper."

Berit laughed and handed the glasses to Lauren to load into the dishwasher. "In case you didn't know, she's not really my type. Stem glasses always go on the bottom rack."

Lauren did as instructed. "A business crush—oh! A business boner. You totally have a business boner for Harper." Lauren couldn't control her giggling.

Berit shook her head but didn't deny Lauren's accusation. "Shut up and get back to work. You still have a lot to learn."

Lauren saluted Berit and followed her the rest of the night, wishing she'd had the foresight to bring a small notebook so she'd remember every tidbit of information.

By the time Lauren fell into bed that evening, her feet were screaming and she was exhausted. Her time behind the bar was spent ducking flying bottles of liquor and retrieving bottles of beer when needed. Her one-on-one interactions with Berit were minimal after Harper and Genevieve had left, but each had taught her something new. Berit was very professional, which was the biggest surprise of the night. Lauren knew Berit from both a customer and employee perspective, and she enjoyed watching the bartender's dynamic shift and sway as she worked. Lauren's eyes grew heavy and she dozed to the memory of Berit's smile.

CHAPTER NINE

Lauren survived her first day and first weekend at the Dollhouse, barely. By the time Monday rolled around, Lauren was aching with exhaustion. She rolled around her queen-sized bed, trying to stay in that fuzzy comfort of near sleep, but her body was still clinging to being a morning person. She was used to waking up at seven in the morning, not finally falling asleep at four.

Every noise in the house irritated Lauren more. She needed more sleep, and her lower body was killing her. Going from a desk job to standing for the majority of an eight- to ten-hour shift was not friendly on your back, legs, or feet. Lauren rolled and cracked her ankles before flopping to her other side. Again. The sound of her bedroom door creaking open got her attention. Jorge's curiosity had probably gotten the best of him. It was worrisome when the other breadwinner in the house stayed home for days at a time.

"Go away," she said, her sleepy voice mimicking the croak of a frog.

"Oh. I'm sorry." The low voice was much more feminine than Jorge's.

"Rebecca?" Lauren uncovered her head and stared at her ex-girlfriend with one open eye. Her hair was disheveled and covered her face like a web. She fought to blow the strands from her sight. "What's up?"

"Nothing, sorry." Rebecca started to leave.

Lauren sat up. "Wait. You obviously came in here for

something." The blankets fell around her waist, revealing the thin, loose tank she wore to bed, but Lauren didn't care about her state of undress. Rebecca had seen it all before.

"I just…" Rebecca picked at a chip in the doorframe. "Sometimes I come in here to sleep once you leave for work." She looked embarrassed to share this confession. "It's way more comfortable than the couch."

The small window above Lauren's bed illuminated Rebecca. She was wearing a large sweatshirt and not much more. She had the longest legs Lauren had ever seen. They were smooth and tempting. Lauren took a deep breath and rubbed at her puffy face roughly. She pulled back the corner of the covers and said, "Get in, but don't move around too much. I'm trying to get another couple hours of sleep." Lauren fell to her side, facing the wall.

"Thank you." Rebecca settled into her usual side of the mattress and remained still, much to Lauren's delight. The sound of lawn mowers and birds filled the still room. Lauren felt her body relaxing, closer and closer to the point of sleep. "Why aren't you at work?"

Lauren opened her eyes and stared at the wall. "I got a different job. I work nights now." She didn't want to give up many more details. She wasn't embarrassed by her new job, but she enjoyed having this secret life with a new friend she didn't have to share with anyone else. Lauren closed her eyes, and Rebecca didn't say anything more.

The mattress shifted as Rebecca moved. Lauren sighed and pulled the covers around her more tightly. Her eyes flew open when Rebecca pressed her body against hers. Lauren loved the intimacy of being in a relationship, not just the sex, but the touching and caressing, the little things no one else was privy to.

"I don't think Savannah would be happy right now." Picturing her helped Lauren resist the urge to push her backside into the welcoming bend of Rebecca's pelvis.

"There's nothing wrong with cuddling," Rebecca said sleepily.

So many things were wrong with them cuddling, but Lauren was too tired to care. Rebecca threw her arm around Lauren's waist and nuzzled her neck. Lauren hated melting into her touch so easily.

She didn't want Rebecca. Lauren just wanted someone to hold her when her life was spinning out of control.

Lauren held out hope Berit would stay true to her word and find her someone. She was ready to forget how well she fit into Rebecca, and how quickly Rebecca had moved on from her.

❖

Berit sat on the small balcony of her apartment, her bare feet stretched onto the railing. She scribbled in a small notebook with a black pen; a red pen was tucked behind her ear. She was working on drink specials for an upcoming theme night. Berit loved theme nights, but they took so much organization, she didn't throw them often. She tossed the pad onto a small table beside her chair and stood to stretch out her back.

Since she'd been planning on a lazy Monday afternoon, Berit wore her most raggedy jeans, a sports bra, and a muscle tank. The sun had finally taken the morning chill out of the air. She checked her phone as she walked into the kitchen for a coffee refill. She poured the last drops from the French press and added a teaspoon of sugar before taking a sip. Berit found herself floating between busy and bored. She drank her lukewarm coffee and looked out the open sliding door. The city was awake, but she didn't feel like going out. She wasn't in the mood to work on a new recipe or continue planning a theme night. Her Nook was filled with unread books, but none of them called out to her. The DVR was nearing capacity, but that wasn't enticing either.

Berit wondered how Lauren was spending her day off. Berit was sure she'd be tired today, but it was just after noon, so she dared to send a quick message. She slid her phone over and typed, *Good afternoon. How are you?* Berit stared at her phone, waiting impatiently for any sign of life on Lauren's end. Three minutes was too long. She started typing again. *Hope you're enjoying your day off.* Berit drummed her fingers on the countertop beside her phone. Crumbs stuck to her fingertips. She stood up straight and looked down at Hugo, who stood faithfully by her feet.

"When was the last time I cleaned this place?" Hugo tilted his head in thought. "Guess I found something to keep me busy."

Berit's apartment was small but had enough space for her and Hugo to live happily. The appliances were new, the hardwood floors had been refinished before she'd moved in, and the open floor plan allowed her to use the entire apartment as a living space. Her bedroom and the bathroom were the only separate rooms. A smaller apartment meant less time cleaning, whenever Berit actually got around to it. She turned on her favorite playlist before grabbing the vacuum, dusters, and cleaning spray from the closet.

By the time the area rugs were dog hair free and the kitchen peninsula spotless, Lauren had finally answered her.

Hey, I'm a little slow to get up, but good. You? Berit smiled knowingly at the screen. Lauren had had to make a lot of adjustments as of late, but her sleeping schedule had to be the hardest to get used to. Berit was a natural night owl, but not everyone was.

I bet you're exhausted. The first week is always the hardest. I promise it'll get easier.

And if it doesn't?

Berit laughed. She could picture Lauren's disbelieving face. *You'll be even more motivated to get back to an office job.*

What have you been up to? Berit read Lauren's message and looked at the notepad she left on the balcony. She walked and grabbed it before plopping down on the couch. She read over the list of drinks again and came up with an idea.

I was working and cleaning. Do you have plans today, and if not, are you opposed to seeing your boss on your day off? Berit was smirking. She really enjoyed referring to herself as Lauren's boss.

I'm not opposed to seeing you, but I'd prefer to stay out of the bar for the day.

Consider it done! Berit nearly jumped with excitement. *I'll send you my address. Come over around three. We'll have a study date. I'll make lunch.* Berit was already getting herself and Hugo ready for the short walk to the store.

You want me to come over to study?

And for lunch, yes.

Berit...

Berit knew she was about to be scolded. *Just come over at three and stop having a dirty mind.* Just for fun, Berit decided to add a winking face. She didn't even read Lauren's reply before leaving for the grocery store.

Berit didn't mind that Lauren showed up closer to three thirty. "Hi," she said as she swung the door open. Lauren looked phenomenal in a simple blue oxford and dark jeans. "Come in. Hugo couldn't wait to see you again." Lauren stepped around Berit wordlessly and stopped just inside the apartment. Her face was blank and she held on to her purse with a death-like grip. "Are you okay?"

"I'm fine," Lauren said, crouching down so Hugo would come running over to her. "Just an odd morning. Now I'm tense and in a weird mood."

"What happened?" Berit knew Lauren's living situation wasn't great, but she also knew it wasn't her place to pry. "You don't have to tell me if you don't want. Sit down." She motioned to the couch and stopped in the kitchen. "Would you like a drink? I have a little bit of everything, nonalcoholic beverages included."

Lauren sat stiffly, her hands never straying far from Hugo's head. He jumped up on the couch to sit beside her. "I'll just have a water for now."

Berit strode into the living room with two bottles of water and sat not too far from Lauren. Hugo was delighted to be sandwiched between the two women. "He's going to forget all about me if you keep scratching behind his ears like that." Lauren flicked his big, upright ears playfully. "Is everything okay at home?"

Lauren took the bottle of water, removed the top, and drank a quarter of it before answering. "Just as weird and uncomfortable as ever. What are those?" she said, pointing to two stacks of notecards on Berit's coffee table.

"Those are study materials."

"You weren't kidding about studying."

"Why would I be kidding about studying? The first set contains various liquors with a quick description and few popular drinks made with them. There's also a few wines and beers that are good to know. The other stack is recipe cards for the drinks we make the most at the Dollhouse. I'm going to help you learn as much as you can in one afternoon. And I'll feed you, of course."

"Would you mind feeding me first? I haven't eaten yet today, and my brain will be useless if I don't eat soon."

"Sure." Berit jumped up from the couch and rushed to the refrigerator. "Is there anything you don't eat?"

"There's a lot of things I shouldn't eat, but I can't think of anything I don't eat," Lauren said over her shoulder.

Berit wondered if they'd ever have a conversation where Lauren didn't manage to pick at herself or put herself down. Between Berit's friendship and a date with someone great, Berit hoped to bolster Lauren's spirit. "I made us fresh mozzarella sandwiches." She walked back to the couch with the sandwiches she'd prepared minutes before Lauren arrived. Hugo perked up, but at Berit's firm glance, he lay back down. "They have fresh basil and roasted red peppers with a little balsamic on the bread."

"Thank you." Lauren took a bite out of her sandwich without a second of hesitation. "You have a really cute place. It's cozy."

Berit waited until she was done chewing to talk. "It's just enough space for me and my man. I love it here."

"What's it like living alone?"

"It's great." Berit winced. She shouldn't brag. "I do get lonely sometimes, but that's a rare occurrence with this rug rat running around." Berit nodded toward Hugo.

"I'm sure Bellamy helps too," Lauren said with innocent eyes.

Berit almost choked on her sandwich. "Bellamy?"

"Don't even try to deny it. I saw the way she was looking at you. You're definitely not just her boss. So what's going on there?"

Berit took another bite of her sandwich to buy her time. She wasn't going to lie to Lauren, but she didn't feel comfortable with complete honesty either. She swallowed and decided to play it vague. "We spend time together."

"And you're both happy with that arrangement?"

"Very," Berit said emphatically. This topic was uncomfortable. She wanted Lauren to see her for who she really was, not the playgirl she assumed her to be. "Bellamy actually has feelings for someone else."

"Really?" Lauren seemed genuinely shocked, which made Berit feel good. "Someone at the bar?"

"She refuses to tell me." Berit shrugged. She noticed Lauren's empty plate. "Wow, you weren't kidding about being hungry."

"Yeah, I probably should've warned you my appetite is the least ladylike thing about me."

Berit couldn't contain the warm smile she shot Lauren. Lauren's charm level just went from a ten to an eleven. Berit's chest felt pleasantly tight, a feeling she recognized immediately. She was smitten, but she had to annihilate that because being smitten usually turned into having a crush, and a crush led to feelings. Feelings developed into... "Love this sandwich. Did you want more?"

"No, I'm fine now. Thank you." Lauren handed Berit her plate and reached for a stack of notecards. "I haven't used flashcards since college."

Berit dropped the dishes in the sink and ran to grab the cards from Lauren's hands. "Hey, hey, hey! Give those to me. You're not allowed to peek. That's cheating." Berit tapped the cards on the table and sat up straight to mimic a talk show host. Lauren's giggle made her weak inside. "Okay, Lauren, let's talk about rum, baby."

For over four hours, Berit and Lauren talked about liquor, work, and life. Berit didn't learn much more about Lauren's personal life than she already knew. Berit played along, worrying more about Lauren's comfort than anything else. She tried to keep the conversation light while giving Lauren the opportunity to get to know her better.

"Growing up in a house with five kids is a challenge. I thought for sure my parents were done at four, but then Matthew came along...oops." Berit relaxed against the arm of her couch and smiled to Lauren as she mirrored her exact position on the opposite end.

"Matthew?" Lauren said. Berit nodded. "Matthew Matthews?"

"Yes. Matthew Matthews is my youngest brother. In my parents' defense, they had already named four kids. Can't really blame them for their lack of creativity."

Lauren giggled. "I guess. What other names did they come up with?"

"They started strong with me and named the first boy Jeffrey Junior after my dad, but we all call him JJ. I'm just happy I wasn't the first boy. I would not do well being named after my dad." Berit took a sip of her Guinness she had opened earlier to use as an example during their study session. The dark beer had since grown warm, but Berit couldn't let it go to waste.

"Strained relationship?"

Berit gave Lauren a thumbs-up. "We have a rocky history, one that almost killed my chances of owning a business." Berit felt her mood start to nosedive and shook it off. "But that's no fun to talk about. Let's get back to the names from the zoo I grew up in."

Lauren laughed. "I already know Lou."

"Lou is actually short for Louise, and if you really want to piss her off, say 'Jeez Louise' around her. It's hilarious."

"I'll do no such thing," Lauren said with a shake of her head. "I adore Lou."

Berit rolled her eyes. "Of course you do."

"And what about the other boy in the family?"

"Bartholomew."

"You're kidding."

"Why do you never believe me when it comes to names?"

"Because you're funny and a tease."

Berit held Lauren's stare for a second before looking at her beer. She found herself struggling to remain friendly and not flirt. "You're not wrong, but I'm not kidding, although I'm sure Bart wishes I was. He was teased mercilessly throughout school."

"I think Bartholomew is classy and old fashioned."

"Bart the fart," was all Berit said. She drank the rest of her beer as Lauren fell into a fit of giggles. Berit knew she'd have to find Lauren the most incredible woman on planet earth to date, because that was who she deserved. Berit started to ache at the prospect but forced herself to smile for the rest of the afternoon.

When Lauren announced she was going to hit the road, Berit slipped Hugo into his harness so they could both walk Lauren outside. Berit and Lauren stood beside her car in the cool, early night. Berit watched the streetlights dance in Lauren's dark eyes. She wasn't ready to say goodbye, but she knew Lauren wouldn't, shouldn't stay any longer. Hugo was sniffing around them. He was the perfect distraction from the awkwardness.

"He'd spend every minute sniffing the sidewalk if I'd allow him."

"Can you blame him? There's probably so much information built into every sniff. For all we know he could be picking up the number for a cute Yorkie right now."

"I think he's more of a poodle guy, but what do I know?" Berit watched Lauren's face. She seemed lighter than when she arrived. If nothing else, Berit was happy she could do that for Lauren. "Today was fun, Lauren. I think you'll be on your own behind the bar in no time."

"Not too soon. I still have a lot to learn, but you're a great teacher. You really know your stuff. If I didn't know any better, I'd say you loved your job."

The light breeze pulled Berit's wavy hair back from her forehead. "I do," she said with pride. "I loved bartending even before I owned my own bar. I get to be surrounded by people and let my creative side loose, and coming up with new cocktail recipes satisfies the mad scientist within. I couldn't imagine doing anything else with my life."

"The Dollhouse is a great place, and now I see why. Good management goes a long way." Lauren reached out to squeeze Berit's colorful forearm as she spoke. "As devastated as I was to be fired, I'm happy for the opportunity be a part of such a place. Thank you, Berit."

Berit was taken by the emotion in Lauren's eyes. She'd seen her cry before, but this wasn't sadness. "I'm happy I can help. I'll see you tomorrow, at work."

As quickly as the storm of emotion entered Lauren's eyes, it left. "See you tomorrow, boss. Good night, Hugo." Lauren pulled away and got in her car. Berit focused on how cold her forearm felt as Lauren drove away.

Chapter Ten

"Did you check these over yet?" Lauren picked up two stacks of shot glasses. Lou nodded, giving Lauren permission to stock them in the bar. "Berit's attention to detail still amazes me. I don't think I've known someone so conscious of water spots before."

"She's certainly meticulous," Lou said with a laugh. "But only here. Her apartment is usually a wreck. I sound like our mom every time I'm over there. 'Berit, when was the last time you vacuumed? Berit, there's dog hair all over the couch. Berit, dishes don't do themselves.' She brings out the worst in me."

Lauren creased her brow. "Huh."

"Huh, what?"

"I didn't get that impression when I was over there the other day. Her apartment was very clean. I left with minimal dog hair on my clothes." Lauren wiped the surface of the high bar chairs. "Do you think this theme will be successful?"

Lou was unmoving and staring at Lauren. "Yes," she said. "Tropical themes are fun in the summer, and people love drinks with tiny umbrellas. When were you in Berit's apartment?"

She considered Lou's question a bit odd. "Last week. She was helping me learn about drinks and stuff." Lauren felt herself start to get defensive, like she had to explain herself. "She invited me over and I had nothing else to do."

Lou put her hands up. "At least you gave her a reason to clean." Lou's words were innocuous enough, but the seed had been planted. Lauren grew mildly irritated.

She felt like she wasn't allowed to be friends with another lesbian without there being more. "I don't have any background in the service industry, and I've never once considered what goes into the cocktails I drink."

"I was wondering how you were making Bay Breezes already. Great job, by the way. Not one got sent back. That's very good for a beginner."

"Thank you," Lauren said with a frown but obvious pride in her voice. This conversation was confusing her, so she changed the subject. "May I ask you a personal question?"

"You can ask, but I can't promise I'll answer." Lou placed small tiki lights along the bar and on the surrounding tables.

Lauren looked around to make sure they were alone. So far she'd been scheduled only when Berit was working, but she was going through opening procedures with Lou this Friday. "You're not gay?" Lou shook her head. "Or bisexual? Or pansexual or any of the other letters of the rainbow?"

Lou laughed and then sighed. "Nope. As much as I hate men sometimes, I love them. Everything about them," she said, walking closer to Lauren. "I even love their body hair." Lou laughed at Lauren's disgusted shiver.

"Then why are you working here? No offense, of course, I just mean—" What did Lauren mean? "I know Berit is your sister, but I'm curious."

Lou took a seat at one of the tables and encouraged Lauren to join her. "The story of the Dollhouse is for Berit to tell, but when she wanted to open her own business, I knew I'd be there to help any way I could. She's my big sister. I've looked up to her since before I could walk." Lou's eyes were so big with admiration, Lauren's heart swelled. She had never known that kind of sibling bond. "Berit came up short financially, and I stepped in to close the gap. Thirty percent of the Dollhouse is mine."

"You're business partners?"

Lou nodded. "I couldn't imagine a better person to go into business with. Berit is brilliant and driven, and don't you ever repeat any of what I'm saying now."

Lauren zipped her finger across her mouth.

"I knew whatever she was getting herself into, it'd be successful."

"Even if it was a lesbian bar?"

"Even then. Plus, women are gorgeous and easy to talk to. I love working here. When a customer is coming on strong, I still feel safe. The attention I get when I'm working the bar makes me feel great."

"There's definitely some good genes in the Matthews bloodline." Lauren blushed at her own words. "Sorry."

Lou smiled brightly, her teeth as perfect as her sister's. Lauren was envious. "Don't apologize. Being complimented by women has never made me uncomfortable."

"I'll keep that in mind, but I still don't want to sound like I'm hitting on my boss's sister. Wait, if you're Berit's partner, that means you're my boss too, right?" Lauren knew she looked ridiculously confused.

Lou waved her off. "No. I told Berit when we signed all the paperwork that I wanted nothing to do with the administrative side. I just wanted a steady job and a cut of the profits," she said with a shrug.

Lauren could only imagine what those profits looked like. "From what I've seen, you both deserve your success."

"Thank you. Lauren, I know Berit is—"

"Here," Lauren said when she spotted Berit coming in the back door with Bellamy in tow. "With Bellamy." Lauren felt her mood sour slightly, but chalked it up to jealousy because at least one of them was getting laid. "Hey, guys."

"Ladies," Berit greeted with her usual charm. "The place looks great. Are we ready for a tropical getaway?" Berit looked at the decorations: light-up palm trees in every corner, paper lanterns, tiki lights, and tropical outfits. "I know Bellamy is," Berit said, biting her lower lip.

"I plan on making this theme night very profitable," Bellamy said, shimmying out of her shirt to reveal a coconut bra. The natural cups held on to her perfectly perky breasts and nothing but twine secured the piece to her body. Lauren just stared and worried the cups would fall away from her bare skin, but they held on. Bellamy would earn a lot of tips, that's for sure.

"You're looking good," Lou said. "Berit looks like she stepped right out of *Summer School*. Mark Harmon, eat your heart out."

Lauren tore her attention away from Bellamy's bare skin to catch Lou flicking the collar of Berit's Hawaiian shirt. With Berit's sandy blond waves, rolled-up sleeves, and sideways smirk, Lauren knew she would be earning a lot of tips and numbers throughout the night as well.

Lauren looked down at her tank with a singular surfboard screen printed on the front and felt like she'd really missed the mark. "I'm not feeling very tropical anymore."

"I came prepared for this," Berit said, holding up a white shopping bag. She riffled through the contents and pulled out a large fake hibiscus flower. She broke the plastic stem so it was only a few inches and beckoned Lauren to come closer. Lauren stepped into Berit's space and bit back a gasp when Berit brushed her hair behind her ear. Berit tucked the flower into place around her ear and smiled softly as she looked into Lauren's eyes. "There. Now you look like you're ready to serve a mai tai on white sandy beaches."

Lauren's ear was on fire where Berit had touched it delicately. "Thank you," she whispered. She cleared her throat and stepped away from Berit. Bellamy looked amused, and Lou's eyes were on the far wall.

"I'm going to finish hanging the little paper light things behind the bar," Lauren said, trying to escape. Berit grabbed her wrist.

"Wait. I wanted to tell you that I'm giving you Wednesday off."

Lauren went through every upcoming day in her mind and couldn't remember needing the day for any specific reason. "Why?"

"You have a date." Berit smirked, the small upturn of her lips holding mischief.

"A date?" Lauren squeaked. "Who am I going on a date with?"

"A buddy of mine has a sister."

Lauren shook her head so rapidly she nearly gave herself a headache.

"What do you mean, no? Hear me out. I've known them both for years, and Jennifer is definitely the marrying kind. Great job, beautiful, and super sweet." Berit ticked off the qualities on her fingers.

"Oh, Jennifer Kramer?" Lou said with a clap. "She is gorgeous and very funny. Oh, I'm excited for this date."

"That makes one of us," Lauren mumbled.

"Well that's a piss-poor thing to say." Berit's tone was sharp, which made Lauren drop her attitude immediately.

"Fine, I'm sorry. Have you dated Jennifer?" Berit and Lou started laughing. "Why's that so funny?"

"Jennifer isn't really my type. Besides that, I've been friends with her brother since grade school. It'd feel almost incestuous if I went there." Berit had a faraway look in her eyes, like she was trying to imagine it. "Just trust me, Lauren. I think you two will be great for each other."

Lauren looked into Berit's earnest eyes and found herself powerless. She agreed to the date. Trusting Berit wasn't a problem, a fact that was scary enough. But what worried Lauren the most was meeting someone new. What if she didn't like Jennifer and offended Berit in the process? She watched Berit walk away and talk to Bellamy. The last thing she wanted was to lose the first real friend she had made on her own. Lauren swallowed hard and hoped with everything she had that a tropical getaway would be the distraction she desperately needed.

Chapter Eleven

Lauren paced back and forth in front of the small Italian restaurant where her blind date was about to take place. She had been texting Jennifer on and off since Berit had made sure they exchanged numbers. They picked a mutual favorite place for dinner and set a convenient time for their date. Lauren hadn't encouraged much conversation beyond planning for fear of exhausting topics before they were finally in each other's company. Lauren had been on one other blind date in her life; her mother had set her up with a man named Terry from the office. Lauren had sworn off blind dates ever since.

Until Berit looked at her with her soft and caring eyes.

She checked her phone again. Jennifer should be arriving in five minutes, unless she was early. Lauren would appreciate that. She could feel the butterflies in her stomach turning violent. She wondered what Berit had told Jennifer about her. This was why Lauren hated meeting new people. She'd go through the entire date trying to act a certain way when all she'd want was the cheesiest meal on the menu and two desserts. She'd make sure to not say anything too off-color or politically incorrect, and not everyone shared her sarcastic sense of humor. Lauren heard her mother's voice in her head reminding her to be more ladylike and soft spoken. What other parts of her personality should she hide away if she wanted the night to be a success?

"Lauren?"

Lauren jumped at her name and the soft touch on her shoulder.

She turned to find a tall, gorgeous butch woman smiling at her. "Jennifer?"

Jennifer nodded with a growing smile, and damn, it was blinding.

Lauren stuck her hand out awkwardly. "It's very nice to meet you." Jennifer had big hands and impeccable style. She wore a cerulean oxford shirt and kept it untucked over her flat-front black trousers. Lauren was sure Jennifer's black leather loafers cost more than her rent payment. Lauren dropped Jennifer's hand when she realized she'd been holding it for too long. Jennifer was tan with short black hair that fell gently onto her forehead. Lauren nearly swooned.

"Shall we go inside?" Jennifer said, her voice low and raspy.

"Yes. After you." Lauren motioned for the door, but Jennifer stepped ahead to open it.

"Ladies first." She was chivalrous, too, and be still Lauren's heart, Jennifer even had deep blue eyes.

Lauren wished she could hug Berit. No, she wouldn't want Berit there. That'd be weird. Lauren stepped into the small restaurant and walked up to the hostess. They got a small table in a secluded corner, which offered quiet privacy for conversation. Lauren sat and waited for Jennifer to decide on a drink.

"How do you feel about sharing a bottle of wine?" The candlelight highlighted Jennifer's chiseled face.

"Sure." Lauren sat back and allowed Jennifer to order what she felt paired best with the evening to come. Lauren understood why Jennifer wasn't Berit's type. She really needed to stop thinking about Berit, even if she was the reason for the date. "I'm ready to order whenever you are. I know all of my favorites."

Jennifer shot Lauren the warmest smile she'd ever seen. "So do I." They ordered as soon as their waitress arrived, and they fell into conversation the moment they were alone. "Tell me about yourself, Lauren. Berit didn't tell me much aside from how beautiful and witty you are. And she was definitely right about the beautiful part." Jennifer locked her eyes on Lauren's as she sipped her water.

Berit actually thinks I'm beautiful? Lauren shook her head to forget the thought and sipped at her own water to collect herself. "Berit didn't tell me much about you, either, aside from you having a good job and being gorgeous."

"She should've gone into sales."

Lauren laughed genuinely. She was happy Jennifer had a sense of humor. "She should. She was able to get me here. I hate blind dates."

"I do, too, but I trust Berit. We've known each other for a long time, and she's heard about my latest dating struggles. Most eligible women are too overstimulated by technology and dating apps to want to settle down." Jennifer's small shrug looked sad. Her expressive eyes lit up when the waitress placed a basket of warm bread on the table. "I'm a little old fashioned when it comes to relationships. I date one woman until it either doesn't work or I know I want it to work forever."

Lauren's heart skipped a beat. "I feel the same way. Dating is treated like a game, and it's been so hard to find something real." Lauren and Jennifer shared a smile. "This bread looks really good."

"It's fresh and incredible. But it's also the number one thing I should avoid."

"Are you on a diet?" Lauren said, hesitating before filling the tip of her knife with seasoned butter. Just a little wouldn't give the wrong impression.

"Not quite. I'm a personal trainer, so I try to eat the right things and keep active. But bread and Italian food will melt my willpower every time."

Lauren imagined Jennifer sweat slicked and lifting weights. A deliciously distracting image. "From what I can see, you've done pretty well in spite of temptations." Lauren loved the small blush creeping up Jennifer's cheeks.

"What do you do for a living?"

Lauren had been rehearsing for this question. "I'm between things right now," she said coolly. "I'm a paralegal, but my last job didn't work out. I'm working for Berit in the meantime while I search for a law firm that'll appreciate my talent and dedication." Jennifer's face was expressionless. Lauren closed her eyes momentarily, sure her employment status had just killed her chances with Jennifer, then she heard a small, surprisingly feminine laugh. Which was very sexy to Lauren.

"I'm sorry. Are you embarrassed by working for Berit?"

Lauren felt her defensive walls go up. "Of course not. Berit is great to work for, and her business is incredibly successful."

Jennifer appeared unbothered by Lauren's sharp tone. "I'm only asking because you answered me like you were on a job interview." Lauren relaxed and felt a bit ashamed for being so harsh. "What happened at your last job? You don't have to answer if that's a sore subject, but your little speech left me intrigued."

Their dinners came, and Lauren looked at Jennifer excitedly, rubbing her hands together. "I'll tell you about it, but I'm diving into this lasagna first."

Lauren and Jennifer chatted nonstop throughout dinner, talking about Lauren's rocky days and sudden dismissal from her job, and Jennifer shared what Berit was like when she was younger. Jennifer reminisced about the antics of Berit and her brother, and how Berit was her first crush.

"It was only because I knew she was gay," Jennifer said, defending herself. "She could've been an absolute monster, and I would've had a crush on her."

"I'm sure it helped that she's as beautiful as she is." Lauren finished the last drop of wine in her glass, thankful the drink had helped loosen her up. "What about you, Jennifer? Were you always this attractive?"

Jennifer gave her a small, confident smile. "I went through an awkward stage just like everyone else, and I even went through a femme phase."

Lauren gasped dramatically.

"I know, I even shocked myself with that one. But the older I get, the more comfortable I become in my skin. I feel more like myself now than I ever did."

Lauren nodded. "Berit has that kind of confidence, too. I've admired that since I first met her."

Jennifer's brow formed a deep crease between her eyes. "How long ago did you two meet?" she said before taking a long sip from her wine.

"A little over a month ago. She actually hit on me, but I didn't fall for it."

"Why not?"

"Come on, a woman like Berit has 'heartbreaker' written across her forehead. I'm not a casual gal, I don't do flings," Lauren said, pushing aside her plate. "She's definitely a flinger."

Jennifer snorted, making Lauren smile. "A flinger?"

"Yeah, and I totally get why women fall for her, but I'm always looking for loyalty and stability. I can't imagine what it's like to date multiple people. I feel lucky enough when one woman actually likes me back." Lauren covered her face. "I cannot believe I just said that." Lauren felt Jennifer wrap her fingers around her wrist before she opened her eyes and saw Jennifer smiling softly at her.

Jennifer held Lauren's hand on the tabletop. "I can't believe anyone wouldn't like you back."

Jennifer was smooth. Lauren looked at their joined hands shyly. "May I ask you a personal question? On a first date do you…" She looked around before leaning in to whisper, "Go all the way and order dessert?"

Jennifer laughed outright, the hearty sound filling the quiet restaurant. When her laughter subsided, she renewed her grip on Lauren's hand and covered it with her other. "I make a habit of it, actually."

They ordered dessert, different choices but they promised to share. Lauren waited for their coffee and sweets to arrive before diving back into conversation. She was dying to learn more about her date. "How would you feel about a rapid-fire round of this-or-that questions?"

Jennifer eyed her curiously as she stirred her coffee. Jennifer liked her coffee dark, Lauren noted, unlike the fancy cappuccinos Berit nearly melted for.

"We'll get to know some basic likes and dislikes. It'll be fun."

Jennifer looked pensive and thoughtful before agreeing. "Sounds fun. Since I already know I like you, I guess it's important to know whether you prefer dark, milk, or white chocolate."

"Dark is my favorite, milk chocolate is delicious, and white chocolate is just a sad reminder you're not eating real chocolate."

"I agree with you, but I do enjoy the occasional cookies and cream bar. Favorite ice cream flavor?"

"Strawberry bonbon." Lauren jumped when Jennifer slapped her palm on the tabletop.

"I was so certain about pistachio, but I had forgotten about strawberry bonbon." Lauren's heart fluttered at Jennifer's playfulness. "Cats or dogs?"

"If you had asked me this a month ago, I'd have said cats. I love their independence and how quiet they are. We had a few cats who were my best friends when I was younger. Even when they hated me." Lauren and Jennifer shared a laugh.

"So what changed?" Jennifer said. She cut a cannoli in half and offered Lauren the larger of the two pieces.

"Have you met Berit's dog, Hugo?" Lauren bit into her dessert and waited for Jennifer to answer. She nearly moaned. She adored cannoli.

"No, I've not."

"He's so cute and sweet. When I watch the two of them goofing around it makes me wonder if I've been a closeted dog person this whole time."

"I'm not rushing you ladies," the waitress said as she approached the table. She placed the check down and smiled brightly. "Can I get either of you more coffee or anything else?"

"I think we're good, thank you," Jennifer answered for them. Lauren was loving her take-charge attitude. Jennifer looked at Lauren with less of a smile than before. "I have an early-morning client tomorrow." Jennifer grabbed the check before Lauren could make an attempt for it.

"Oh." Lauren checked the time and was shocked to see the time nearing ten o'clock. They'd been together for over two hours, and it felt like no time at all. "I didn't realize it was getting so late. How much do I owe you?" Lauren picked up her purse from its hanging spot on the chair.

"This is my treat," Jennifer said. She smiled broadly, but Lauren wondered why it hadn't reached her eyes in the same way as earlier.

"Thank you." Lauren couldn't say how grateful she really was for not having to max out her last credit card just to pay for dinner. Payday at the Dollhouse couldn't come soon enough. Lauren knew exactly what she'd like to do with the next few extra bucks she earned. "Maybe you'll let me treat you next time?" She threw her desire to see Jennifer again out there. After all, they had more than enough compatibility to explore.

Jennifer waited a beat before answering. "That sounds great. I have a busy week ahead of me, but I'll call you." Jennifer signed the receipt and stood. "Let me walk you to your car."

They walked side by side, bumping against one another ever so often. Lauren resisted the natural urge to hook her hand into the crook of Jennifer's elbow. Lauren's belly filled with the jitters that always accompanied the end of a first date. Would they kiss? Did Jennifer *want* to kiss Lauren?

"Tonight was great," Lauren blurted awkwardly. She stopped beside her car, trying not to focus on how embarrassingly old it was, and stared up at Jennifer, who stood at least two inches taller than her. "I'm actually surprised by how great."

Jennifer took Lauren's hands in her own and said quietly, "I'm happy to have surprised you, Lauren." She raised Lauren's hands to her lips and placed a kiss on her knuckles. "I'll call you."

Lauren giggled like a smitten schoolgirl. "I'll look forward to your call." She watched Jennifer walk away, unabashedly checking out her ass as she sauntered to her car. Lauren waited for Jennifer to drive away before heading to the Dollhouse to thank Berit.

❖

"You really need to stop spoiling me, Rosa," Berit said as she took her twenty dollar tip from the bar and shoved it into the overflowing glass behind the bar.

"You deserve it. You make me a perfect martini every time I'm here. Consistency is hard to find these days." Rosa chewed on one of three olives from her martini as she watched Berit closely. "You're very quiet tonight."

Berit let the comment roll right off her. "It's been a busy night."

"You're usually at your most energetic and talkative on busy nights." Berit eyed her curiously. "I'm here a few times a week, I notice things," Rosa said with a shrug. "Is everything okay?"

"I'm fine." Berit patted Rosa's hand and threw in a wink for good measure. "Let me know if you want another. It's buy one get one free martinis tonight."

"Is it really?" Rosa perked up noticeably.

"For you it is," Berit said. She walked to the back of the bar. Some paperwork had to be finished. Berit still had to work out payroll hours and how much cash to give Lauren. Lou knocked on the doorframe.

"We're running low on Grey Goose and Fireball. Do we have some on order?" Lou shoved off the wall and took a seat.

Berit checked her order history. "Both are on order and should be here Tuesday. Think we'll be good until then?" Berit didn't look at her sister before going back to her work.

"I think so. Is everything okay with you?"

"You're the second person to ask me that in the last ten minutes. I'm fine, really. Just in a weird mood. Probably PMS-ing or hangry or something." Berit waved off Lou's concern. She wasn't ready to examine the reason for her foul mood.

"Hey!"

Berit winced the moment she recognized Lauren's voice behind her. She looked at Lou blankly and turned to find Lauren smiling brightly.

"What brings you in tonight? I thought you like to stay out of the bar on your days off." Berit didn't mean to sound like she wasn't happy to see Lauren. She had a feeling she'd always be happy to see Lauren, but tonight had been enough of a struggle without having her around.

Lauren leaned her head against the doorframe and giggled. "I'm in a very good mood and didn't want to go home."

"I, for one, am glad to have some good vibes around," Lou spoke up. "Berit has been—"

"Busy tonight." Berit turned back to glare at Lou.

"Well, I just wanted to thank you for setting me up with Jennifer. You were right, she's amazing and funny and *really* sexy." Lauren looked to Lou and started fanning herself.

Berit smiled meekly. "You're welcome." She felt a little more of her inner light dim. "See? I can be a good friend." Lauren nodded and bounced out of the office. Berit slumped into her chair with a heavy sigh.

"I forgot her date with Jennifer was tonight," Lou said. Berit could hear the shift in her sister's tone. "That explains your sour mood."

"I'm fine." Berit grabbed her phone. "Two friends of mine hit it off and will live happily ever after. I'm great," she said drolly. She stood in the small doorway and looked out into the bar. She typed out a message to Jennifer.

Hope it's not too late. I just wanted to see how your date went. Berit tried her damnedest to list reasons why Jennifer and Lauren wouldn't work out, but she came up with nothing. Jennifer answered her message almost immediately.

I had a good time.

Berit frowned at her phone. She looked up and easily found Lauren's smile in the crowd around the bar. *That's it? No details?* She typed back.

There's not much more to say.

Berit was getting a distinctly different vibe from Jennifer than she had from Lauren. But how could she tactfully ask about their date without giving away Lauren's giddy presence? *Will there be a date number two?*

"I have to get back to work. Thanks for draining my break of all its fun." Lou stormed past Berit and back to the bar. She always had a flair for the dramatic.

You two have never been together? At all?

Berit's eyes went so wide, her phone screen seemed to brighten. *Me and Lauren? No. Why?*

Because she talked about you all night. Maybe you ought to give it a go.

At one time Berit would've thought the constant mention of her meant something. She'd feel hopeful about a future for her and Lauren, but not now. Berit watched as Lauren laughed with Dee from across the bar. She'd never seen Lauren that happy. She'd been unable to make her that happy. Berit had tried for weeks to put the same kind of sparkle in Lauren's eyes, and Jennifer was able to do it in one night. She had to tamp down her jealousy and muster up the kind of support a true friend would show.

There's nothing to "give a go." She talked about me because I'm common ground. She was nervous to meet you. Berit sent the message and closed her eyes. When she reopened them, she typed one more message. *Take her out again. I already know she really likes you.*

Berit swallowed back her sadness when Jennifer replied with a smiley face. She looked at Lauren again and wondered how her feelings had spun out of her control.

CHAPTER TWELVE

Berit couldn't think of anything else in the world she enjoyed more than her mother's mashed potatoes. Lou had convinced Berit to head to their parents' house for Sunday dinner the following weekend, and although family time could be stressful, she needed the distraction. She had suffered through a play-by-play of Lauren's first and second dates with Jennifer.

On some level, Berit was happy for Lauren, but every other level was jealous and somewhat surprised. Jennifer seemed quite boring as a date, but Lauren was positively gaga over her. They had their second date at the beach. Not the boardwalk with the rides and games and ice cream, but just the beach. Berit yawned while Lauren recounted the way they splashed together in the waves.

"Would you like more gravy?" Berit's mother offered her the gravy boat. "The chicken is a little drier than usual."

"Everything is great, Mom. Especially the potatoes."

"I made extra just for you, Berit."

"Wow," Matt said deeply. "It's like the rest of us don't even matter."

Berit's mother, Florence, smiled at her three children who had managed to make it for dinner. "When it comes to mashed potatoes, Berit *is* the only one who matters."

"Ouch." Lou chuckled.

"I'm sorry your father is at the shop so late. He said he'd be home for dinner, but you know how your dad is." Florence shifted the napkin on her lap and reached for more green beans. Berit grabbed the dish first and served her mother.

Berit chose to ignore her father's absence. It was a relief, really. They'd usually butt heads for the whole meal and everyone's appetites would nosedive. But that didn't mean she didn't care for her father. "How's Dad been? Other than busy."

"His cholesterol is high and his knee is bothering him, but he refuses to do anything about either. He says he's too young to make changes," Florence said with a roll of her eyes. "I told him he's old and won't get much older if he keeps this up." Everyone laughed. "How have you been, dear? We haven't heard from you much lately." Florence lightly touched Berit's forearm.

"I'm sorry. I've been so busy with the bar."

"Louise has been busy, but has also made time to check in with me," Florence said. Lou stuck her tongue out at Berit from across the oval table.

"Message received loud and clear." Berit filled her mouth with another forkful of potatoes.

"I make sure I talk to Mom every day," Matt said.

"You live here."

"Still. Every day." Matt stuck his tongue out, too.

"Enough of that," Florence said. "Tell me, Berit, how's life outside the bar? How's my grandpuppy? Are you dating anyone?" She raised her glass and paused before she drank to say, "Finally?"

And Florence wondered why Berit rarely updated her on her life. "No, Mom, I'm not dating anyone." Ever since her eldest brother's second wedding, Florence had been harping on Berit to settle down. She still didn't know what about Jeffrey Junior's second marriage triggered her mom, but Florence was relentless on her quest for Berit to get married.

"I dream of the day you bring someone home. A nice woman that makes you happy. Preferably a woman who'd like some children, too."

"Talk to JJ if you'd like some grandkids." Berit ate the last of the chicken from her plate and pushed it aside.

"Let's make sure this marriage sticks first," Florence said.

Everyone looked at her with wide eyes. "What?"

"Sick burn, Mom!" Matt applauded his mother's cynical display.

"I'm home," Berit's father called out from the front door. He rushed into the kitchen with a broad smile. "Three out of five kids here at once. You'd think it was my birthday or something." His blue work shirt was smudged with grease from the day. Jeffrey Matthews was one of the most trusted mechanics in town. He filled a plate with most of what was left over and sat heavily in the head chair. He looked grayer than the last time Berit had seen him. "Wait, *is* it someone's birthday?" Matt and Lou laughed, but Berit knew he wasn't joking. She shook her head.

"Berit was just telling us why she's still single."

"No, Mom, I wasn't." Berit stood and brought her dishes to the sink.

"She has feelings for someone at work," Lou whispered, but Berit still overheard.

"I do not."

"Tell us about her," Florence said excitedly.

Lou took charge. "Her name is Lauren and she's really smart and pretty, and has absolutely no interest in Berit."

"Get the fuck out of here," Matt chimed in.

"Language," Berit's dad barked. "No cursing at the dinner table. You're twenty years old, you know the rules."

Berit excused herself during the distraction. "I have to go. I'm meeting up with a friend."

Her dad held up his hand. Berit looked at him, annoyance surfacing so easily. "I just got home. Sit with your family a little while longer."

"Imagine all the time you could've had if you were home on time for once," Berit said harshly.

"Berit..." Florence's soft voice and even softer eyes persuaded Berit to sit down. "So why doesn't Lauren like you back?"

Berit's face reddened, and Matt laughed. She shot daggers at her sister. "We're just friends, and I'm okay with that. I actually set her up with Chester's sister, Jennifer. They're really hitting it off."

"But you wish it was you," Lou said, singsong tone louder than ever.

"I swear to God, Lou, I will cover you in gravy again."

"Stop teasing your sister, Louise, and do not pour gravy on her again, Berit. It took forever to get it out of her hair that time." Florence slid the gravy boat away from Berit.

Matt dropped his silverware onto his empty dish loudly. "Jennifer was pretty hot until she started looking like a dude." He wiped his face and stood. "I'm going up to my room. I want to get some *Skyrim* in before I hit the hay. I'm working the morning shift with Dad tomorrow." Matt ran up the stairs.

"If he's gone, I'm gone." Berit stood again and kissed her mother on the cheek. "Dinner was delicious as always. Thank you."

"You're welcome, sweetie."

"Good night, Dad," Berit said, laying her hand on her dad's shoulder and squeezing it. She turned to Lou and said with a smile, "You're lucky you're still alive. I'll see you tomorrow at the bar." Berit walked away, ignoring Lou's middle finger.

❖

"How did you learn to do these things with your tongue?" Bellamy punctuated her words with a low moan. Berit smirked and ran the tip of her tongue across Bellamy's sensitive flesh, focusing her torturously light touch on Bellamy's glistening labia. She wondered if Lauren had slept with Jennifer yet. *No*, she scolded herself, focusing her attention on Bellamy's protruding clit. She sucked just enough to make Bellamy squirm. Would Lauren enjoy Berit's talents as much as Bellamy was? An image of Lauren, aroused with disheveled hair flashed in her mind. Berit sat back and shook her head.

"Is everything okay?" Bellamy sat up from where she had thrown herself across Berit's sofa. Berit knelt on the cushions and stared down at Bellamy's supine body.

"Yeah, of course," Berit said with a reassuring smile. She wrapped her arms around Bellamy's bent legs and pulled her forward. She kissed Bellamy deeply and removed the rest of her clothing.

Berit traced Bellamy's soft skin with her fingertips. Of all her lovers, Bellamy had the most enticing skin. It always seemed to be glowing and tasted sweet. Berit bit at Bellamy's womanly hip. What did Lauren's skin feel like? Did she mind a few bite marks? Berit stopped moving again. Thinking about Lauren was turning her on more than the woman below her. Bellamy ran her fingers through Berit's shaggy hair, encouraging her to continue. Berit brought her left hand to the juncture of Bellamy's thighs. She dipped her fingertips between swollen skin and sank into her hot center. Three of her fingers fit into Bellamy perfectly. She found a good rhythm in and out and kissed along Bellamy's throat. Berit tried to focus on Bellamy's rapid pulse and the feel of her inner walls contracting around her fingers.

Berit was quickly losing the battle of not thinking about Lauren. She crawled down Bellamy's body and sucked her clit into her mouth once more. She sucked and licked ravenously, desperate to make Bellamy come just so she could stop this weird emotional betrayal. Her mind shouldn't be filled with thoughts and images of Lauren, not her smile or laugh. Berit doubled her efforts, pushing Bellamy to the edge. Bellamy came loudly.

Berit stood and backed away from the sofa, wiping her mouth with the back of her hand. What was wrong with her? This was not Berit. She *focused* on her lovers. She could even lose herself in them. Where naked women were concerned, Berit was a willing and captive audience. She felt a little panicked, and though she was no stranger to a random anxiety attack here and there, Berit felt like she couldn't control her breathing.

"Wow," Bellamy said, throwing her long, shapely leg over the back of Berit's couch. She was everything erotic Berit had ever dreamed of. But she wasn't Lauren. "I've never come that fast."

"I can't do this anymore."

Bellamy lifted her head. Her face was glistening with sweat. "What?"

"This," Berit said while motioning between them. She averted her gaze, suddenly shy with Bellamy's nakedness. As if she wasn't just inside her. "I'm sorry, Bellamy. I really am." Berit felt heavy with guilt. She never treated a woman like a second choice or one of many. Even if Lauren thought she did. *Stop thinking about Lauren!* Berit was frustrating herself.

Bellamy started collecting her clothes. "What are you sorry for? You don't owe me anything."

"You're stunning and so, so sexy. But I couldn't—" Berit blew out a long breath. What could she say? "My mind is somewhere else instead of focusing on you."

Bellamy stood and started to slowly walk toward Berit. "Hey, Berit?"

"I'm probably just stressed. They say stress really kills the libido." She threw up her hands and widened her eyes. "Not that I wasn't into this, what we did, but I couldn't quite get to where I usually do." Bellamy kissed Berit, but not passionately. Instead, it was kind and soft. Bellamy pulled back and placed her hand against Berit's cheek.

"We're just having fun, yes?"

Berit nodded.

Bellamy ran her thumb along Berit's pout. "Do you have feelings for me?"

Berit stared into her dark eyes and shook her head.

"Good. Are we friends?"

"Absolutely," Berit said without hesitation.

"Then sit down and tell me what's wrong."

Berit fell onto the sofa. Hugo chose that moment to walk from the bedroom and join Berit on the couch. He must've sensed his mom was having a crisis of sorts. Berit sighed. "I think my casual days are over."

"I'm lucky to have been your last." Bellamy patted Berit's knee. "Does this mean you *do* have feelings for someone?"

Berit swallowed hard. Bellamy was her friend. If she could trust her enough with her body, she should be able to trust her with details of her crush. But something about her feelings for Lauren felt sacred. She placed her hand over Bellamy's and ran her finger along the skin, savoring their last intimate touch. "I think I do. This isn't the first time, of course, but it's the first time I don't know how to handle it."

"That means this is the first time your feelings are real."

Berit looked at Bellamy, obvious terror in her eyes.

"That's a good thing, Berit. Who is it?"

"I'll only tell you if you tell me yours first." Berit smirked.

Bellamy considered this for a minute, her mouth screwed up delightfully. Berit would miss those lips. "I guess we'll suffer in silence together, then."

"Damn." Berit snapped her fingers. "So what do we do now?"

"Exactly what we've been doing, except we stop fucking."

Berit bobbed her head from side to side, thinking about what a platonic friendship with Bellamy would be like. She enjoyed the prospect. She picked up the remote from her coffee table and turned on the television. "I'm going to take a quick shower. Do you want to watch a movie?"

"Yes, but I'll have to shower after you, and you're going to order pizza."

"Oh, am I?" Berit started toward the bathroom.

"Yes. I came over expecting to be fully satisfied. The one orgasm was great, but I need more."

Berit laughed loudly. She pointed toward the bathroom door. "You shower first and I'll order the pizza."

Bellamy leapt from the couch and rushed around Berit. "Half pepperoni and half plain. Thanks."

When the bathroom door shut, Berit felt a sense of peace wash over her. Talking to Bellamy, even vaguely, about her feelings lightened Berit's mood. Perhaps Bellamy's shoulder would be the one she'd cry on when Jennifer and Lauren lived their happily ever after.

Chapter Thirteen

Lauren needed the perfect outfit for her third date with Jennifer. She'd been given specific instructions to dress casually, but every woman knew a third date meant sex. Or at least some guaranteed heavy petting. So while Lauren wanted to follow Jennifer's instructions, she knew at least her bottom layer had to be sexy. Lauren shivered as she pulled lace panties up her thighs. Excitement was a cheap descriptor for how she felt. Lauren hadn't had honest sex, the kind of sex where you lose yourself to your partner instead of their motives, in a very long time.

They'd spent their second date strolling the beach in the early evening. Jennifer had held her hand lightly after their hands had bumped together enough times to make it awkward. They never lacked topics of conversation and even indulged in a picnic of sandwiches and snacks. Lauren enjoyed every second of their time together, even their brief good-night kiss interrupted by the delivery of Jorge's Chinese food. Lauren was ready for more than a peck. Their first kiss was barely long enough to register if Jennifer's lips were as soft as they looked.

Lauren was ready for whatever their third date would bring. She threw on a white T-shirt and skinny jeans before heading out of her bedroom. Rebecca was standing in the kitchen, one hand on the fridge as she watched Lauren walk to the front door. "Where are you heading to?"

"I have a date," Lauren answered curtly. She ignored the shocked look on Rebecca's face, but couldn't ignore her when she called out for Lauren to wait. She had her hand on the doorknob—so close to freedom and getting to kiss Jennifer. "I really have to go."

"I know," Rebecca said, swiping a few stray hairs from her forehead. "I just wanted to check in. You've seemed really happy lately."

"I am." Lauren pulled the door open, but Rebecca pushed it shut.

"Tell me about your new job."

"It's great. I'm appreciated, and my coworkers are wonderful." Lauren had practiced her response for weeks now. She didn't want anyone knowing about her guest spot at the Dollhouse. Every night she worried Rebecca would saunter in with a supermodel on her arm and laugh at what her life had become. "Let me go."

"And where are you working?"

Lauren looked at Rebecca's glittering eyes and to the doorknob. She had to escape and manage to not mention her job before doing so. "I, uh—" Lauren's phone rang. *Thank God.* She turned away from Rebecca and answered. "Hey you."

"Hey yourself," Jennifer said. "You ready?"

Lauren turned and stared at Rebecca defiantly. "Yes. I'm walking out the door as we speak. I'll meet you at the car." She made a show of opening the front door and slamming it in Rebecca's face. Lauren practically ran to Jennifer's car and climbed into the passenger seat before Jennifer could cut the engine. "Hi."

"Hi," Jennifer said, leaning across the console and kissing Lauren's cheek. She pulled away from the curb without another word. She drove for quite some time before speaking again. "You look great," Jennifer said, scanning Lauren's body slowly.

Lauren felt herself blush. "I couldn't look any more plain." She touched her ponytail subconsciously. "I wasn't sure what your definition of casual was, so I just threw this on. Where are we going?" Jennifer remained quiet and mysterious as she drove along highways and back roads for nearly twenty-five minutes.

Jennifer didn't give the slightest indication they were close to their destination until she pulled her Audi into a large parking lot. She got out of the car wordlessly and opened Lauren's door.

Jennifer grabbed Lauren's hand and intertwined their fingers. With her free hand, Jennifer pointed to a large, unmarked building. She smiled softly at Lauren. "We're going roller skating."

"Oh, dear God."

"What?" Jennifer looked confused and slightly fearful for a brief moment. "Bad idea?"

"No, not a bad idea. I just can't remember the last time I had wheels strapped to my feet. I'm not the most steady or smooth person."

"Do you trust me to catch you if you fall?"

Jennifer's smile beamed, the dimple on her left cheek on display, and Lauren was powerless to its charm. Lauren nodded.

"Great. I'll protect you."

Lauren swooned. "I bet you will." She tugged Jennifer's hand slightly to keep her in place. She looked up into Jennifer's eyes before staring at her lips. Jennifer leaned down and brought their mouths within a whisper's distance, but before Lauren got the kiss she was craving, a child bumped into them.

"Sorry," the little brat called out before running off toward the restaurant that shared the roller rink's parking lot. At least he had manners.

Lauren growled in frustration, which made Jennifer laugh. "Come on," she said to Lauren. She tugged her toward the skating rink. "We can pick that back up later."

"You seem pretty excited. Are you some sort of skating aficionado? Wait, don't tell me. Roller derby."

Jennifer laughed. She opened the door to the rink and ushered Lauren inside. "I'm not tough enough for roller derby. I have a friend who's part of a local team—those women do not mess around."

Lauren's eyes grew wide when she spotted the large rink. Singles, couples, and groups weaved about and skated around. Some were more talented than others, but all seemed smooth and steady. She heard Jennifer say her name. "Huh?"

"What size skates do you need?" Jennifer pointed to her feet. "I'm a size nine and usually wear an eight in skates."

"I'm a seven and a half," Lauren said in a daze, completely

entranced by everyone skating. She watched Jennifer run up to the rental counter and come back with two sets of skates. Her broad smile was contagious and calming. Maybe Lauren wouldn't die today.

Jennifer must've noticed Lauren's apprehension because she sat closely and touched her hand tenderly. "I used to skate every day. My family lived closer to the country than the city, and the only thing for kids to do was roller skate or swim. One of those activities was much easier to do year-round. Also, mostly girls were into skating." Jennifer winked, making Lauren's insides quiver.

Lauren's eyes fell to Jennifer's biceps as she tightened the laces of her skates. The short sleeves of her navy blue button up hugged the muscles tightly. Lauren cleared her throat and secured her own skates. "You're very sexy," she said in a quiet voice, but Lauren was still proud of her boldness for saying what she was thinking for once. If she wanted a relationship to be successful, she knew she'd have to dig deep for confidence.

"Yeah?" Jennifer stood and held out her hand. She pulled Lauren so their bodies were flush. She ran her hand down the length of Lauren's back and came to rest on her hips. "You're pretty sexy yourself."

Lauren was more focused on her unsteady wheels than the woman holding her. "This is a bad idea," she blurted.

"Come on." Jennifer guided her toward the smooth wooden floor of the rink. Most skaters kept to the worn, darkened ring along the perimeter. "I got you, remember? You can do this."

Lauren looked into Jennifer's eyes and soaked up her assurance. She nodded. "I can do this."

One hour and two tender spots from a collision with the wall later, Lauren was laughing as they walked from the rink. Jennifer had stayed true to her word and caught Lauren every time her balance wavered. Lauren knew Jennifer's hands had been all over her, but she was too preoccupied with fear to focus on that feeling. This led Lauren to the realization that she hated roller skating. What fun was being taught if you couldn't fully enjoy your instructor?

Jennifer opened the car door for Lauren and waited for her

to get in before getting behind the steering wheel and starting her car. She licked her lips, an action Lauren watched keenly. "Are you hungry?" Jennifer asked, making no move to put the car in drive.

"Now that I'm no longer terrified, I think I am starting to feel a little hungry. Did you want to try that place?" Lauren pointed to the restaurant.

"I was thinking," Jennifer said, shifting nervously in her seat. Lauren found the sight adorable. "I'm not the best cook, but if you like pasta and jarred sauce, I could make us dinner."

Even if Lauren was allergic to pasta, she'd still have said yes. "Let's go, then," she said, placing her hand gently on Jennifer's forearm.

Lauren quickly realized Jennifer wasn't kidding when she said she wasn't much of a cook. Jennifer ordered her to stay out of the kitchen while she prepped their meal. She took the time to explore the first floor of Jennifer's Craftsman-style home. The large great room was filled with artwork and odds and ends. Jennifer liked floral art and nonfiction, judging by the books on one shelf. Lauren was happy to see she had a vast Blu-ray collection with movies spanning every genre. This gave Lauren hope Jennifer would enjoy lazy movie nights as much as she did.

The sound of the smoke detector broke Lauren away from her character study.

"It's okay!" Jennifer called out from the kitchen. "Just a little burned bread. Pasta's ready, though."

Lauren sauntered back toward the kitchen just in time to catch Jennifer standing on a kitchen chair fanning the smoke away from the detector with a magazine. Finally, the beeping stopped. "I promise I didn't burn the sauce."

"I know the number of an Italian place nearby if you did."

Jennifer hopped down from the chair and walked over to Lauren. She stood in Lauren's space and smiled. "You do strike me as the kind of person who's prepared for any situation."

Lauren wanted to laugh in her face. "Not quite," Lauren said. "But when it comes to food situations, I do like to have a few backup plans. Nothing can ruin a night like bad food."

Jennifer looked back toward the smoking stove with a grimace. "Maybe you should call that Italian place."

An hour later they sat, quietly finishing their takeout dinner. Lauren kept her dinner light, a salad of fresh mozzarella and tomatoes, knowing the anxiety of spending alone time with someone new would wreak havoc on her stomach. She could feel her palms grow sweaty as she pushed her plate aside. "I'm sure your pasta would've been good, but that was delicious."

Jennifer took one last bite of her cavatelli. "You're right." She stood and cleared the table quickly, shooing Lauren away when she tried to help. Lauren brought their wine to the living room and waited for her there.

Lauren sat on the large, plush couch and counted as she breathed. She was anxious but excited. Her time with Jennifer had been wonderful. Jennifer seemed normal and laid back, exactly what she needed in a woman. Now she just had to relax. Jennifer walked into the room. "All cleaned up?"

"Dinner one *and* dinner two." She sat beside Lauren, pressed against her side. Jennifer put her arm across the back of the couch, offering a wordless invitation to get closer.

With a subtle deep breath, Lauren placed her hand on Jennifer's thigh. She melted the moment she felt how hard the muscle was. "Do you want to watch a movie or something?" Lauren tilted her head to look at Jennifer.

Jennifer ran her fingers through Lauren's hair and whispered, "Or something." Jennifer leaned in slowly, her nose barely touching Lauren's before their lips met.

Lauren concentrated on the firm pressure of Jennifer's soft lips. Lauren opened up willingly to Jennifer, allowing her tongue its first tentative taste. Jennifer moaned. She felt along Jennifer's toned arms, each muscle of Jennifer's upper back flexing beneath her palms.

Lauren felt…she felt…nothing.

She lay back as Jennifer encouraged her onto her back and cradled Lauren's head. Lauren focused on the firm dominance of Jennifer's body as she reclined beneath her. She was more aware of her surroundings; the scent of dinner in the air, how velvety the surface of the sofa was, and the sound of a car passing outside. Lauren couldn't snap into the moment.

With her right hand, Lauren reached for Jennifer's skin in hopes of shocking her brain into feeling something. Jennifer's hips ground into her the moment Lauren touched her bare lower back. Lauren opened her eyes. She saw Jennifer's eyes closed tightly; her face was flushed and she was clearly enjoying their time together. Lauren wondered if her own body, or mind, was broken. A gorgeous woman was on top of her, but she felt not a flicker of desire.

How was this possible?

Lauren kissed Jennifer again, grabbed her firm ass and pulled Jennifer into her. She broke the kiss, her head falling against the sofa, when she continued to feel blank. Lauren huffed in frustration.

Jennifer pressed her forehead to Lauren's and said, "I'm sorry, I got carried away. I wasn't kidding earlier when I said you look great." Jennifer's breathing was labored, but she spared a laugh. Lauren didn't feel a fraction of how Jennifer looked—aroused and happy.

Lauren wanted to crawl into a hole. How was she not into this incredible woman? She ran her hands up Jennifer's sides, intent on feeling every incredible dip and flex, before framing Jennifer's face with her hands. She kissed her again, slowly, and surrendered to the fact that she didn't feel a sexual spark with her. It seemed as if the butterflies had all died the moment their relationship turned physical.

"I should be the one apologizing," Lauren said, sitting up. All the anxiety she expected earlier came at once, but for a different reason. "I had a wonderful time, *you* are absolutely incredible." She pushed her hair out of her face. Lauren couldn't meet Jennifer's eyes.

"But…"

Lauren looked in her wide, curious eyes. What was she going to say? She searched her brain for the kindest, most honest response. "I think we make better friends," she said, holding back the wince she wanted so badly to show.

Jennifer stared blankly for a moment before saying, "Really? We're into each other, right? Because I felt something here," she said while waving between them. "Obviously."

A thousand thoughts flew through Lauren's head. *Was I into her? How into me can she possibly be? Why don't I feel anything? Am I freaking myself out? Did Rebecca ruin me?*

"I'm sorry." Lauren stood and wiped her damp palms on her jeans. She gathered her purse and turned back to Jennifer who'd yet move from the couch. "It's just—"

"Berit," Jennifer said with a nod. Lauren backed up a step.

She shook her head and her mouth opened and closed several times. Lauren was flabbergasted. "What does Berit have to do with any of this?" Her stomach turned.

Jennifer stood and placed her hands on Lauren's shoulders. "I figured you had a crush on her or something when you couldn't stop talking about her."

"She's a mutual friend."

"Yeah, I believed that for a brief moment, too."

Lauren scratched at her neck and then her forehead. She fought to find her next words. Jennifer's idea was crazy, and Lauren wanted to shut her down nicely. "I just don't feel like we have physical chemistry, and if I stay and try to feel it, I know it'll be for the wrong reasons." Jennifer's hands fell from Lauren's shoulders. Lauren felt a flash of guilt.

Unexpectedly, Jennifer pulled Lauren in for a hug. "I would never want you to *try* to feel anything for me," she whispered in Lauren's ear. When she pulled back, a sad smile lit up her face. "But there *are* some people we can't help but feel things for."

Lauren opened her mouth, ready with a giant denial, but Jennifer stepped away and walked toward the door. "What the fuck is going on right now?" she muttered to herself.

The drive back was tense. Lauren replayed the entire day over and over in her head, along with every moment from their past dates. Why couldn't her body respond to Jennifer the way her mind had? But above all else, Lauren couldn't understand why Jennifer had to say Berit's name.

CHAPTER FOURTEEN

Lauren didn't sleep a wink after returning home from Jennifer's. She mostly tossed and turned, but she also spent too much time dodging Rebecca's incessant questions about her new girlfriend. Lauren didn't have any answers because she loathed to admit she didn't have a new girlfriend—at least to Rebecca. She was still tired when her five o'clock shift started at the Dollhouse. She shuffled sluggishly through the back door into the stockroom. She was grateful to hear an acoustic band playing, conjuring the memory of Berit mentioning an acoustic night coming up. Lauren's memory had been suffering from stress-induced lapses, something she hoped would fade soon. She needed to relax.

"Hey, Lauren." Berit's voice was a little too loud for Lauren's exhausted mind. She cursed her body for feeling like it was hungover when all she had was a glass of wine the night before. Emotional hangovers were a thing, apparently. "Are you okay?"

"Yeah, I'm fine. I'm just really tired. I had a hard time staying asleep last night." Lauren turned in to the small employee room and tucked her purse into the small cubby designated just for her belongings. She clocked in, but she could feel Berit's eyes on her as she moved about.

"Acoustic night isn't shaping up to be as popular as I had hoped."

Lauren laughed lightly. "It's only five. How many songs have been played? Two?"

"We're covered out there if you need time, that's what I'm

trying to say." Berit stepped closer to Lauren and touched her forearm gently.

Lauren looked at Berit's hand, and Berit pulled back.

"I know it can be hard to adjust to the hours," Berit said quietly. "I don't want you to run yourself into the ground. I can always work the schedule around to make sure you're okay."

"And get special treatment from the boss?" Lauren joked half-heartedly. She did mean it. The last thing Lauren wanted was for her coworkers to think she was treated differently. Berit's eyes bored into her, her kindness a chokehold. "I'll be fine." Lauren stepped around Berit and walked out of the employee room. She subconsciously touched her arm where Berit had laid her hand.

"I would do the same for any of my girls."

"Your *girls*?" Lauren said, turning around so fast her hair flipped over her shoulder. "Is that what they are to you?"

Berit's eyebrows rose.

"Those *women* are not yours. They are very hardworking employees." Lauren stepped back. Her eyes widened as her mind caught up with her mouth and was thoroughly embarrassed by her outburst.

Berit took in a slow breath, her face impassive. "I know you don't think very highly of me as a person," Berit said. Lauren's heart sank instantly. "But I'm positive I've never given you a reason to think I treat my staff unfairly or inappropriately." Berit's tone was unlike anything Lauren had ever heard. She sounded tense, thoughtful, and a little hurt.

Lauren's shoulders slumped. "I'm sorry, you're right. I don't know what's gotten into me today. I'm so grumpy."

Some of the warmth returned to Berit's smile. "It's okay. We're all entitled to our bad days. I'm wretched when I'm grumpy or mad, especially mad."

"I doubt that." Lauren stepped up to Berit and poked her shoulder, a move driven by a flash of flirtatious energy, something that seemed to catch both Lauren and Berit off guard.

Berit looked curiously from her shoulder to Lauren, a cocky smile lighting up her face.

Lauren cleared her throat. "I just mean that, uh, you're always in a good mood." She felt awkward but made no move to leave Berit's space. Her body and mind were at war. *What is going on with me?*

"And let's hope that's the only side of me you see. Otherwise, you may hate me more than you did the first time you met me."

"I didn't hate you," Lauren said seriously. "I could never hate you."

Berit licked her lips as she seemed to be searching Lauren's face for something, dishonesty maybe? Lauren wasn't sure, but she must've passed the test because Berit nodded and stepped back. She motioned toward the door. "We should get to work."

"We should." Lauren stepped around Berit, feeling more than a little off balance. She spotted Cynthia by a back table and started that way.

"Where do you think you're going?"

Lauren froze at Berit's question. For the past week, she had been on table duty with Monica, and she assumed today would be the same. "To check on tables?"

"Forget about tables. You're behind the bar with me tonight." Berit laughed at Lauren's gaping mouth. "Like I said, it looks like it'll be a slow night. I think tonight is a great night for a full bar shift, so you get a real feel of the flow back there."

"I don't think I'll be much help back there," Lauren said emphatically. She didn't usually decline a boss's request, but something told Lauren she needed to avoid Berit for the night, or at least until she stopped hearing Jennifer's words. "I'm exhausted and really sluggish—body and mind. I'll just be in your way."

"Thank you for the warning. If I start to feel that way, I'll send you out to the tables." Berit made a sweeping gesture toward the bar with her arms. "But for now, I'd like to teach you a little bit about what I love to do and why."

Lauren shook her head as she followed Berit. She walked around the bar and surveyed the interior of the Dollhouse. Berit was right, it was rather slow. Several small groups sat as close to the singer as possible, but the rest of the bar barely had occupants.

Two women who weren't together occupied the bar, paying more attention to their phones than anything else.

"Why *do* you love bartending so much?" Lauren asked before she could stop herself. She'd seen many people act passionate about their profession, but Berit was in a different class.

Berit pulled several shot glasses from under the bar. "I like to compare it to cooking. Chefs work with ingredients and try to come up with new recipes and presentations all the time." She grabbed a bottle of rum and a cocktail shaker. "I do the same, but with cocktails. And with cocktails, your customer has a front row seat to a show." Berit launched the shaker into the air, and it spun several times before she caught it upright on the back of her hand.

Lauren smiled in delight, still impressed with Berit's skills and confident hands. She watched her flip the cup a few more times before saying, "I hope you don't expect me to do anything like that."

Lauren sucked in a breath when Berit grabbed her hand. She watched in a daze as Berit flattened it out, palm down, and felt along the length of each finger. The sensation traveled throughout her body. Berit placed the metal cup on the back of her hand and smiled triumphantly when it didn't immediately topple off. "Pure luck," Lauren said. She moved the cup and shook out her hands. Why did she feel dizzy all of a sudden?

"You really need to give yourself more credit." Berit tossed Lauren the bottle of rum and laughed when she caught it awkwardly. "You have good reflexes. Pass that from hand to hand."

"Like this?" Lauren passed the bottle from one palm to the other. The glass hung in the air for less than a second during each toss.

"Farther," Berit said, her voice taking on a deeper tone. She leaned back against the counter and crossed her arms over her chest. Her loose T-shirt clung to her shoulders, highlighting how broad she was.

Lauren wondered if Berit was a swimmer because her body was slight but solid, long and lean. She admired the way Berit carried herself and often caught herself wondering how dominant

Berit could be. Lauren dropped the bottle, and it hit the floor with a loud thud. "Oh, my God. I'm sorry. I told you this was a bad idea."

Berit picked up the bottle with a chuckle. "Do you have any idea how many bottles I dropped when I was starting out?" Berit grabbed a bottle of Svedka and handed the bottle of Bacardi back to Lauren. "A lot. I even paid for anything I broke. Which is why I made sure to get these," she said, toeing the rubber flooring. "These are the top recommended rubber mats for bartending. Bottles and thick glasses are less likely to break when they're dropped. Delicate glasses like martini and champagne are a different story. So let's not throw any of those around." Berit winked at Lauren.

In that brief moment, a butterfly rose from the dead deep in Lauren's stomach.

Lauren cleared her throat and stared at the bottle of rum in her hands. She started tossing it back and forth again. "How long have you been doing this?"

"Since I could. Here," Berit said with an extended hand. She motioned for Lauren to throw the bottle to her. She returned the bottle to Lauren a second after she caught it, initiating a game of catch between them. "I started as a barback when I turned eighteen and started mixing drinks as soon as they'd let me. Everything about bartending came naturally to me, and I knew this was what I wanted to do." Berit must've noticed Lauren's dominant hand was her left, because her next toss was to her right. The bottle bounced off Lauren's palm and onto the floor.

Lauren was less apologetic this time. She picked up the bottle and kept up with the game. She grew determined to not drop the bottle again, for the sake of ego and to make Berit proud. Lauren tucked her left hand behind her back and shot Berit a challenging smirk. She caught the next one seamlessly.

Berit smiled brightly. "Impressive."

"How many bars have you worked at?" Lauren was thirsty for all information regarding Berit, and it was neither professional nor innocent curiosity. The distraction of the flying bottle made it easier for Lauren to speak her mind and ask all the questions she'd normally be too shy or self-conscious to ask. "Were they all gay bars?"

Berit flipped the glass bottle before throwing it back to Lauren and nodding for her to try the same. "I've worked at three bars, all gay. I worked at the third one for the longest time and learned everything I could about alcohol's flavor spectrum and flair."

"Flair?"

"This," Berit said as she threw the rum bottle high into the air, spun her body, and caught the bottle nozzle down in the metal mixing cup she grabbed from the bar in one smooth motion, "is flair."

"Oh." Lauren's mouth remained in a small *O*.

Berit poured the rum from the cup into a shot glass. The liquid came exactly to the rim. "Relax. We'll start slowly, and I'll give you a little kit to take home and practice with. Sometimes it's easier to pick up without an audience. You'll even get your very own Dollhouse pint glass." Berit shot Lauren a proud smile. "Now I'm going to teach you how to pour multiple shots and how to mix one of your favorite drinks."

"Which one?"

"The Dolly, also known as a Leg Spreader." Berit laughed loudly when Lauren dropped the bottle again.

"Dammit." Lauren picked up the bottle, placed it on the bar, and backed away with her hands up. "I get why you stick to calling it the Dolly."

"I put a spin on the original recipe, so it truly is a Dollhouse original, and a secret recipe." Berit arranged the four shot glasses on the bar. "We use one- and two-ounce shot glasses here, but we stick to the one-ounce for mixing. It makes counting your measurements easier. One, two, three, four—that's all you'll need to know." Lauren eyed her skeptically. "A four-count pour fills a one-ounce shot glass. Got it?"

"Uh, sure."

Berit started counting again, this time pouring a darker liquid into another shot glass. On the count of four, the glass was full.

"This shot happens to be one of my top fantasies." Lauren didn't want to know and she didn't ask, but Berit answered with a smirk anyway. "Twin sisters."

"You're disgusting," Lauren said, pushing at Berit's shoulder. She pulled her hand back quickly and swallowed hard. The desire to touch Berit again was overwhelming and unexpected.

Berit's eyes remained on Lauren's, and she grinned wickedly. "I'm just kidding. I'd prefer to be able to tell them apart. Things could get awkward otherwise." She grabbed a small can of Coca-Cola from a mini fridge under the bar and a small pitcher of lime juice.

Lauren opened her mouth, willing a witty response to come to mind, but she fell flat and said, "Har har."

Berit spared an amused laugh. "Light rum," she said, holding up the clear rum before pouring it into the metal cup. She did the same with the darker rum. "Spiced rum, the good stuff, and a dash of both real Coke and lime juice. Add a little ice…" Berit dumped a scoop of ice into the shaker and secured a glass over it, checking the seal before handing it to Lauren. "Shake it, baby."

Lauren put her hand over the glass and kept her grip tight on the shaker, moving it back and forth. Berit shook her head and grabbed Lauren's hands along with the shaker. "A few times, up and down, quickly." She moved Lauren as if she were her puppet. "Now hit the glass gently with the heel of your hand to dislodge it."

After removing the glass, Lauren stared at Berit, waiting for her next instructions. Common sense told her it was time to pour, but Lauren never really knew with Berit. Her brown eyes grew wide when Berit turned her to the bar and stepped behind her. She wrapped her arms around Lauren and placed her hand over Lauren's on the metal shaker. Berit's warmth permeated the back of Lauren's shirt, and she soaked it up.

"Slowly," Berit whispered into Lauren's ear. She guided Lauren's hand, pouring the liquid into two waiting shot glasses, moving seamlessly from one to the next without spilling. The liquor rose in the glasses along with a torrent of goose bumps along

Lauren's skin. Lauren took in a deep breath, trying to keep her hands steady and her stance calm. "Slow and steady will give you a perfect pour every time."

Lauren watched the final drop of liquor ripple the surface. Berit had yet to move, and being boxed in like this would normally make Lauren feel claustrophobic, but not one negative feeling coursed through her body. Everything she felt was good, *too* good. Reacting this way to Berit was all Jennifer's fault. "Son of a bitch," Lauren mumbled.

"What?" Berit stepped back and looked at the shots. "They're perfect." She picked one up and held it out to Lauren. "Want a taste?"

"No. I'm going to work tables for the rest of the night if that's okay." Lauren marched out from behind the bar without giving Berit a chance to voice her approval.

"Okay then," Berit said as she watched Lauren practically run away from her. She blew out a large breath, puffing out her cheeks. She handed the shots off to the two closest patrons, who were elated by free drinks.

Lou stepped up behind her to input drinks into the register. "What was that all about?"

Berit's mind reeled. "Be more specific."

"You and Lauren were getting cozy back here."

"I was teaching her basic flair."

Lou chortled. "I've seen you teach Flair 101, and that was not it."

Berit sighed. She checked everyone's glasses at the bar and knew she'd have a few minutes before the next refill request. "I thought she gave me the signal."

"The signal?" Lou said with a raised eyebrow.

"Yeah, the signal. We were in the back and she was acting weird and grumpy, and then she went out of her way to touch me and she blushed."

"And *that's* the signal?"

Berit recognized every bit of mockery in her sister's face and tone. She clenched her jaw. "When was the last time anyone shot you the signal? Would you even recognize it?" Lou opened her mouth, and Berit raised her hand to stop her. "And bar patrons don't count."

Lou glared at her. "All I'm saying is don't read too much into it. You obviously came on too strong just now, and she ran for the hills. You also seem to have forgotten that she's dating Jennifer, whom you set her up with."

Berit's face fell. The melancholy that always accompanied the harsh truth filled her chest. She'd never wanted someone so unattainable that she'd fabricate their interest. She let out a small, sad laugh. "You're right. Thinking back, I don't think it was a signal. Why would it be? She's already dating the perfect woman." Berit pulled the dish towel from her back pocket and threw it on the counter.

"That's not what I—"

"I'll be in my office if you need me." Berit chastised herself for the rest of the night. Lauren had made her feelings toward her clear. She'd never go for a woman like Berit.

Chapter Fifteen

I don't know if it's a mental breakdown or my mind playing tricks on me, or maybe it's even a midlife crisis. I feel like everything I should want is on the 'no' list for me, and everything I never, ever wanted is screaming 'yes' at me and I'm really worried." Lauren bit her thumbnail, turning the once-smooth corner jagged. She paced her room, waiting to hear a token of good advice come through her eerily silent phone. She peeked at the screen to make sure the call was connected.

Amber mumbled something unintelligible into the phone. Lauren could hear a commotion in the background. "Lauren, I have no idea what you're talking about, and I'm at work."

"My life," Lauren nearly yelled. She paced back and forth in her bedroom. Today was one of the rare days where she was home alone for a few brief moments before work—a workday she wanted to avoid like a wet kiss from your grabby aunt. "Everything is turning upside down, and I don't know how to stop it." Lauren wanted to know what angle Amber was holding her phone at because she heard the entire breath Amber released at her. "Don't be like that."

"Hang on. I'm trying to sneak out for a smoke break."

"You don't smoke."

"If the smokers can take ten from time to time, I can take time to talk my friend out of her spiraling craziness and breathe some fresh air while I'm at it. Even if it is humid as hell today."

Lauren tilted her head in consideration. "I always assumed hell would be a dry heat."

"Okay. Upside-down life. You have five minutes—go."

"You know how when people go through a big life change or traumatic experience, something in them can snap? I think something in me snapped or is at least a little frayed or broken."

"When was the last time you saw your therapist?" Amber's question sounded so instant and dull, Lauren wondered if her friend even heard a word she had said.

"It's been a few months. I haven't been able to afford it since most of our utilities went up." Lauren checked the clock on the far wall of her bedroom. Her shift started in thirty minutes.

"Promise me you'll make an appointment soon. I'll even give you the money. You always feel better when you see her regularly."

"I promise, but I need your help right now." She resumed her pacing.

"What's first?"

"I like my job," Lauren admitted quietly.

Amber laughed lightly, the sound nearly carried away by the breeze that crackled in the phone. "Why is that a bad thing?"

"Because I'm a paralegal; I went to school for it and always wanted to work in law." Lauren's head fell back. She looked at a small water spot on the ceiling and saw dollar signs for a moment but decided she didn't have the energy to worry about that, too. Not yet, anyway. "I shouldn't be okay with being a bartender or waitress or whatever I am right now."

"Why not? Both are very valid occupations. My cousin has been bartending for nearly twenty years and has more designer shoes and handbags than I'll ever own. She drives a BMW she bought new."

"The money can be good, but I feel like I'll be giving up on what I've worked for my whole life."

"You sound like your mother, which leads me to believe you're more worried about what other people will think of you."

Lauren hung her head. "What if I do?"

"Don't," Amber said instantly and forcefully. "You are responsible for your happiness and *just* your happiness, Lauren, no one else's. You should work the job you want to, period."

"You are right." Lauren took the first full, deep breath her body had allowed since the beginning of her anxious episode. "I'll start looking for a paralegal position when and if I'm ready."

"Good. Was that it? Because I have to get back—"

"Do you remember Jennifer?" Every time she thought of the way things had ended between her and Jennifer, Lauren felt like her insides were shrinking in embarrassment.

"The woman you're dating? The eleven on a scale of one to ten? Yeah, I can still hear you bragging about her."

"We're not dating anymore." Lauren went back to chewing her thumbnail in hopes of smoothing out her earlier damage. "We weren't sexually compatible." God, that sounded so much simpler than it felt.

"You describe her like she was some sexy stud superstar. I can't imagine the sex was that bad."

Lauren recalled the way her body refused to react to Jennifer. "We didn't have sex, *I* couldn't have sex *with* her. She didn't turn me on, and I know how crazy that sounds. She's perfect on paper and in person, but I didn't feel lust or desire or anything when things started to get hot and heavy. I actually think my vagina's broken or dead."

"You're exaggerating, maybe, how hot was she?" Amber's voice was strained, like she was really trying to figure out Lauren's recent sexual lapse.

"An eleven out of ten," Lauren said wistfully. "But that's not what's got me really messed up. Jennifer asked me if it had anything to do with Berit."

"Well, does it?"

Lauren sat at the end of her bed and played those three words over and over in her head. "I don't know. I didn't think so, but then we were really close yesterday and...I don't know if I'm feeling something because Jennifer planted the idea in my head."

Amber laughed very loudly into the phone. "Honey, the mind is a powerful and dangerous weapon, but if you couldn't get wet for Jennifer, I don't think you can convince yourself to get hard for Berit, either."

"Thanks for making that truth bomb as vulgar as possible."

"Anytime. Listen, I have to get back to work, but I'll stop by the bar later and we'll talk. Hang in there, bud."

"Thanks." Lauren tossed her phone into her purse. Her protective case faced upward, the bold print reminding her to keep calm and carry on. She laughed. "Yeah, right."

❖

Lauren's shift started smoothly and progressed with little issue. No awkwardness hung between her and Berit, and everyone at the Dollhouse was in a cheery mood. Bellamy shared stories of her weekend away with family, Monica danced to every song that played, and Berit instructed Lauren to work the bar with Lou, showing trust in Lauren's abilities—no matter how shaky. For over three hours, Lauren poured shots and mixed drinks with Lou. Berit was at the other end of the bar, shouldering most of the crowd while Lauren and Lou worked a little more slowly. Lauren couldn't stop wondering why Berit placed her with Lou. Had she made things uncomfortable for Berit?

"Want to learn how to make a Redheaded Slut?"

"Make her what?" Lauren's counter was met by a brilliant smile from Lou.

"You know, you're funny. I say that like it's a surprise because it is. When you first started, you seemed kinda stiff. But you're all right."

"I wasn't at my best a month ago." Lauren tossed a runaway ice cube into the sink.

"And now?"

Lauren considered the question with a deep breath. Something within her had shifted since working with the spectacular women at the Dollhouse. "I'm happier," she said honestly. "I thought I had lost control of everything—my job, my relationship, my home life…" Most of her list was still in disarray, but she somehow breathed easier. "I'm a mess, but I'm a happier mess. I'm actually thinking about having her put me on the books and make my position more permanent."

Lou nodded and brushed a few stray strands of hair from her face. "That's great. I'm very happy to know you're sticking around. Berit is a pain in my ass but a very good judge of character. She saw something special in you right away."

Lauren's stomach quivered, and she fought to keep her feelings off her face. Lou, Berit's *sister*, could not know about Lauren's turmoil. She cleared her throat roughly and grabbed her bottle of water from the back counter. After two long swallows, she spotted Berit making her way over.

"No drinking on the job," Berit said with a wink.

Lauren laughed loudly. Too loudly. Her chuckling was prolonged and awkward, carrying on until Berit disappeared into her office. Lauren's face fell. Lou punched her shoulder.

Lauren smoothed her hands over her dark hair nervously and picked up a rag to wipe down the bar, ignoring the fact that Lou had already cleaned the same spot.

"Lauren, I may be Berit's sister, but you can talk to me. So seriously, talk to me. Do you have a thing for my—for Berit?"

Lauren winced. This moment was uncomfortable. Thankfully, a line of customers sidled up to the bar. Lauren mouthed "later" to Lou, and they served the group. Lauren chatted casually with a young couple that brought along their best guy friend. He spoke highly of the Dollhouse and its friendly, inclusive atmosphere. Lauren took the time to advertise their upcoming fellas' night and mentioned there'd be a stud night for the ladies. Everyone's eyes lit up with excitement, and that was when Lauren's heart dropped.

Through the crowd, she spotted Rebecca walk through the door. Lauren took a second too long to react, and Rebecca saw her. She waved excitedly as Lauren looked around for help.

"Lauren!" Rebecca's voice was shrill, even in the loud space as she rushed over to the bar.

Lauren didn't even try to fake enthusiasm. "Hey, Rebecca. Do you want a drink?"

"I want to know why you didn't tell me you were working here." Rebecca crossed her arms over her chest, the way she always would when Lauren acted like an independent person. "And I'll take a shot of tequila, whatever's fine."

Lauren purposely grabbed the cheapest bottle on the shelf and poured a shot. She placed a lime wedge atop the small glass and pushed it toward Rebecca. Lauren's face had yet to change from stoic. "I work here, it's great, and that's all you need to know."

"I know stooping to bartending can't be comfortable for you, but you should've told me."

Lauren clenched her jaw. Her face flushed with anger, but she kept it in check. She was on the clock and a front-row representative of the Dollhouse. "I'm not stooping—"

"You're not talking to me, you're hiding your job and your new girlfriend from me. I'm hurt. It's like we're not even friends."

We're not, Lauren's inner voice screamed. "I'm sorry you feel that way."

"So tell me about her," Rebecca said, pulling out a barstool and getting comfortable.

Lying never came naturally to Lauren. She fumbled with a response. She didn't want to give Rebecca the satisfaction of knowing her latest relationship had failed. "I can't. We're…" Lauren thought long and hard about how to handle herself. In her peripheral vision, Lauren saw Berit laughing. "We're not out at work yet."

Rebecca gasped. "No way. It's someone here."

"Yeah. It was all very unexpected." Lauren's heart started to beat a little faster.

"Who is it?" Rebecca spun around in every direction. Lauren worried she'd topple from the stool. "Is it her?" she said, nodding in Talia's direction. "Her?" She pointed to Dee. Rebecca must've passed over Berit four times in her attempt to find Lauren's secret girlfriend.

Lauren smiled and excused herself. She fidgeted with her hands during the short walk to Berit's side. Berit was unpacking napkins. Lauren chewed at the inside of her cheek while she waited for Berit's attention. "Hey, Berit, would it be okay for me to take my break?"

"Yeah. You know you don't have to ask me. I trust you know when it's a good time to go and when it's not."

Lauren envied how relaxed Berit was at all times. Her nerves made her hands tingle and her legs feel like cement pillars. "I also need to ask a favor of you. It's a very weird, huge favor."

That got Berit's full attention. She put the napkins down and faced Lauren fully. With a tilt of her head she asked, "What's wrong?"

"Look over my shoulder." Lauren waited a beat for Berit to do so. "See the really cute, petite woman with curly black hair at the bar?" Lauren hated Berit's natural reaction to smile at a pretty girl. Rebecca didn't deserve Berit's positive appraisal. "That's my ex."

Berit's face turned serious. "*The* ex?" Berit took a breath. "The not-so-nice one?"

Lauren nodded.

"Do you want me to have Danny escort her out?"

Lauren's tension eased a bit at Berit's concern and the image of Danny, the muscular stone butch, carrying Rebecca out by her collar. "Not exactly. Would you...can we...uh," Lauren stuttered. "She asked me about my new girlfriend, and I don't want her to know I'm not seeing Jennifer anymore."

Berit looked shocked. "You're not?"

"No, but that's not important right now. Will you pretend to be with me? Like, *with me*?" Lauren cringed, closed her eyes and dropped her head. Her plan sounded stupid once she said it aloud. "This is ridiculous," she mumbled. "I'm sorry. I'm an adult and can handle this." Before she could walk away, Berit grabbed Lauren's wrist and pulled her back into her. Their faces were an inch apart. Lauren's knees weakened.

"I think we should do it," Berit said, looking into Lauren's eyes. Lauren saw nothing but sincerity and security shining back at her. "Why give her any kind of satisfaction? If you decide to tell her we broke up tomorrow, that's fine, but at least it'll be on your time."

Lauren felt chills as Berit placed her hands on her shoulders and ran them the length of her arms. She gripped Lauren's hands as she leaned in to whisper in her ear. "And I'll make it very convincing."

Lauren swallowed hard as she stared at the pale, flawless skin of Berit's neck. It'd take no effort at all to taste it. But Lauren didn't want to send mixed signals. She knew Berit was out of her league, and she was far below Berit's standards. They made great friends. She pushed back and said, "I appreciate this, but no funny business." She turned and walked back to Rebecca, knowing Berit was only a step behind her.

"Rebecca," Lauren said with a prideful smile that came a little too easily. "This is Berit, the owner of the Dollhouse and the woman I've been dating." Lauren turned back to Berit and felt damned when she saw her charming smile slide into place. Berit reached out to shake Rebecca's hand. Rebecca's jaw was nearly on the floor.

Berit played right along. "Not what you expected, huh? Me either. But Lauren is persistent. She knew she wanted me from day one and just kept coming on to me. Eventually, I gave in, and I'm so happy I did." Berit snaked her arm around Lauren's waist and pulled her close.

"Berit, I thought we decided it was best to not be out at work." Lauren watched Rebecca's reactions closely, trying to focus on the ruse instead of how good it felt in Berit's arms. Rebecca's eyes bounced between Berit and Lauren like a ping-pong ball.

Berit chuckled low and slow, and Lauren found the sound to be incredibly sexy. "I know, I put that rule in place as your boss," Berit said, turning her face and looking directly at Lauren's lips. Lauren felt panicked. "But I think it's okay. Everyone will be happy for us."

"Wow. How did this happen exactly?" Rebecca said.

"We were friends first." Berit answered immediately, not giving Lauren a second to jump in. "I had met Lauren here and she hit on me a few times, but I told her I'm not really interested in being picked up by a customer and treated like a one-night novelty." Berit's eyes met Lauren's briefly before she looked to Rebecca again. "I'm sure you could imagine that happens a lot around here."

Rebecca twirled a long tendril of her hair around her index finger and looked Berit up and down. "I know I'd try to take you home with me."

Berit shifted closer to Lauren. Lauren's hand was now around her waist possessively. Fake girlfriend or not, Lauren wasn't about to let Rebecca talk to Berit like that.

"You're not really my type. Anyway," Berit said, dismissing Rebecca, "when Lauren lost her job, I offered her one for however long she'd need it." The hazel of Berit's eyes seemed to deepen the longer she looked at Lauren. "Ever since then, she's proven my first impression of her was wrong."

Lauren mentally skimmed Berit's small speech. She knew it had a hidden meaning, a secret message. But the serious moment and her focus vanished a second later when Berit pulled her flush against her body and placed a kiss on her temple. She leaned into the kiss, not even trying to resist the pull she felt.

"I never knew Lauren to be so aggressive in pursuing someone. When we were together, she could barely make a decision for herself."

"I would've if I had the chance."

"You two were together?" Berit held Lauren tighter. "I guess I should thank you for letting this one go." Berit leaned in slowly, giving Lauren more than enough time to pull away if she wanted.

Lauren stayed put and welcomed Berit's unbelievably soft lips on hers. Her stomach tensed at the feel of Berit's warmth, mouth, and her comforting scent. Before Lauren could lose herself to the undeniably amazing sensation, Berit pulled away. Lauren stared up at Berit like she was seeing her for the first time. The look they shared was playful, but something more serious simmered beneath the surface.

"I should go," Rebecca said, breaking the moment. She reached into her purse, but Berit stopped her.

"It's on the house, as a thank you." Berit's smile was nearly lethal.

Rebecca threw a ten dollar bill on the bar. "I insist." All the sugar had drained from her tone. She grabbed her purse and started off, but not without looking at Lauren once more. "I'll see you at home."

Lauren and Berit broke out into a fit of giggles as they watched Rebecca storm out. She looked around, relieved to notice not one staff member but Lou in the area. "You were great. God, that was so fun."

"It was, wasn't it?" Berit still stood within Lauren's space. Lauren knew she wasn't talking about teasing Rebecca. "What did she mean when she said she'd see you at home?"

Lauren swallowed the lump of embarrassment and worry forming in her throat. "She moved in before we were together. It was supposed to be a temporary thing, but she's still there and we kind of need her to make the rent each month." Lauren was scared to meet Berit's eyes, afraid to catch a hint of judgment, but she saw no such thing.

"That has to be awful for you."

"I told you my home life is uncomfortable."

"Hey guys, I hate to break this up, but we need a little help at the bar," Lou called out. She waited until she caught Lauren's eye and sent her a wink.

Lauren laughed. She gave Berit a playful shove. "You heard your sister. Get back to work."

"Should we pick this up later? My place?" Berit said cheekily as she sauntered away. She made a show of shaking out her towel before tucking it back into her pocket.

Lauren could never let Berit know just how tempted she was. "No we shouldn't, but thank you for playing along." Over Berit's shoulder, Lauren spotted Amber walk into the bar. A welcome visitor. She tried to step away, but Berit placed her hand on Lauren's forearm.

"I'm always here to help."

Lauren tried to stop herself from falling into Berit's eyes and smile, an impossible task. She nodded and rushed off toward her friend, hoping to continue their earlier conversation. Even though Lauren knew exactly where her best friend stood on the matter of Berit.

CHAPTER SIXTEEN

Rebecca is such a bitch," Amber said before downing the rest of her drink. Her fourth of the night. "And your hot girlfriend makes these better than you." Amber shook her glass, making the ice cubes rattle loudly.

Lauren took the glass and shook her head. "She's not my girlfriend, and don't say that too loudly. I can only imagine what everyone here is thinking after our little display before." Lauren was happy Lou hadn't teased her any more, and not even Dee or Bellamy said a word.

Amber slapped the bar top, signaling she was ready for another round.

"You have no bar etiquette," Lauren said.

"Only when you're bartending."

"I also think you've had enough. You usually stop after two anyway. What gives?"

Amber huffed. "Remember the woman I'm seeing?"

"Yes. You've told me nothing about her, but I know who you're talking about. Things aren't going so great?" Lauren split her attention between Amber's wallowing and shaking up a martini for Rosa, who showed up right on time as always.

Amber twirled a cocktail napkin between her fingers. She looked sadder than Lauren had ever seen her. "Her name is Annalise and she has great legs, like these." She pointed to the embossed logo of legs over the bar's name on the napkin. "I also just found out she has two kids."

Lauren almost dropped the cocktail shaker. "Haven't you been dating for over a month? How did you just find this out?"

"Because I was blinded by a talented tongue." Amber covered her face in shame.

"Hang on," Lauren said as she poured the martini into a chilled glass and garnished with three olives. "Here you go, Rosa." She slid the cocktail to everyone's favorite customer. "I apologize in advance if it's not as good as you're used to, but Berit is insisting I handle mixing drinks on my own."

"You're doing wonderful, dear." Rosa spoke like a socialite in her fifties, looked like she was in her thirties, and never told anyone her actual age. Rosa took her first sip and wasn't hesitant. "It's delicious, just as I suspected it'd be. Berit has incredible taste in women."

Lauren's eyebrows shot skyward.

"The women she hires, I mean." Rosa smirked.

"You're beautiful," Amber mumbled drunkenly to Rosa. "My girlfriend is beautiful like you and so good in bed. She's made me dumb."

"Okay." Lauren clapped her hands. "It's time to get you a ride." She looked at Rosa apologetically and picked up Amber's phone.

"She has pictures of them everywhere." Amber's head fell back, and she continued talking to the ceiling. "I just assumed she was a proud aunt or something. Not a mother of two who has an ex-husband in Pennsylvania. Ugh." Her head lolled forward. "This is a mess. *I'm* a mess."

Lauren slid Amber's phone into her purse and walked around the bar to assist her friend. "You're a mess right now, but not always. You're brilliant and sweet." Lauren wrapped her arm around Amber's waist. Berit must've spotted her struggles, because she was at her side in an instant.

"It's Lauren's hot girlfriend to the rescue!" Amber extended her hand. "I'm Ambler."

Lauren looked at Berit apologetically. "You've met my friend *Amber* before. I told her about the incident with Rebecca earlier."

"Gotcha. Does she have a ride?" Berit grunted as Amber twisted, seemingly reluctant to allow anyone to help her.

"Yeah. The driver should be here any minute. You can head back in." The three stood outside beside Danny.

Berit looked back to the door. "I have a few things to finish up before closing. Are you sure you're okay out here?"

Lauren smiled at Berit's never-ending concern. "We're fine, especially with Danny. You can go." Berit reluctantly left Lauren and Amber. Lauren's skin became tacky from the humidity and the ends of her hair flipped.

"You really need to climb that tree."

"What 'tree'? What are you talking about?"

"Her," Amber said loudly, pointing her finger in no certain direction. She looked at Lauren and then up to Danny, who towered over both of them. She reached out and touched Danny's firm bicep. "Not you. Although you are a pretty fine tree also."

"Amber, stop." Lauren slapped at Amber's wandering hand.

"I'm serious, Lauren." Amber was almost a full whine. "Rebecca is awful, and you should be happy. Berit is so, so nice and really hot. Have fun because you're still young and before you know it, you'll find out there's two children hiding in Pennsylvania. Boom. You're left with the choice of an instant family or dying alone." A black sedan with a ride service sticker in the window pulled up.

"Go," Amber called over her shoulder as she opened the car door. "Climb that sexy tree." Amber fell into the car and off she went.

Lauren looked up at Danny and said, "She's drunk and has no clue what she's talking about."

"Mm-hmm." Danny stood tall and quiet. She barely passed Lauren a sideways glance.

"You don't say much, do you?" No answer came. Lauren patted Danny's bulky shoulder and opened the door to the Dollhouse. As the door closed, Lauren could swear she heard Danny tell her to start climbing.

"Did I just hear Danny yelling?" Lauren jumped at Bellamy's sudden closeness.

"We were just joking around while I was waiting for my friend to get picked up."

"Danny makes jokes?"

Lauren erupted in laughter, the control over her emotions finally snapping and leading her to hysterics. Thankfully, Bellamy joined in.

"Let's close up," Berit shouted to her employees. The only customer left in the Dollhouse was Rosa.

The day had been a hell of a roller coaster, and Lauren felt exhausted. "I'm ready to pass out," she said as she helped Berit push in and stack chairs.

Berit took a chair from Lauren with a nod of thanks. "You're handling two in the morning better than you did in the beginning."

"You mean when you had a zombie working for you?"

"A cute zombie."

Lauren's first instinct was to not engage a comment like that from Berit, but she decided to throw caution to the wind. After all, they had already kissed that evening. "Only you would think calling a woman a cute zombie would be a compliment."

"Did it make you feel good?"

"Yeah," Lauren said, taking all of Berit in and considering her own feelings throughout the night. "It felt really good."

"You're doing great." Berit turned back to the bar and signaled for her sister. "Lou, will you finish up here? I'm heading out and can't wait to do this all again tomorrow. Good night, Lauren." Berit made her way to the back and presumably out of the bar.

Lauren was confused by Berit's sudden exit. She had thought the entire night had only affected her, but what if Berit hadn't been comfortable? What if Lauren had compromised anything that could've been between them by acting like the mess she always was?

Lauren took a deep breath and made a decision. She was going to finish cleaning up and then go climb a tree.

❖

Berit threw Hugo's large plush frog for the tenth time and watched him run and grab it, her smile just as big when he returned with it as it was the very first time he figured out how to play fetch. "Just a couple more throws, and then it's time for bed. Mama had a very weird day and she's tired." Hugo grinned at her from his place on the floor. She threw the frog again.

Hugo started barking at the knock on the door. It was nearly three in the morning, and Berit definitely wasn't expecting visitors. She crept up to her door quietly, wanting to take a peek in the peephole before opening the door. She'd seen plenty of horror movies to know better, but no movie prepared her for this. She opened the door.

"Lauren?" Berit felt exposed in her thin tank, no bra, and boxer briefs. She crossed her arms over her chest to hide her nipples. "What are you doing here?"

"I'm sorry for just stopping by." Lauren's voice was so small, Berit strained to hear her and struggled with the desire to wrap Lauren in her arms. "It's poor manners to show up without calling, but if I'd called I think I would've chickened out."

"Lauren, stop and come in." Berit waved into her apartment and shut the door behind her. Lauren's posture was rigid, and she seemed uncomfortable. "Is everything all right?"

Lauren clenched and unclenched her fists before meeting Berit's eyes. "Here's the thing, I don't want to be stuck between an instant family or dying alone."

"Well, those sound like terrible choices. Would you like something to drink?"

"No, thank you." Lauren knelt and started petting Hugo. "I'm sorry for upsetting Hugo. I'm sure he's used to you having late-night guests, but not ones who just show up."

Berit ignored the small insult. "You apologize too much."

"I just—I feel bad and guilty for doing things that make other people uncomfortable or for causing any problems. I was raised to be proper and considerate, and I find it incredibly frustrating because I always end up putting what I want last on the list." Lauren narrowed her eyes at Berit's wide grin. "Why are you smiling? I'm ranting like a lunatic, and you're just smiling."

"Your accent comes out when you're ranting, particularly when you say 'frustrating,' and I think it's adorable."

"I'm not adorable."

"You're not *just* adorable."

"I'm frustrated."

Berit's smile grew impossibly larger. She felt the shift between them. The change started earlier, but in this room and this moment, Berit knew all preconceived expectations of their relationship had fallen away. "You're frustrated because you rarely do what you want. What is that, exactly? What do you want, Lauren?" Berit let the question hang between them. She didn't move or speak again. She had handed the next move to Lauren on a platter, and Berit's heart beat rapidly as she waited. The anticipation was suffocating her.

"I want..." Lauren's voice shook. She stepped closer to Berit and said, "I want to tell you why things didn't work between Jennifer and me." She reached out and took Berit's hand and touched her arm lightly.

Berit watched the contact, enthralled by Lauren's pale fingers tracing her colorful tattoos. "I wanted to ask, but I don't like to be nosy."

"She's gorgeous and successful. Her body was amazing, and we always had things to talk about."

Berit thought of the phone call from Jennifer and her complaint of hearing too much about Berit during her date with Lauren. She swallowed thickly when Lauren touched the inside of her bicep.

"But what I felt when she kissed me couldn't even compare to what I feel when you barely even touch me." Lauren's words brought a throb to life between Berit's thighs. "Even right now, I'm more turned on from this than I was when I felt her body against mine."

Berit buried the jealousy she felt at the imagery Lauren painted. She grabbed Lauren's hand and laced their fingers together. "Lauren, do you really want this? I need to be sure because you've told me no…a lot." The small joke lifted a bit of the tension between them.

Lauren placed her palm against Berit's cheek. "That was when I saw you as someone who'd never really be interested in me."

"And what do you see now?" Berit held her breath.

"I see someone who's kind, generous, and incredibly sexy. Someone with borderline terrible jokes and a sweet dog I want to steal. I guess it's a lot like what you said to Rebecca. My first impression of you was proven wrong."

Berit closed the distance between them and looked into Lauren's dark eyes. She had resigned herself to knowing this moment would never happen, even as she waited for it. Lauren was the first woman she'd met in a long time who made her consider what she had to give as a person and as a partner. Berit tilted her head slightly and brought her lips within a breath of Lauren's. She reveled a moment in the closeness, the anticipation, the turning point of their relationship. Berit never had to prove herself for a woman before, but she was ready to do so for Lauren until she had nothing left to prove.

"I've thought about kissing you more times than I can count," she confessed against Lauren's waiting mouth. She heard Lauren swallow.

"You don't need to use any more lines on me."

"It's not a line." Berit touched the tip of her nose to Lauren's cheek. The delicate touch combined with Lauren's breath against her lips sent a shiver up Berit's spine. "Your lips, your smile, and your accent make your mouth like a forbidden fruit for me."

Lauren placed her hands high up on Berit's chest before wrapping them around the back of her neck. She pressed their foreheads together. "Says the woman with the most lethal smile on the planet."

Berit leaned back and flashed that smile at Lauren. She tucked a strand of hair behind Lauren's ear and said, "I have no expectations for tonight, except a lot of kissing starting now." Berit framed Lauren's face with her hands and kissed her slowly at first, allowing herself time to enjoy the supple, pillow-like texture of Lauren's mouth. All the details she forbade herself from noticing earlier in the night were more delectable than she thought possible. Lauren's upper lip fit perfectly between Berit's.

Lauren tugged the hem of Berit's shirt until their hips and breasts met. She moaned as Berit traced her bottom lip with her tongue. "I need a couch or a bed or even a chair because I swear my knees are about to give out."

"Glad it's not just me, then." Berit ran her palms along Lauren's sides and grabbed the belt loops of her jeans with her fingers. "Come on," Berit said, bringing her to the bedroom. She turned on a small lamp on the nightstand, only to have Lauren turn it off again. Berit stared at her in the dark.

"In case we…you know." Lauren seemed so unsure of herself now.

"Above all else, I want you to feel comfortable. But I'd also like to see you."

"What if you don't like what you see?"

Berit kissed Lauren deeply, hoping the passion she felt could help assuage Lauren's insecurities. Berit knew she had no immediate cure, but hopefully they'd make small strides together. She stepped back to catch her breath and pulled her shirt over her head. "I'm not wearing a bra," she said in a husky voice, her throat tight with desire. Berit took Lauren's hand and placed it on her chest. "I want you to see me, like how I want to see you."

Lauren touched from Berit's collarbone to the center of her chest, and brought her hand down to rest on her stomach. "I'm not perfect," she whispered.

"I think you and I have different ideas of perfection." Berit kissed Lauren's cheek and then her brow. She ran her fingers through Lauren's hair, letting her nails scratch gently along Lauren's scalp to help relax her. Berit sucked in a breath when Lauren's hand descended her abdomen and grazed the top of her boxers. She hadn't experienced that kind of sensitivity in a long time. It took her by surprise.

"You're already driving me crazy." She laughed lightly. Berit reached out as Lauren stepped away, searching the dark. "Where are you?"

Lauren turned the light on. "It occurred to me that I see these almost every day," she said, reaching out for Berit's arm. She traced along the lines of the tattoos, following waves and flower petals etched in muscle and sinew. "You probably have a few more I've yet to see." Lauren looked down between their bodies. She reached out to touch a mermaid that swam along Berit's ribs, her hair flowing along the curve of Berit's breast. "Why a mermaid?"

"I spent a lot of time at the shore with my family when I was younger. I was always in the ocean and frolicking in the waves, even when everyone else complained the water was too cold or rough." Berit captured Lauren's free hand and brought it to her lips. She kissed her palm. "Now the ocean scares me, so this is a permanent reminder that at one time I was fearless."

"You seem pretty fearless to me."

"I'm terrified of so much, but I've realized life is about what you do with your fear." Berit gripped the bottom of Lauren's T-shirt, her eyes never faltering from Lauren's steady gaze. Berit noticed every small detail of Lauren's face—a small mole next to her eye, the wrinkle of intensity between her eyebrows, and a faint scar at the center of her forehead. "You're beautiful." Lauren kissed Berit before she helped her take her shirt off. Berit was sure she'd never seen anything sexier than Lauren's pert breasts encased in a burgundy lace bra. Her mouth hung open.

Lauren covered herself with her arms. "Please don't stare."

"I'm sorry, but it's the truth when I say I can't help it." Berit wrapped her arms around Lauren and held her close. She whispered in her ear. "Would it make you feel better if we took off your pants and got right under the covers?" Berit felt Lauren nod against her. She unbuttoned Lauren's jeans and pushed them past her hips. Against temptation, Berit never looked at the newly exposed skin as Lauren crawled beneath her gray comforter.

Lauren pulled the covers up and stretched out on her side facing Berit. She patted the mattress beside her. "I'm kinda lonely."

Berit slid between the covers and gently rolled Lauren onto

her back. "Hi," she said before kissing Lauren soundly. She gently spread Lauren's legs and situated herself between them. Every point where their bare bodies made contact set Berit's skin on fire. Her hips started a slow seduction of their own. She kissed Lauren's jaw and tried to memorize her scent.

Lauren let out a long, low moan when Berit palmed her breast. "Kiss me," Lauren said, her voice straining.

Berit dove in, filling Lauren's mouth and meeting her growing passion head-on. They kissed the same, like they already knew one another and had done this a hundred times before. Berit whimpered as Lauren nibbled her bottom lip. She slid her hand beneath the lace of Lauren's bra and rolled her hard nipple between her fingers. Lauren raised her hips off the mattress. Berit met the movement with her own hips, pushing forward to apply pressure to Lauren's mound.

"God," Lauren said between heavy breaths. "This is happening so fast."

Berit pulled back. "Do you want me to stop? I don't want to rush you."

Lauren pressed two fingers against Berit's lips. "That is the opposite of what I want." Lauren replaced her fingers with her lips, kissing Berit until she needed to breathe. "I just meant my body… I'm going to come really, really fast."

Berit smiled smugly. "The remedy for that is making you come more than once." Berit kissed Lauren hard before pulling her bra off. Again, Berit was shocked into silence. Lauren's nipples were dark and begging for attention. Her breasts were small, but their curve and soft skin were enticing. "I'm going to stare," Berit said. She pulled back the covers to look at the rest of Lauren's body. Her eyes barely made it past where Lauren's thighs were pressed together. "You're breathtaking. Are you really here?" Berit asked goofily, touching Lauren's face all over.

Lauren held Berit's face in her hands and said, "Berit, I love your jokes." Berit's heart fluttered. "But what I'd love more is for you to touch me." Lauren spread her legs wide in invitation.

Berit followed Lauren's demand immediately. It's poor manners to leave a woman waiting. She slipped her hand beneath the waistband of Lauren's panties to find Lauren's clit pronounced and ready for attention. Berit circled it once with her middle finger before dipping into Lauren's soaked entrance. Lauren's whole body twitched at the sensation. She kissed Lauren's lips, her neck, and her chest. She circled Lauren's nipple with her tongue, mimicking the motion of her fingertip along Lauren's most sensitive skin. Berit felt herself grow wetter with every small noise that escaped Lauren's parted lips.

"What do you like?" Berit said between the open-mouthed kisses she was leaving along Lauren's breasts.

"Two fingers." Lauren moaned loudly as Berit entered her slowly with her middle and ring fingers. "*Fuck*. Like that. Now lick me." Berit's pussy clenched at the command.

Berit kissed down Lauren's abdomen, getting distracted by a wayward freckle that beckoned for her attention. She withdrew her fingers for a brief moment to strip Lauren of her panties, laughing when Lauren voiced her dissatisfaction at the loss. She reentered Lauren a little more roughly, and Lauren's brilliant smile told Berit she didn't mind a little roughness during moments of passion.

She settled between Lauren's thighs and ran her tongue along the crease where thigh met hip. Lauren's breathing grew more rapid. Berit twisted and curled her fingers slightly before teasing Lauren's fleshy hood with the tip of her tongue. She sucked Lauren's clit into her mouth, and her back bowed off the mattress.

Lauren was gorgeous in her wild abandon. Berit didn't stop her pleasurable ministrations, not when Lauren's grip in her hair turned painful and especially not when Lauren begged her to never, ever stop what she was doing to her. Berit was awestricken by the woman writhing around her. For someone who assumed an average role in this world, Lauren was exceptional in every way.

"Berit, don't stop, I'm so close," Lauren growled. Berit's head bobbed up and down as she sucked Lauren's clit and fucked her furiously with her fingers. Lauren ran her hands through Berit's hair and down to frame her face the best they could. Her hands felt small and feminine against Berit's flexing jaw, and the action made Berit feel sexier than she ever had.

Berit knew Lauren was on the brink of orgasm. Her inner walls had started to contract, and her legs were shaking, but Lauren refused to let go. She continuously chanted, "Not yet, not yet."

Berit licked a long, firm stroke along Lauren's clit. "Let go, Lauren," she said before latching on again. Instantly, Lauren bucked her hips off the bed as she shouted a stream of expletives combined with Berit's name. Berit continued to taste Lauren after the final tremors of pleasure had subsided. She wasn't ready to surrender the feel of Lauren's silky skin against her tongue, but Lauren had other ideas. Berit found herself being tugged by her hair and guided up Lauren's body.

"You," Lauren said as she kissed Berit. "You are fucking amazing. No wonder women throw themselves at you." She kissed her again before Berit could respond. "But now it's my turn." Lauren grabbed the waistband of Berit's boxers and said, "Take these off and then I want you up here." She signaled to her mouth. Berit's eyebrows rose, and she knew her face mirrored her excitement. For their first time, Lauren was confident and sure of what she wanted. Now Berit knew what Lauren had meant when she described herself as an active bottom.

"Yes ma'am." Berit moved at lightning speed to strip and position her soaked center over Lauren's waiting mouth. "This is one of my favorite positions." Berit's mind went blank when Lauren's hands caressed her thighs and ass. Her short nails felt divine scraping along her heated skin.

"Mmm...mine, too. The view is incredible." Lauren rubbed up Berit's abdomen and squeezed her small breasts. "You have perfect tits," Lauren said as she tugged at the small barbell running horizontally through Berit's right nipple. "This is a nice surprise."

"Heightened sensitivity is the biggest perk." Berit took in a long, steady breath. The anticipation was killing her, but feeling Lauren's breath against her as she spoke was a delicious sensation on its own. Berit didn't want any of it to end. The first touch of

Lauren's tongue to her waiting skin exploded behind Berit's eyelids in vivid colors. "Holy shit, that's good."

Berit moved round and round, assisting Lauren in reaching every millimeter of her skin. Every sensation radiated from her center, up to her chest, and back into her toes as she rose higher and higher toward mind-numbing pleasure. Lauren's moan vibrated against Berit's clit, and Berit felt the first pull of an orgasm. She gripped the headboard with a fierce hold and looked back at Lauren's body.

Lauren buried her right hand between her own thighs, working her clit feverishly. Berit could hear Lauren's wet flesh being touched, which was the last bit of stimulus needed to send her into the most pleasurable oblivion.

She made small noises as she held on to the headboard for dear life, not wanting to fall on Lauren or away from her pleasure-giving mouth. Berit pressed her forehead against the wall and tried to catch her breath. Her orgasm shook her with unexpected and powerful tremors when she felt Lauren gasp as her own orgasm hit. Berit felt Lauren giggle against her pussy before she smacked her bare ass.

Berit fell to her side and turned off the lamp. She was taken with Lauren's easy smile bathed in dim moonlight. Lauren wiped her mouth against the sheets before leaning in for a kiss. Berit kissed Lauren sweetly, wanting the last moment they both experienced before falling asleep to be one of tenderness instead of passion.

Understanding washed over Berit. She'd known Lauren was different after the first time they met, and she always saw the potential of what they could be together. Now Lauren was finally seeing that as well.

CHAPTER SEVENTEEN

B erit woke up to Hugo's nose in her ear. The sun brightened her bedroom with early-morning energy. She buried her face into her pillow, and Hugo stood on her back with his front paws.

"Okay, Hugo, I know it's time for your walk. Give me a minute." She turned onto her other side, and her heart sank. Lauren was gone. Berit sat up quickly, her floppy hair falling onto her face as she scanned the floor for Lauren's clothing. Not one piece was left behind. She got up and went to the bathroom and then into the kitchen, not at all surprised to find both rooms empty. Berit pulled on the first pair of sweatpants she grabbed from her dresser and threw on the tank from the previous night. How had she missed Lauren's escape?

She hooked Hugo into his harness and trudged downstairs and out to the street for their morning walk. On gorgeous mornings like these, Berit usually soaked up the sunshine and lost herself to the tunes the neighborhood birds performed. But this morning felt different. She felt sad, but more importantly, disappointed. She was looking forward to waking up with Lauren and spending the morning together, but Lauren clearly didn't want the same thing, and Berit didn't know what Lauren was thinking.

"What do you think?" Berit said to Hugo as he circled a tree, tangling his leash along the way. "Maybe she had plans and couldn't stay, or maybe she's not a morning person and wanted to save me from her grumpy side." Hugo looked over his shoulder and tilted his head at Berit. "You're right, I'm probably way grumpier in the morning." They walked another couple blocks before turning around and heading back to Berit's apartment. Berit released Hugo's leash and let him lead her up the stairs. She walked into her kitchen and started a pot of coffee. "Hugo." She called him back into the room. He stared at her with an open-mouthed smile and panted. "Do you think she regrets last night?"

Hugo closed his mouth and whined a bit. He shook his head at her and ran up to stand on his hind legs with his front paws on her thighs. She scratched behind his ears and thought about her night with Lauren. The sex and the connection they shared had been fantastic. How could Lauren regret any of it? Berit grabbed her phone from the bedroom and felt another bit of her heart ache when she didn't see any messages or calls waiting for her.

By the time she prepared her coffee and a small breakfast, as well as a meal for Hugo, she had convinced herself to resist messaging Lauren. She couldn't read her mind or assume what she needed. Berit would wait to talk to her, face-to-face like an adult. They both had work later and they'd have to address this thing eventually. Berit tossed Hugo a small piece of toast with peanut butter. He enjoyed the morsel much more than his own breakfast.

"Do you want to go to the park today?" The P-word was almost as recognizable as the W-word. Hugo started his dance of excitement and ran to the door. A day out in the fresh air would be good for both of them. Berit changed into a more appropriate outfit before heading out with her dog. She'd consider what the hell she was going to say to Lauren while giving her favorite companion the attention he deserved.

Berit arrived at the Dollhouse a little earlier than usual, citing the need to do inventory, while knowing she needed to see Lauren. She felt nervous and checked her phone continuously, worrying Lauren would call out if she was trying to avoid Berit. She took a deep breath in preparation. Berit had worked through every scenario in her head and felt ready for confrontation. Lauren wouldn't get away with disappearing. The back door to the bar opened and closed, and Berit waited eagerly to see who'd walk past her office door. If it was Lou, her plans would be compromised. Berit couldn't wait to see who the slow footsteps belonged to and she called out, "Hey." Lauren peeked around the doorframe shyly. Berit released a relieved sigh.

"Hi." Lauren fidgeted with the shoulder strap of her purse. She was dressed in all black, and Berit's heart stuttered as she took her in.

"You were gone this morning," Berit said, cutting to the chase before her physical reaction could overshadow her emotional turmoil.

Lauren's shoulders slumped. She tossed her purse onto Berit's desk. "I wasn't sure of the proper protocol."

Berit searched Lauren's tone for sarcasm or mockery, but Lauren was serious. "What protocol?"

Lauren leaned against Berit's desk with her hip. Berit stood in front of her. "Morning-after protocol. I've never woke up in someone's bed after a—you know, one-night thing or fling or whatever. I didn't know what to do, so I just left. It seemed like the safest choice." Berit tried to quell her growing frustration, but she was getting mad. "I came to you last night, clearly ready for whatever might happen, but I just didn't think it all the way through. I'm sorry if that's not what you usually do."

Berit rubbed at the center of her chest. She had never shied away from her playgirl reputation, but hearing how Lauren still saw her as a hit-and-run hurt. She was shocked to feel her throat tighten and eyes sting. When was the last time a woman made her cry?

"Yeah, you're right. I usually make sure they're gone before I go to sleep. I guess we both did something we're not used to last night. Time for work." Berit grabbed her clipboard and stormed out of her office. She waited until she was surrounded by unopened cases of liquor to breathe.

"What the hell, Berit?" Lauren was hot on Berit's heels.

The back door to the Dollhouse opened and Lou walked in, noticing the obvious tension immediately. She raised her hands in innocence and walked past Berit and Lauren.

"Why are you acting so shitty?"

Berit ripped open a case of whiskey. "You want to know why *I'm* acting shitty? That's rich coming from you."

Lauren put her hands on her hips and looked up. "Wow," she said, leveling Berit with a stone cold stare. "If this is how it's going to be, I guess last night was a mistake." Lauren turned to leave, but looked back to Berit one more time. "For the record, I thought you were more mature than this."

"Yeah? Well, for the record, I didn't want it to be like this. Not with you."

Confusion pinched Lauren's features. "What?"

"I thought I made myself clear." Berit wiped her face roughly in frustration. "I didn't want a fling with you," she said with her hands outstretched. "You know, Jennifer called me after your first date and asked me what was going on between us because you wouldn't stop talking about me."

Lauren looked shocked.

"I told her nothing, and that you were sticking to common ground conversation topics because that's just who you are, but when I hung up, all I could think about was how I wished it was true. I wanted it to be true. I wanted to be on your mind as much as you were on mine." Berit looked away from Lauren as tears started to blur her vision. "And then you stood in front of me last night and said how your first impression of me was wrong. I thought you finally saw me for me." Berit wiped at her wet cheeks and took a long, shaky breath. "It really sucks being wrong."

"Berit, I..."

"Let's just get back to work. We've wasted enough time." Berit made her way back toward her office, leaving Lauren alone in the receiving room.

❖

A million thoughts buzzed around Lauren's head as she went about her shift, but she wouldn't allow herself to focus on any of them. She couldn't risk a stray tear as she served someone a fun cocktail, and service without a smile didn't get many tips. She tried several times to grab a minute with Berit so she could ask one of the hundred questions she had, but Berit had managed to expertly dodge her all night. Lauren even went as far as waiting in Berit's office while she took her break in hopes of Berit strolling in, but she struck out.

The Dollhouse was nearing last call when Lauren felt herself start to crack. Berit had followed Bellamy into the stockroom, and Lauren felt overwhelmed with unjust jealousy. She was torn between storming back there and declaring Berit hers, and escaping out the front door with a bottle of tequila to shut her mind off for the night. She opted for the mature option and went back to work.

After Berit didn't return from the stockroom for nearly thirty minutes, Lauren turned to the one person she hoped could help her. "Hey, Lou," she said shyly while joining Lou behind the bar. She moved around some glasses as Lou counted the register. "Can I talk to you for a minute?"

"Sure. What's up?" Lou zipped up the deposit bag for the night.

"I did something I'm not proud of, and I don't know how to make it better."

Lou stared at her, clearly waiting for actual details.

"I upset Berit, and I don't want to tell you everything since you're her sister."

"You should also take into account that I'm more inclined to beat you up for hurting my sister."

Lauren grimaced. "I did think about that, but I believe you're less likely to because I know I'm an idiot and I want to make things better. I did a lot of assuming, and it got me into trouble. Please help me." Lauren pressed her hands together and smiled the largest grin she could conjure up.

"Fine."

Lauren started to cheer loudly.

"Okay, keep it down." Lou checked their surroundings. "The worst part of all of this is that I want to know so much more, but I won't ask for fear of being scarred."

"Let's say I treated her a little like a one-night stand and keep it at that."

Lou cringed and said, "You're a dick."

"I know."

"She really likes you."

"I'm starting to realize this." Lauren felt even more ashamed now.

Lou watched her intently for a minute. "Berit's a good person and deserves someone as good, if not better. Is that you, Lauren?"

Lauren thought long and hard, the contemplation her way of showing Lou how serious she was about making things better with Berit. "I want to be," she said honestly.

Lou nodded before heading to the large fridge and returning with a six-pack of craft ale. She set the beer on the bar. "Berit has a place she likes to go when she's upset. Ever since we were kids, if someone pissed her off she'd run away and hide until she calmed down. Are you familiar with Lewis Park?" Lauren nodded. "There's a stone wall overlooking the lake near the north entrance."

"Should I check her apartment first?"

"How upset is she?"

Lauren thought of Berit's tears, and her stomach twisted. She couldn't bring herself to say the words. She lowered her head and said, "Very."

"She's there, trust me. Bring these." She pushed the bottles to Lauren but kept her hand on them. "Are you sure about this?"

Lauren thought about every wayward moment from recent weeks, and not one negative thought could overshadow the good she'd felt seep into her life the night before. She needed Berit to be okay, to forgive her, and to recapture the feeling that surged between them less than twenty-four hours before.

"Without a doubt."

Lou nodded and released the beer. "Good luck."

Lauren took a deep breath. She knew she was going to need all the luck she could get.

❖

The drive from the Dollhouse to the lake took fifteen minutes. Finding the north entrance took another ten for directionally impaired Lauren. She was relieved to see Berit's Jeep parked in the lot. Lauren got out of her car and started to walk slowly with the six-pack in hand. It was after two in the morning. She was tired, but she'd never be able to rest with this discontent between her and Berit. Lauren followed the worn path and let out a sigh when she saw Berit sitting on the stone wall. The lights illuminated her sandy hair. She approached loudly, not wanting to scare Berit.

"You're too beautiful to look so sad," she said into the quiet night. Berit barely shifted, but Lauren gave her some time before stepping closer. "You know, that line actually got me when you said it, but I made sure you couldn't tell."

"Did Lou tell you I'd be here?" Berit kept her back to Lauren.

"Yes."

"Traitor."

"She also told me to bring you these." Lauren held out the six-pack. The condensation had turned the cardboard damp.

Berit turned just enough to eye the offering.

"Maybe we could share a drink and talk?" Lauren said, setting the beer on the stone wall and leaning against it. She didn't feel steady enough to sit above the water like Berit did.

Berit grabbed a beer, twisted off the cap, and took a long pull from the bottle. "This is one of my favorite beers."

"Why?"

"Because it's made in a small, local brewery, and they put a lot of attention into the details. The flavor is layered and magnificent. Try it."

Lauren pulled a bottle from the case and removed the cap. She was slow to taste it, wary of beer in general. The first sip was a surprise. She tasted citrus and a sweetness that saved her tongue from the bitterness she had associated with beer for so many years. "This ain't bad. I normally hate beer."

Berit didn't respond. She just turned back to look at the lake.

"I'm really sorry, Berit."

"We had different expectations. It happens all the time."

"I hurt you, and you're the last person I'd ever want to do that to." Lauren reached out but pulled her hand back before she could touch Berit. "Our expectations weren't all that different. We wanted the same thing."

Berit looked back at Lauren incredulously. "Clearly we didn't."

"We did." Lauren moved the beer over in order to slide closer to Berit, and her jeans caught on the rough surface of the wall. She faced the trees while Berit stared out onto the water. She turned to look at Berit's profile. The moon and the streetlights highlighted Berit's strong jaw. Lauren could still feel it flexing in her hands. "You were everything I shouldn't, *couldn't* want when I first met you. You were sexy and gorgeous, and you were capable of charming me right out of my skirt." Lauren watched a small smile pull at Berit's lips. "But when I told you no, I told myself no, too."

Berit looked at Lauren. "Why?"

"Because I didn't think my heart could handle you. I convinced myself you weren't looking for the same thing as me, and I turned off any attraction I felt for you. I was terrified of liking you too much."

"Why be scared?"

"When I was younger, a woman like you would never go for me. My heart was broken so many times because I'd fall for the unattainable. I'm nothing more than a boring business suit—a beige one at that. Thinking about having someone as amazing as you interested in me is scary because it'll hurt so much more when I ruin the relationship." Lauren felt ridiculous for admitting so much. "Someone who can have anyone never settles for someone like me." A tear ran down Lauren's cheek. Berit turned to face her fully and held her hand. "I felt so much for you last night, and I panicked."

Berit abandoned her beer and took Lauren's hand. She played with her fingers and felt each knuckle. She turned it over to trace every line she could see on Lauren's palm. The delicate touch felt inexplicably intimate. Berit brought Lauren's hand to her lips and kissed it.

"I had a girlfriend during my junior year of high school," Berit said after a long stretch of silence. "Our families were very close, and we just sort of fell into one another. We were each other's first everything, but our parents caught us eventually."

Lauren gasped and covered her mouth with her free hand. "Oh no," she said between parted fingers.

"It actually wasn't that bad. Very embarrassing, yes, but our parents were pretty cool about it. No one turned homophobic or treated us differently, except for sleepovers, of course." Berit nudged Lauren's shoulder. "I felt like a million dollars because I was madly in love with my first girlfriend and could be open about it."

Lauren listened with rapt attention, anxious for more information about a young Berit Matthews. "So what happened?"

"Remember when I told you how I had a hard time opening the Dollhouse?"

"Yeah," Lauren said dismissively, wanting to get back to the good stuff.

"My first girlfriend was Ashleigh McCarthy, Michael McCarthy's daughter."

"*Mayor* McCarthy?"

Berit nodded. "While our families were close, my dad would constantly try to get Mike to invest in a hundred different startup companies. One right after another would fail, and Mike wasn't an idiot. He saw the way my dad kept my family barely above poverty level because of these investments.

"Then one day, my dad put on a whole presentation about his latest investment, and Mike fell for it. In my dad's defense, which is something you'll rarely hear me say, the company was a surgical robot manufacturer."

"That sounds like a brilliant investment, especially at that time," Lauren said.

"It would've been, if it wasn't a total scam. Within days, all of my dad's contacts at the company disappeared, along with thousands of dollars. Mike's money and my college fund included." Berit picked up her beer and took another healthy swig. "Her dad's still holding a grudge and is determined to make my life with the Dollhouse a living hell."

"Wow. Did Mike forbid you from seeing Ashleigh after that?"

"He tried, but we were too old to control. We broke up because she was going away to the college we both dreamed of attending, and I was stuck here. Thanks to Ashleigh, I knew what it was like to be crazy about someone, so I never bothered to pursue something serious unless I felt that. I've only experienced it a few times since."

Lauren ran her fingertip along the stone wall as she tried to decide whether her next question was appropriate. "Do you still…"

"Still what?" Berit searched Lauren's face. "Still love Ashleigh? No, that was a lifetime ago. She's married to a Marine now and has four kids. The moral of the story is I know what it feels like to have a connection and chemistry with someone, and I'm not going to pursue someone if I don't feel it."

Lauren moved her body so she sat flush against Berit's side. She placed her hand on Berit's thigh and drew shapes with her fingertips. "You feel a connection and chemistry with me?"

Berit looked from Lauren's lips to her eyes. "The real question is, do you feel it, too?"

Instead of answering, Lauren leaned in and kissed Berit sweetly. Passion simmered quietly as adoration fueled the slow kiss. Lauren let her heart lead her actions as the crickets sang around them.

Chapter Eighteen

Lauren fell back and into a fit of giggles. "You're not crushing me," she said. She adjusted her legs to accommodate Berit more comfortably between her thighs. Berit had been lying lazily atop her for some time now, making no move to get off. Lauren loved Berit's weight and her long limbs wrapped around her. She felt secure and wanted, two things that hadn't come easily to Lauren recently. Berit's skin was warm and smooth beneath her palms. "You didn't strike me as a cuddler."

Berit fanned her hot breath across the side of Lauren's neck. "I think we've already established that most of your assumptions about me were wrong." She continued to make small movements with her pelvis, even though they were both oversensitive. The uncontrollable nature of the movement was intimate.

Lauren smiled. "Most, but not all. I knew you'd be phenomenal in bed."

Berit raised her head. "Phenomenal?"

"Outstanding," Lauren said, kissing Berit deeply before releasing her with a loud pop. "But you already know it."

Berit kissed Lauren softly before rolling off to the side and propping her head in her hand, elbow planted firmly on the mattress. "Just because I've never heard any complaints doesn't mean I'd assume I was good in bed. Everyone is different."

Lauren saw so much in Berit's lazy smile: happiness, satisfaction, and not a care that the sun was about to rise. "A girlfriend once told me I needed to slow down because I always made her feel rushed." Lauren remembered the incident like it was yesterday. It had taken her years to shake the thought every time she was in bed with someone.

With her index finger, Berit traced a line from Lauren's lips straight down to the center of her chest. She wiggled her finger playfully between Lauren's breasts. "As your girlfriend, I'd tell you no such thing. Your pacing is perfect and allows me to come again and again without waiting." Berit pressed her front against the length of Lauren's body.

Lauren felt herself warm all over at the contact. Berit's body was a marvel, but she couldn't focus fully on skin and muscle. Was this Berit's way of declaring their relationship more significant than casual or simply dating? "Are you sure?" Lauren whispered before she could stop herself.

"About your pacing? I'm sure." Berit ran her lips over Lauren's collarbone. Lauren tried to gather her scrambling thoughts, but her desire was winning.

Lauren ran her hands over the short hairs on the back of Berit's head before tangling her fingers in the mess of loose curls at the top. She tugged lightly. Lauren was out of breath by the time Berit's eyes met hers. This type of passion was new to her.

"You'd say that *if* you were my girlfriend?" Lauren said, her heart racing and her vision hazy, "or are you saying it *as* my girlfriend?"

Berit froze, sparking panic within Lauren. Tense, motionless seconds passed before Berit so much as blinked. She kissed Lauren's inner wrist and said, "I didn't realize people still had these conversations."

"Probably because it's been a while since you've made it to this point with a woman." Lauren held Berit's stare, meeting her challenge head-on.

"That's fair. Rude, but fair." Berit's small smile told Lauren she wasn't truly offended. "By girlfriend, you mean exclusive?"

Lauren nodded.

"I'd be the only one allowed to touch you, to see you like this?"

Lauren sucked in a breath as Berit traced the underside of her breast with her soft lips, and she scratched her short nails across Berit's back in response. "And only you'd have me this way?"

Lauren's framed Berit's face with her hands and pulled her up so their eyes met. "Relationships aren't easy for me, and I'm terrified, but I can't do this any other way. For me, this is all or nothing."

Berit's grin was blinding. "Lauren Daly, I wouldn't want to share you with anyone else."

"And you're okay with monogamy?"

Berit's smile fell away, and she lay back against her pillow. A cold distance grew between their bodies.

"I'm sorry. My track record with relationships isn't good, and with Rebecca…" Lauren felt tears sting her eyes.

"What happened between you two?"

Lauren shook her head at the deceptively complex question. "We were on and off again more times than I can count. She'd either cheat on me or find someone better and prettier to spend her time with. But when things didn't work with those women, she'd come running to me."

"And you'd take her back?" Berit said, grabbing Lauren's hand and lacing their fingers together.

Lauren let out a strangled laugh, her grip on Berit's hand tightening. "My reasons for that are pretty shallow."

"Tell me," Berit said, gently encouraging Lauren to open up.

"You saw her. She's way out of my league, and I couldn't understand what she ever saw in me. I was a sucker for the validation having her on my arm gave me."

"But she seems pretty terrible on the inside."

"Like I said, shallow." Lauren turned on her side and buried her face in her pillow. "I can't believe I just admitted that to you," she said in a small, muffled voice. "I've never told anyone that. I always used the excuse of taking her back because I loved her."

"Did you love her?" Berit's voice came out louder, more earnest than before.

"I was madly in love with the version of Rebecca I forced

myself to see, but that faded quickly. The love we felt, what I felt, was never real."

"Are you with me for shallow reasons?"

"No." Lauren gasped at the touch of Berit's fingertip along her inner thigh. "You know how beautiful and sexy you are, and you also know we would've been in bed after you served me that first night if I was in this for shallow reasons." Berit's smile crackled to life in her ear. Berit toyed with the curls at the apex of Lauren's thighs before spreading her open and rubbing along her growing wetness. Lauren moaned.

Berit grazed Lauren's ear with her teeth. "Is that so?" she said in a purr. She slid her middle finger into Lauren slowly, too slowly, before bottoming out with her palm pressed against Lauren's clit.

"Yesss," Lauren hissed. "I won't do that again. I deserve more." She was trying to stay of sound mind, but Berit felt so good.

Berit pulled back and looked down at her with shining eyes. "You do, and don't you forget it." Berit kissed her deeply, her tongue mimicking the way her finger moved and explored Lauren's depths.

Lauren's feelings for Berit were anything but shallow. She gripped Berit's slender hips as her pleasure began to mount. Real feelings were scary, but Lauren's heart was finally ready to welcome them.

Lauren watched Lou approach her slowly toward the end of her shift. The night had flown by, groups of women coming and going faster than Lauren could keep track of. She had already engaged with nearly every patron who walked into the Dollhouse. She hadn't gotten much sleep, but she felt energized and knew the smile on her face told a story.

"Hey, Lou," she said loudly, straining to be heard over the music and chatter in the bar. "Busy night."

"Saturdays usually are." Lou looked her up and down, a knowing smirk on her lips. "You look happy. Safe to assume everything between you and Berit worked out for the best?"

Lauren's cheeks warmed. "I think so." She focused on collecting tips from the bar and checking the glasses lined up in front of her for any refills. Each action had become second nature. "We're good." Lauren could barely contain her smile at just how good they were.

"I can tell. Ready to start closing up?" Lou switched on the last call light. "I'm happy for you and my sister. I think you're a good match," Lou said. She didn't add another word on the matter and went back to work.

Together, they took several more drink orders. Lauren filled the ones she knew and handed the more complex drinks over to Lou. Her confidence behind the bar had grown substantially. She mixed up martinis and mojitos with precision, and even managed to perfect the Tom Collins and Manhattan. She'd never bothered to try those drinks in her life, but she now crafted them with ease.

"Will you run to the stockroom and grab me a bottle of José Cuervo and a bottle of Jack?" Lou called out over her shoulder to Lauren.

"You got it." Lauren wiped her hands on a towel she kept with her, a tip she'd learned from watching Berit, and tossed it onto the back counter. She marched toward the back while repeating Lou's order to herself over and over. She walked past Berit's office, startled when Berit reached out and pulled her in. She pinned Lauren to the wall next to the door and kissed her deeply before she had the chance to register anything else.

Berit pulled back and breathed heavily. "Hi."

"Hi." Lauren felt her way up Berit's loose black T-shirt. She traced the underside of Berit's ribs lightly and laughed when Berit jumped from a tickle.

"I didn't think this would be so hard."

"What?" Lauren gave Berit's sides a squeeze before touching her face. She ran her thumbs along Berit's cheekbones and over her plump lips. "What's so hard?"

"Not being with you while being around you. I always want to be touching you," Berit said while gripping Lauren's ass. "I want to talk and learn more about you."

Lauren's heart melted. "Unfortunately, I was on my way back

to grab a few things from the stockroom. Maybe we could steal a few hours after work?"

Berit's hot gaze turned apologetic. "Some of the girls are hanging around for a few drinks after lockup. Join us?"

"Of course." Lauren moved forward for a kiss but held back a second to relish the warmth of Berit's mouth near hers. "I can't promise I'll keep my hands to myself."

"I'd hate that kind of promise." Berit bit at Lauren's lower lip. "If you're worried about the staff knowing about us, don't be. They'll be cool. I know it."

"I'll follow your lead. One request, though."

"What's that?"

"Will you make a drink for me?"

"Anything you want."

"I've mixed about twenty mojitos tonight and now I want one," Lauren said with a salacious smirk.

Berit pressed into her body. "Top, bottom, or switch?"

Lauren's hips had a mind of their own as she ground her pelvis into Berit. "You already know the answer to that." Lauren indulged in one last, long kiss before pushing Berit away. "Let me get those bottles for Lou." Lauren sauntered away, trying her best to ignore Berit's low comments about what she'd rather be doing with Lauren.

An hour later, Lauren sat with Bellamy, Lou, and Monica around a small table and laughed with drinks in hand. She loved listening to tales from the Dollhouse. The bar had seen its fair share of shenanigans over the years. "For some reason, brief nudity doesn't shock me around here," Lauren said before sipping her mojito. The subtle peach flavor settled on the back of her tongue.

Bellamy held up her hand. "This wasn't brief nudity. The woman walked out of the restroom with her skirt pushed up around her waist. Completely commando."

Lauren looked at Monica, who was red in the face and had tears in her eyes. "Drunk or promiscuous?" Her question was met with more laughter.

"A combination of both," Bellamy said confidently. "A stone butch walked out right before her and was wearing a huge shit-eating grin. I think that woman was drunk and fucked senseless. The last thing she was thinking about was her skirt."

"Does that happen often? Sex in the bathroom?" Lauren tried to feign innocence as she drank, but her mind was alive with pictures of Berit taking her against the stall. She shivered when Berit tangled her long fingers into the back of her hair.

"We catch people fairly often," Monica said, "but more often than not we just let them be. As long as they're not breaking anything, making a mess, or keeping other people from using the bathroom, who am I to stop two people from getting some?" She downed the rest of her beer and started to twirl her long blond ponytail.

"Fair point," Berit chimed in, clinking her beer bottle against Monica's.

"So, Lauren, I hear you're from England," Lou said.

Lauren wasn't expecting this turn of conversation. She wasn't always comfortable being the center of attention. "Yes, uh, Birmingham to be exact."

"Really?" Monica sat up straighter. "How long have you lived in America?"

"My family moved here when I was six. Now it's just me and my mum." Lauren made sure her accent grew thick, knowing it made Berit's knees weak. "My parents divorced when I was twenty, my dad went back to England and my brother followed."

"That must've been hard for you," Bellamy said sympathetically.

Lauren shook her head. "Not really. I was an adult and had established so much of my life by then, and I was always a little closer to my mum than my dad. I love him, and our relationship is good, but my mum and I have always been like friends."

Lou leaned on her elbows and asked, "Do you ever think about going back?"

"Only for vacations."

"Do you miss it?"

"No," Lauren said with certainty. "I'm American. I love this country and its people, even when they're not at their best." Everyone laughed. "I do miss one thing about England."

"What's that?" Berit said.

"They have beautiful botanical gardens. We spent a good portion of every summer exploring them all. I guess I miss that time more than the actual gardens, although being surrounded by so much greenery and color was spectacular."

"I'm happy you're here." Berit held Lauren's gaze. Her eyes seemed a darker shade of hazel in the dim lighting.

"Me too," Lauren said quietly, intimately.

Monica and Lou went on to talk about their favorite flowers and the power a perfectly crafted floral arrangement held. Lauren heard bits and pieces of the conversation, but her attention was mostly on the way Berit's fingertips teased the nape of her neck. Berit's arm was around the back of her chair so casually, Lauren felt at home. She closed her eyes for a moment, relishing the therapeutic touch, and when she reopened them, she realized they had an audience. She had hoped the other women would let her and Berit's closeness go unacknowledged, but Bellamy had other ideas.

Bellamy watched Berit and Lauren over the rim of her tumbler glass. She drank straight whiskey, a drink Lauren thought suited her perfectly. "This is new." She pointed to the cozy couple.

Lauren felt worried embarrassment. She considered Bellamy's past with Berit and grew concerned their connection was more than an innocent hookup on Bellamy's part, but Bellamy's smile soothed her apprehension.

"Is this her?" Bellamy said directly to Berit with a tilt of her glass toward Lauren.

Berit nodded shyly. "This is her."

"Her who?" Lauren felt like she'd been shut out of some exclusive joke.

"Berit told me she had someone on her mind." Bellamy took a long sip of her whiskey, her eyes never wavering from Lauren. "I'm happy it's you."

Lauren was shocked to see Berit blushing. "I was on your mind?"

"You always are," she said in a whisper so the sentiment remained between them. "And have been for a while."

"I thought something was up the other night. You guys are so cute," Monica said.

Lou added a gag. "And disgusting."

"We should call it a night," Bellamy said as she tossed back the rest of her drink. "Leave these lovebirds alone."

Lauren was disappointed. They'd been having so much fun. It'd been a long time since Lauren felt like she was part of a group. "Really? It's still so early." Lauren checked her watch and her eyes nearly bulged when she noticed it was closer to four in the morning than she thought.

"Time flies with us," Lou said with a wink. She stood and stretched.

"Good night," Berit said from where she remained seated. "I can't wait to do it all again tomorrow."

Lauren followed Berit's lead and made no move to get up and leave. "Good night, everyone." Lauren watched as they all placed their glasses in the dishwasher and filed out the back. She looked back to Berit just in time to catch her hazel eyes on her. "You really told Bellamy about me?"

"Not in so many words," Berit said. "She knew I had feelings for someone. We were planning on spending the night together, but I couldn't stop thinking about you."

Lauren held her hand up. "Wait."

"I know. I'm sure that's not the detail you wanted to hear. I'm sorry for that."

"No, that doesn't bother me." Lauren almost laughed at the confusion on Berit's face. "I'm trying to understand this. You were with Bellamy—gorgeous, sexy Bellamy, and you couldn't stop thinking about *me*?"

"You shouldn't sound so surprised. Instead of Bellamy, I was thinking about gorgeous, sexy *you*."

Lauren snorted.

"Stop that," Berit said as she gently ran her fingers through Lauren's hair. "Believe me when I tell you you're incredible to me, inside and out."

Lauren felt her emotions swell. She wanted to cry because of Berit's kindness, while her body ignited at Berit's touch. She stood and threw her leg over Berit, lowering herself to straddle her. Lauren poured every emotion she felt into a kiss because the words were too scary to say aloud. She pulled back and said, "I think you're pretty incredible, too."

Berit caressed and massaged Lauren's thighs before moving up to her lower back. She pulled Lauren's body flush against hers. "Stay with me tonight," Berit said breathily.

"I can't." Lauren's tone was filled with dismay. "I have so much to do at home." She wished she could avoid her house forever, but she hadn't seen Jorge in over a week, and her laundry had been piling up. If she didn't check in soon, who knew what she'd go home to next.

"You can go home early in the morning." Berit felt under the hem of Lauren's navy tank top and skimmed the plane of her back.

Lauren smiled against Berit's mouth. "You know that won't happen."

"Go out with me tomorrow night instead, then. I already know you don't have work." Berit kissed Lauren again.

Lauren was losing the war against Berit's persuasion. "Okay." Suddenly, Berit lifted her and placed her onto the table. Lauren was very surprised by Berit's leg strength.

"Tomorrow night we'll go on a date, but I need a small taste before then." Berit unbuttoned and removed Lauren's jeans.

"What if someone comes back?" Lauren's concern was only halfhearted as she spread her legs willingly for Berit.

"They won't. Trust me." Berit wiggled her eyebrows and licked her lips.

Lauren felt Berit's tongue tease her inner thighs before diving into her. The last thing Lauren saw before losing herself to pleasure was the rainbow of colors behind the bar. The sight was beautiful, but nothing in comparison to the woman between her legs.

Chapter Nineteen

B erit blew into her hand to check her breath and second-guessed the action immediately. She laughed and rolled her eyes at herself. After popping a mint in her mouth, she rang Lauren's doorbell. They had agreed to a six o'clock date, but Berit showed up twenty minutes early thanks to the nervous excitement building in her. She straightened her light green button-up and ran her damp palms along her slim, dark jeans. Berit didn't know why her nerves were kicking in now, but she guessed it had an awful lot to do with the woman leaving her to wait on the doorstep.

The door cracked open a fraction. "Can I help you?" a deep voice said.

"Hey, hi, is Lauren around?" The door opened an inch more. Berit saw a chubby man's face clearly now. "I'm Berit. You must be Jorge." She held out her hand.

He smiled. "I hope you've only heard good things." Jorge ushered Berit inside. She surveyed her surroundings, noting the general disarray of the space. A woman stood with her back to Berit, searching through the cabinets with a huff. "I'm embarrassed to admit, Lauren hasn't told me much about you, but she's also not around much." Berit looked to her left and recognized Rebecca, sprawled across the couch channel-surfing. "I guess you're the one responsible for her working so much."

"She works full-time just as she would at any other job." Berit's attention was still on Lauren's ex-girlfriend, when the woman in the kitchen grew louder.

"Why do we never have snacks around here? Has Lauren even bothered to go to the store recently?" Her voice sounded entitled. Berit despised entitled people. "She's off all day now."

"Briana, babe, come here and meet Lauren's boss—girlfriend." Jorge looked at Berit with a question twinkling in his dark eyes. "Boss *and* girlfriend?"

"I'm here as her girlfriend tonight, so let's just stick with that." *Where is Lauren?*

Briana peeled herself away from the empty cabinets, shuffling in her oversized sweats to where Berit stood with Jorge in the hall separating the living room from the kitchen. "You must be Bridget."

"My name's Berit," she said evenly in spite of her growing frustration.

"Oh." Briana seemed clueless and nearly lost. Like she had to count the facts in front of her on her fingers. "But Rebecca told me your name was—"

"Nice to see you again." Rebecca appeared at Berit's side.

Berit hardly spared her a glance. "Hi, Rebecca. Could someone direct me to Lauren's room? I'd like to tell her I'm here."

"I'll tell her," Rebecca said, sauntering off toward the back of the house and letting herself into a closed room. Berit took a deep breath to calm herself, her nostrils flaring widely.

Jorge clapped Berit's shoulder, and she swayed slightly from the force. "Can I get you something to drink while you wait? Could be a while. Women, am I right?" His full cheeks grew with a smile.

Berit reminded herself this guy was Lauren's friend before answering. "I think it's flattering to know a woman is taking her time getting ready to see me." Against her better judgment and control, she shot a quick glance at Briana in her sweats. "There's something sexy and respectful about the person I'm with making an effort." These people brought out the worst in her. "I'm actually going to wait in the car. Just let Lauren know I'm here." Without another word, Berit left the house and nearly ran for her Jeep. She leaned back against the passenger side door and waited. Her mind was running a mile a minute with all she'd witnessed and experienced in the short five minutes she'd been in Lauren's home.

A slug made its way along the sidewalk, and Berit found its slow and steady pace soothing. She felt sad for Lauren, infuriated by the people taking advantage of her, and jealous of Rebecca for acting like a rightful owner of a piece of Lauren's life. The front door creaked open, putting an end to Berit's turmoil.

Berit raised her head to catch her first glance of Lauren. She licked her lips instantly. Lauren was wearing a long, flowy skirt that had a tie-dyed pattern of every earth tone you could imagine, and she'd paired it with a simple navy blue T-shirt. You'd never expect these articles of clothing to work perfectly together, but they did. The tightness of Lauren's shirt showcased her breasts and midsection, and Berit wanted to run her hands along the soft material. Lauren yelled something into the house before closing the door and approaching Berit. She touched her hair subconsciously.

Every other feeling left Berit's chest once Lauren stood before her. She was left only with awe, admiration, and desire. "Wow," she said breathlessly.

"Wow, yourself." Lauren leaned in and pecked Berit's lips, but Berit pulled her in for a much deeper, sensuous kiss. She pulled back, dazed, and said, "Again, wow."

"You look incredible." Berit ran her fingertip along Lauren's clavicle. "And you cut your hair." She fingered the ends of Lauren's chestnut hair, which was now just below her chin and tucked behind her ears. Lauren's new style included blunt bangs that ran straight along her brow line, adding a new intensity to her dark eyes. "I love it."

"I was worried it wasn't me, but I wanted something new for our first date. Rebecca said the bangs make me look twelve." Lauren began to lower her head, but Berit grabbed her chin and encouraged her to meet her eyes.

"The bangs make your eyes even more dangerous and sexy than they were, and I think I hate Rebecca."

"You could never hate anybody. Your heart is too good for that," Lauren said as she snaked her fingers between Berit's buttons and caressed the skin between her breasts.

Berit melted at the touch. She gripped the handle behind her and opened the door. "Let's get out of here before I either take you in my back seat or march back into your house to give Rebecca the finger."

Lauren smiled and climbed into the Jeep. "Where are we going?"

"You'll see."

After a forty-five minute drive, Lauren became restless. She started to fiddle more with Berit's right hand, resting on her thigh. Lauren's legs bounced up and down countless times, and she couldn't stop changing the song on the radio. Normally, this type of behavior would irk Berit, but she found it endearing with Lauren. She wondered when or if anyone had surprised Lauren.

"We're almost there." Berit took another sharp right.

"Finally. We've been driving forever."

Berit laughed at Lauren's exaggeration. "Hardly." Berit steered her car up a long driveway and parked in a nearly empty lot. She cut the engine and sat silently, waiting for Lauren to notice the signs around them. The wait was worth it when Lauren's eyes grew wider and brighter than Berit had ever seen them.

"We're at a botanical garden?" Lauren couldn't get her seat belt off fast enough. "I didn't know we had any so close."

"It's a large public garden, but I'm sure it's not as fancy as the ones you had back home."

Lauren paused before opening the door. She turned back to Berit and smiled sweetly. "America is my home. England is a small place in my heart that holds memories. Come on," she said excitedly as she jumped out of the Jeep.

Berit followed and held Lauren's hand the moment she caught up. She couldn't recall the last time she was on a real date. She tried to remember walking hand in hand with a woman, leisurely strolling and insisting on paying for each other, but she kept coming up blank. She tightened her grip on Lauren's hand.

"Which way should we go first?" Lauren said, glancing over the pamphlet she was handed at the donation desk. She struggled to open the folded paper because she wouldn't let go of Berit's hand, melting Berit's heart in the process.

"Whichever way you want to go."

Lauren looked up at Berit with a bright smile. "Let's head to the bamboo forest." She tugged Berit along.

They weaved between natural exhibits and artistically plotted and planted displays. Lauren would stop at every other place of interest to read facts from a plaque or share a memory from her flower-filled childhood. Berit soaked up every second and made sure she forced Lauren to stop, kiss her, and literally smell the roses. Berit stood with Lauren in front of her, holding Lauren close as they stared out at a small pond. Dusk had fallen, painting the sky with raspberry and orange hues, and they knew their time at the gardens was drawing to a close.

"This is beautiful," Lauren said quietly, her voice peaceful.

"The way you feel right now as you look at the sunset and all of these flowers is exactly how I feel when I look at you."

"Berit..."

She held Lauren tighter. "I mean it, Lauren."

"I know you do." Lauren took a deep breath and settled back into Berit's embrace. Minutes of silence passed, punctuated by the sound of crickets coming to life. Lauren looked up into Berit's eyes.

Berit knew this was the perfect moment to share her huge feelings. Right then, in front of the sunset and the pond with picturesque lily pads. Berit wanted to tell Lauren she was falling into that deserted territory labeled love. She took a breath and opened her mouth, but she wasn't quick enough.

"Why are you so nice to me?" Lauren said first, deflating Berit's bravado and breaking her heart simultaneously.

"What?" Berit said, nearly squawking.

"No one has ever cared like you or treated me the way you do. I'm not even talking about the sex." Lauren's smile did nothing to soften what she was saying or hide the tears in her eyes. "I was used to being treated a certain way and figured it's what I deserve."

Berit placed her fingertip on Lauren's lips. "Please stop." She kissed Lauren's nose. Her heart and mind were at war with how to answer Lauren and her big, doelike eyes. "No one has cared for you or treated you the way I do because none of those people were me."

Berit tucked a single runaway strand of hair back behind Lauren's ear. "Sometimes it takes meeting the right person to see your true self."

Lauren didn't say another word. She just kissed Berit deeply before leading them back to the Jeep. Once they were buckled in, she turned to Berit. "Take me straight to your apartment."

"What about dinner?" Berit asked, not really caring about food when Lauren wore such a devious smirk.

Lauren leaned across the space between their seats, pressing her lips to Berit's jaw and then ear. She nipped at Berit's earlobe and said, "Make love to me first, food after."

Berit put the car in reverse, her hands shaky from Lauren's tone and words, and stepped on the gas. "Yes ma'am."

❖

Berit leaned against her kitchen counter in a loose tank and sweatpants, holding out a bowl of chocolate chip ice cream to Lauren. She waited patiently while Lauren filled her spoon to capacity. Lauren, dressed in Berit's green shirt from earlier that evening, sat at the bar, looking more delectable than their dessert.

"I really have to get ice cream the next time I go to the store," Lauren said, licking her spoon clean and going back for more. "I usually skip it to save money, but I do love it so."

"You can eat my ice cream any time you want, and you can stay in my apartment any time you want."

"Thank you. I'll definitely take you up on that."

"The ice cream or the apartment?"

Lauren eyed Berit oddly. "The ice cream. I do have to go home from time to time, no matter how wonderful it is here and how charming your dog is." Hugo was sleeping belly up in one of his many beds.

"I don't understand why you have to go home." Berit knew she sounded childish.

"Because it's my house."

Berit stabbed at the ice cream aggressively.

"Okay, whoa, stop murdering the ice cream." Lauren placed the bowl on the counter. "Where is all of this coming from?"

"Your roommates are jerks," Berit blurted out. "I know Jorge is your friend and supposedly cares about you, but the whole thing with Briana is fucked up. She was more concerned about *you* going to the store so she could have snacks than making a nice first impression with me, the woman dating her sugar daddy's friend. And don't even get me started on Rebecca."

Lauren hung her head. She looked ashamed and embarrassed. "How long were you in my house?"

"No more than five minutes. Rebecca didn't tell you I was waiting?" Lauren shook her head. "There's a shocker."

"She came into my room to make a comment about my bangs and said a car was waiting out front. I assumed it was you. I'm sorry."

"You have nothing to be sorry for."

"I'm sorry for the way they acted and for everything you saw. You know how much I hate living there."

Berit pushed the bowl onto the counter and moved closer to Lauren. She had to choose her next words wisely. "It's not healthy for you to live there."

"I've tried to talk to Jorge—"

"You should move out."

"I can't," Lauren said, her voice raising an octave. "I pay over a third of the rent."

"Jorge will have to pay more, which he should be doing now."

"He can't afford it."

"What about Rebecca?" Berit was growing to hate the name.

"She wouldn't go for it."

"Because she's only living there for you," Berit said without thinking. Not only did she sound accusatory, but she also sounded a little too jealous for her liking. "I'm sorry." Berit rubbed her face roughly and ran her fingers through her slightly knotted hair. Lauren had yet to relax. Oh, how she wished she could go back in time to the beginning of their dessert. She'd approach this topic much more carefully.

Lauren let out a sigh. "I do think it's a control thing for Rebecca, but we can't afford to lose her income, and it's difficult to find a roommate willing to live on a couch."

"Move in with me," Berit said, as if the solution was so simple and obvious.

"Hell, no." Lauren's quick answer cut Berit like a dull razor.

"Not even taking a minute to think about that one, huh?" Berit took the bowl to the sink and began washing it out. "You live with grown adults who leave their dishes piled up in the sink. Jorge and Briana's clothes are stained, which I guess is a sign they're soul mates, and the barely responsible one is your ex who sticks around to control you." Berit emptied the bowl, flinching at the water that splashed back at her. "I see how I'm the worst choice out of the two."

"You're not." Lauren's voice came from surprisingly close over Berit's shoulder. Berit dried her hands and turned to catch Lauren looking at her with wide, earnest eyes. "You're the best choice, my favorite choice without hesitation, but that's the problem."

Berit looked at her blankly, her mind lagging behind.

"I won't U-Haul with you," Lauren said.

"I'm not asking you to U-Haul."

"You *are*." She cradled Berit's face. "And that makes me feel weak inside, but I'm not willing to risk what we have by moving in with you. What I feel for you is big and growing at a scary fast rate, but it's not a feeling I want to use as an excuse to avoid the mess I've gotten myself into over the years."

Berit hated that Lauren made sense. She nodded. "Okay." She puckered up when Lauren leaned in slowly.

After a soft kiss, Lauren said, "Being with you makes me feel like maybe I'm strong enough to face the mess, though."

Berit smiled. "Good. I hate seeing people I care about get taken advantage of. It happens all too often. Lord knows it's happened to me enough for one lifetime."

"What do you mean?"

Berit finished cleaning up quickly and prepared for what was never a quick story. "When I started planning for the Dollhouse, I had different ideas in place and I was looking at several locations. The first was a larger lot, which allowed for more parking and interior space. I would've had to build, but I was confident I could get the money through loans and investors."

Lauren slid her hands into the large arm holes of Berit's tank and tickled her ribs. "Do I even want to know what you had planned for all that extra space?"

"A dance floor and exotic dancers."

"You're not kidding."

"I'm not. I wanted to take the lesbian world by storm, and what better way than to bring crafted drinks, hot dancers, and the club scene to them in northern New Jersey? Imagine dancers of all shapes, sizes, colors, and looks catered to queer women and not clichéd male fantasies." Berit heard her voice turn all business, which happened every time she told the story of the Dollhouse. "But the newly elected mayor had other plans."

"Does the mayor even get involved with things like that?"

"Not usually, but for me he made an exception."

"Because of the bad blood between him and your father?"

"Bingo." Berit reached out to smooth the crease between Lauren's eyes. "At first, he approached me directly, using my father's mistakes against me in order to guilt me into looking for a new location or giving up altogether. But eventually he realized I wasn't going away."

"What did he do then?"

"He wined and dined city council members and spoke directly to townspeople about how this city didn't need that kind of sin."

Lauren's crease grew deeper. "I thought you said he was fine with you dating his daughter."

"He was, but he was also willing to play the role of Jesus-worshiping homophobe to get people to shut me down." Berit shrugged and started to turn off the lights. Hugo jumped up and followed them into the bedroom, where he took his rightful place at the foot of Berit's king-size bed.

Lauren pulled up the covers from where they lay in a discarded ball beside Hugo. "How did you finally open the Dollhouse?" She fluffed her pillow and set her alarm. The easy, natural move wasn't lost on Berit.

Berit stripped and slid between the covers, holding her breath that Lauren would do the same. She smiled broadly when Lauren undid each button slowly and let Berit's shirt fall to the ground before she joined her. She pulled Lauren close and continued her tale. "I downsized my plan, picked a different location, and presented it myself in front of the city council, as well as at a town meeting. I lied a teeny bit in my description of the bar." Berit held up her hand, index finger and thumb no more than millimeters apart.

Lauren pressed her naked back into Berit's front. "What did you say?"

"That I wanted to open an artisanal bar that would be a safe space for women."

"Not much of a lie."

Berit reached back and turned off her bedside lamp. "It was a lie by omission. I didn't clarify it'd be a safe space where women could meet other woman for casual and not-so-casual sexual encounters." Lauren giggled in her arms, the sound a soothing lullaby for Berit.

"The Dollhouse was and always will be a safe place for me," Lauren said in a sleepy voice. "Just like you, Berit."

Berit kissed Lauren's neck lightly. "I want to be the safest of all the places for you."

"You are," Lauren mumbled. "The more I fall in love with you, the more you are."

Berit lay wide-awake long after Lauren's breathing evened out. Lauren's confession played over and over in her head and made its way into her heart moments before she drifted off into a peaceful slumber.

CHAPTER TWENTY

M ake sure the longneck craft beers are fully stocked. I have a feeling those will be the biggest seller tonight." Berit made a check on her paperwork. Stud Night was her idea, building off their successful Femme Night in the winter. Not much planning went into the event, just the right amount of advertising on social media and the promise of drink specials for boyish women and their partners. Berit loved big theme nights, but simple nights like these were her favorite.

"Don't forget the most important rule," Berit said to Lou and Dee, her main bartenders for the night. "Studs and butches are the stars tonight, but anyone walking up to the bar gets special pricing."

Lou smirked and pulled her hair back. "I love nights like these."

"Because butch women love you." Dee pinched Lou's bicep.

Lou flipped her ponytail, the small motion underlining her femininity. "They really do."

"One more thing." Berit held up her index finger. "If you notice a bulge," she said, pointing between her own legs, where her tight jeans were noticeably fuller, "give your customer a wink and an extra dollar off their drink."

"So we should stare at everyone's crotch tonight?"

"Yes, Lou, grab 'em, too." Berit rolled her eyes. "No. If you happen to notice, you notice. I'm going to check on Lauren. You two get organized and prepare yourself for a busy night. I pushed Stud Night *hard.* I'm hoping it pays off." Berit stalked off to the stockroom where Lauren was checking their on-hand inventory. She adjusted herself discreetly. Lauren had no idea Berit was packing, and Berit wanted to introduce her to the fact slowly. But when Berit found Lauren bent over, all her control slipped away.

She approached Lauren quietly, getting little to no reaction when she placed her hands on Lauren's hips, but when she pressed her firm cock against Lauren's ass, Lauren jumped up with a yelp.

Berit was torn between arousal and worry.

"Hi, Berit," Lauren said, her breathing rapid from being startled. She checked over Berit's shoulder and whispered, "What are you doing with *that*?" she said, appearing more concerned than interested.

"It's Stud Night," Berit said as if it was the most obvious fact on earth. "We've talked about it all week." She stepped closer, just wanting to share Lauren's space. "Five-dollar craft beers, and packing's encouraged."

"I remember the drink specials."

"Maybe I forgot to mention the other thing." Berit snaked her arms around Lauren's waist and pulled her close.

"You most certainly did not mention anything about wearing your dick to the bar."

Berit's expression turned from playful to serious. She pulled back slightly and said, "If it bothers you, I'll take it off. I just thought it'd be good to lead by example."

Lauren pulled Berit's hips in to meet her own. "I was surprised, but I definitely don't want you to take it off." She thrust her pelvis forward. The pressure on the silicone cock sent a jolt to Berit's clit. "What're you packing here?" Lauren grabbed Berit's bulge slowly. "Six or eight inches?" She stroked Berit firmly, nearly sending her to her knees.

Berit licked her lips. "Six." She whimpered when Lauren increased the speed and pressure of her stroke. "Eight inches wouldn't be as discreet." Berit watched, completely entranced as Lauren bit her lower lip.

"Hey, guys." Lou's voice sent them flying apart. Berit knew her face was flaming red, and Lauren was in even worse shape. Lou averted her eyes and said, "I don't even want to know, just hand me a bottle of Johnnie Walker Black."

Berit handed it to her and gave her a nod. She looked back at Lauren once Lou left and blew out a long breath. "Are you wet?" Lauren's dark eyes flew open. "Are you?" If Berit wasn't so turned on and in tune to Lauren's every move, she would've missed Lauren's barely perceptible nod. She grabbed Lauren's hand and led her to her office. Shutting the door, she locked it and pushed Lauren toward her small desk. "We don't have much time."

"We probably shouldn't do this."

"I'm the boss."

"What if someone comes looking for us?"

Berit kissed Lauren deeply, moving her hands from Lauren's hair to her breasts and finally coming to a stop on her ass. Berit encouraged Lauren to sit on the edge of the desk. "They're busy." She unbuttoned Lauren's jeans and tugged them down her hips. Berit's fingertips went right to Lauren's core. "You're soaked," Berit said as she stroked Lauren over her panties. Her warmth and moisture permeated the cotton barrier.

"What can I say?" Lauren shut her eyes as Berit toyed with her covered entrance. When her eyes opened again, they were darker than Berit had ever seen them. "I must have a thing for a woman with a big cock."

Berit grinned wickedly. "Take off your pants," she said in a low, demanding voice. Lauren obeyed and kicked her jeans to the side and started on Berit's. Berit watched Lauren undo her belt. That sight alone ratcheted the pulse between her thighs to high. Lauren caught the purple phallus in her palm when it sprang free from Berit's jeans. Berit swallowed hard as she watched Lauren's hand move up and down the shaft.

"I can be quick," Lauren said. She reached lower into Berit's pants, sliding her middle finger into her briefs and swirling it through her wetness. Berit sucked in a breath. "Can you?" She removed her finger to smear Berit's juices on the head of the dildo.

"You're so incredibly sexy. Like, really fucking hot." Berit knew her voice and knees were shaking. Lauren was bringing a page of her unwritten fantasy diary to life. "You're pretty wet, but if you need more—"

Lauren pushed Berit back slightly and dropped to her knees. She ran her tongue around the head before taking Berit's length into her mouth. Berit damn near fell over when Lauren locked her innocent eyes on hers and started to bob her head up and down. Berit's clit ached, her breathing grew labored, and her heart was about to pound out of her chest.

Lauren released the dildo from between her swollen lips and said, "I think it'll be plenty wet now." She stood and sat back on the desk.

Berit swallowed hard and nodded dumbly. She was so turned on, she felt paralyzed, like she might come just from blinking too hard. "I—I'm…"

"Fuck me, Berit." Lauren's command shook Berit out of her stupor.

Berit lined her silicone cock up and sank slowly into Lauren's ready pussy, kissing her deeply as the dildo disappeared between them. Once she was deep inside Lauren, Berit pulled back to look into her smiling eyes. "Are you okay?"

"I'm great, but I'd be even better if you started moving."

Berit started to piston slowly, listening to Lauren's breathing for any hints of pain. All she heard were sounds of pleasure. She found a rhythm Lauren liked and stuck with it before palming Lauren's breasts roughly. She encouraged Lauren to rub her own clit and knew in an instant Lauren wasn't far from orgasm. Berit kissed her, swallowing her growing cries.

Lauren tore her mouth away and whined, "I'm so close, Berit, oh!" Lauren pulled at Berit's hair, holding her face against her neck. Berit could feel Lauren's pulse racing against her lips. "Harder, fuck me harder." She whispered the words fiercely, and they slammed Berit into action.

Berit moved her hips faster and with purpose. Sweat collected on her brow, and the sounds of their skin slapping together filled the office space. She brought her lips to Lauren's ear and placed a sweet kiss there. "Come for me," she said in a deep voice.

Lauren let go, her thighs shaking around Berit's thin frame and her cries muffled by Berit's red T-shirt. She slumped forward against Berit. As Berit tried to step back, Lauren grabbed her ass and held her in place. "Not yet," she said. The small whimper warmed Berit's heart.

Berit pulled out after a minute, missing the closeness immediately. "We'll have to do that again when we have more time."

Lauren was already standing on unsteady legs while she pulled on her jeans. "More time so I can return the favor."

Berit grabbed paper towels from a nearby shelf and cleaned herself up. She tucked the dildo away and winked at Lauren. "I can think of a few ways you can return the favor later."

"Anything you want." Lauren gave Berit a tender, promising kiss.

Berit pulled back and smiled. "I have something to give you."

"Are you sure you didn't just give it to me?"

"I was talking about this," Berit said, reaching into the bottom drawer of her small desk. She pulled out a small dish towel that had an American flag in one corner and the flag of England in the other. She handed it to Lauren and rubbed the back of her neck nervously as she watched Lauren look it over. "It's a silly gift, but it's nice to have a towel of your own around here and—"

Lauren cut her off with a hard kiss. "I love it. I love…" Lauren's eyes were so dark and deep. Berit felt the moment grow between them. "I really do love it, and I can't wait to use it tonight." Lauren unlocked the door. "Thank you," she said just before walking out of the office.

Berit couldn't keep her eyes off of Lauren's slightly affected stride. She laughed and ran her fingers through her hair.

Within an hour, the bar was filled almost wall to wall. Berit knew they'd be pushing maximum capacity soon enough. Nights like these made the Dollhouse feel like an extension of Berit's beating heart. She stood at the back of the bar and watched people move about her space. The energy surrounding her made Berit's skin feel electric. She watched Lauren work tables full of captivated women. Everyone loved Lauren—the patrons, the staff, and the boss.

"Hey, Berit," Dee shouted as she approached. "I want to take a quick smoke break."

"You need to quit."

"True, but I'm not quitting right now. Mind if I run out back?"

Berit checked her watch.

"I'll be quick," Dee said.

"Take your fifteen and get Lou to go with you. You're both due for a break." Berit raised her hand and waved to Lauren for her to come up to the bar. "Lauren and I can handle the bar while you're away."

"You summoned me?" Lauren's face was set in a satisfied, if not smug, smile.

"You and I are on bar duty for a bit while Lou and Dee take their break." Berit tucked her dish towel into the back pocket of her pants and took her place behind the bar. Lauren was close behind with her own towel in hand.

"What about the tables?"

"Bellamy and Monica have it covered with Cynthia and Talia. Hey, Rosa," Berit said as the regular took a seat across from her. "The usual?" Berit already had a bottle of top-shelf vodka in her hand.

"Please. And can you do an extra little dance with it? I had a terrible day today." Rosa placed her small purse on the bar top and slumped forward. "My ex is fighting me for custody of our golden retriever."

Berit put on her most charming smile. "Anything to make you happy." She tossed the bottle into the air and did a spin. She caught the bottle behind her back, flipped it once in the air, and started to pour just the right amount into the metal cocktail shaker.

"Why do martinis taste better when a hot woman flips around while she makes it?" Rosa said to Lauren as she watched Berit's moves.

Lauren popped the tops off four longneck bottles in a row. "I think it has more to do with the hot woman than it does her tricks." Lauren carried two bottles in each hand down to a group at the end of the bar.

"Here you go." Berit filled a martini glass and placed a toothpick filled with olives into the glass. "First one's on the house."

Rosa threw a twenty on the bar. "I'm only having one tonight. I'm meeting someone later, and I want to have all my wits about me."

Berit hitched up her eyebrow.

"Don't give me that look. I'm not telling you any more, just like how you're staying tight-lipped about what's going on between you and the girl next door." Rosa tilted her head toward Lauren.

Berit felt the heat of a blush rising in her cheeks. She took another order before going back to Rosa. "Fair enough," she said. "That one's still on the house. If you'd like another, just flag me down."

"You're amazing."

"Don't inflate her ego any more than it already is, Rosa. I can barely stand her now," Lauren said as she passed.

Rosa grimaced. "Good point."

Berit looked between Rosa and Lauren incredulously. "I'm right here, you know."

"I know." Rosa smiled sweetly. "Thank you for the drink." Rosa took a sip and winked at Berit over the rim of her glass.

"I'm back." Dee clapped her hand onto Berit's shoulder with an alarming amount of force. "Lou's in the break room shoving a frozen dinner down her throat. Can you please go back there and tell her to slow down? It's bad for her health."

Berit snorted. Dee had no idea Lou just happened to eat that way. Ever since they were little, she'd shove food into her cheeks faster than their mother could serve it. Berit always thought it was the curse of living amongst five children—a race to get the food before nothing was left. "She's fine," Berit said reassuringly. "I'm more worried about her eating a frozen dinner." She shuddered and walked to the back.

Berit found Lou sitting by her lonesome at the small square table in the center of the break room. Berit hated the break room. She wished she could offer her employees a more plush resting area. They deserved top-notch amenities, but they only had so much space and money to work with. "Where's your food?" Berit said knowingly from the doorway. She leaned against the frame with her arms crossed over her chest.

"That measly thing? Long gone." Lou waved her hand in the air. "Sit," she said forcefully and kicked out a chair.

Berit sat, eyeing her sister suspiciously.

"There's five minutes left to my break, and we need to talk," Lou said.

"Since when do you keep track of your breaks?"

"Since a line started forming to get into this place."

Berit's chest puffed out with pride. "Pretty cool, huh? I knew Stud Night would be a hit, but this is blowing my mind. Next month we should—"

"Monday is Dad's birthday."

Berit slumped into the chair, all excitement draining from her body. Her chest filled with the same detached feeling she'd come to associate with her father. "I know. It's the same day every year."

"We're having dinner and cake."

"Just like we do every year," Berit said with growing frustration. "It'll be roast beef because that's his favorite, and he'll be late to dinner. Mom will make a cake from the box, probably double chocolate because Bart loves it and doesn't come around as often as the rest of us. If for some reason you think I've forgotten, I haven't."

Lou sat calmly even as Berit stood and started to pace. "I think you should bring Lauren to dinner. And I think it's time for you to forgive him."

Berit froze. She turned slowly toward Lou. "Oh you do, do you?"

"Yes, Berit, I do. The man is going to be sixty, and I think you've dragged this on for long enough."

"Well, I don't think I have."

"Of course you don't, because you're just as stubborn as he is. I have to get back to work, which means I don't have enough time to listen to your lame excuses for hanging on to a grudge for nearly two decades." Lou got up and walked past Berit to the break room door. She paused and looked hesitant for a second. "Remember how close we all were?"

Berit lowered her head, shame making it hard for her to meet Lou's eyes. "It's not my fault we're not anymore," she said in a harsh whisper.

"I never said it was. But you hold the power to bring some of that back. You have a successful business now, a *very* successful business you should be proud of. Whatever happened in the past has brought you here, to this moment with all of us and the Dollhouse."

"*We* have a successful business," she said.

"I can't take any credit even if I wanted to. This is all you, and you should be really proud."

"I am."

"Then share that with your family and your *girlfriend*." Lou dragged out the last word, sounding like a second grader on the playground.

Berit looked at her sister and tried her best to picture it all. Her family would be sitting around their huge dining room table with little space to spare. They'd be doting over Lauren and ribbing Berit for finally finding a girl who met her impossible standards, all while she denied their every word. They'd all ask Berit how she managed to convince Lauren to finally like her back, and she'd get to talk about the Dollhouse and this latest successful night. Berit's mother would squawk with pride, and Berit would look to her father for approval.

Berit nodded at Lou. "If Lauren is free, I'll bring her to dinner."

"And…" Lou's eyes were wide with hopeful anticipation.

"And I'll work on it." Berit didn't need to say anything more specific. She rolled her eyes at her sister as she skipped from the break room.

When Berit walked back into the crowded bar area, she was pleased to see the hustle and bustle moving along just as it had before. Familiar and new faces filled her bar. Lou was right. She had built a successful business in spite of the rocky start handed to her by her father. If she had already moved on professionally, maybe it was time to move on personally. Plus, she shouldn't introduce Lauren to a tense family. Berit watched the woman who'd been on her mind and in her heart for a while now. She wanted her family to get to know Lauren because she was exceptional, a game-changer, and the exact kind of woman Berit had fantasized about since she was a daydreaming teenager.

Berit's mouth curled into an indulgent smirk as she watched a fresh-faced woman flirt with Lauren, who handed her and a friend two beers. Berit's smirk and the warm feeling in her chest fell away, replaced with panic as she watched what happened next.

The once-flirty woman got pulled away from the bar.

Another woman flashed Lauren a badge.

Two uniformed officers walked through the doors.

Berit swallowed hard when all the pieces came together. Lauren had just served an underage drinker.

CHAPTER TWENTY-ONE

Lauren stood immobile. Shock, shame, and nausea paralyzed her. How could this have happened? How could she have done something so stupid? She felt herself be jostled by the people around her. Dee had tried talking sense while Lou attempted to keep the other patrons distracted. The conversation between the police and Dee turned heated by the time Berit rushed over. Lauren tried to read her face, but Berit's eyebrows were knitted together deeply and her normally warm eyes had turned chilly. When Berit looked at Lauren, she felt as if Berit had looked through her.

"Berit, I'm—" Lauren's apology halted the moment Berit raised a hand and shook her head. If only Lauren could tell whether her actions meant they'd talk later or never talk again.

"Were they sent in by you, or did you receive a call?" Berit said to the police officer in charge of writing up the fine.

The burly cop barely raised his head when he began speaking. "I think it's fair to assume you don't normally serve underage people in this bar?" He motioned to the two young women being interviewed.

Lauren studied Berit's reaction carefully. The muscles of her jaw flexed, and she balled her hands into fists. Berit was angry. Berit stepped forward, and Lauren was happy a bar stood between her and the officer. She was sure Berit would have no issue standing nose to nose with him. Lou tried to intervene by placing her hand on Berit's shoulder, but Berit brushed it off immediately.

"I won't dignify your stupid question with an answer."

"Answer the question, ma'am," a female officer said. Lauren did a double take when she recognized her as a customer. Lauren opened her mouth, but shut it the moment her mind caught up with her emotions. Maybe the cop wasn't out at work, or maybe she had other personal reasons for siding with the imbecile she'd been partnered with. Lauren knew speaking up would only make the problem worse.

"No," Berit said. The deep timbre of her voice matched that of a growl. "We have a very strict process. Customers are carded once at the door and then again upon ordering."

"And somehow your strict system failed both times," the female cop said. Lauren squinted to catch the name on her shiny name tag. *Markey.*

Berit crossed her arms. "I'll be looking into what happened on both occasions, I can promise you that."

Lauren took a breath and spoke up in her defense. "I didn't realize—"

"Neither of you answered my question," Berit said, cutting Lauren off again, like she wasn't even there. "Were the underage drinkers sent in by law enforcement to check on us, or did you receive a call?"

The male officer, whose name tag was too weathered, smudged, and tilted for Lauren to read, made a show of ripping the paper from his pad. Lauren waited for either cop to answer, wondering why Berit felt compelled to ask the question, and then it hit her: Berit figured Mayor McCarthy was behind this. The cop lifted his head, his eyes never straying from Berit's as he handed over the fine.

"Pay it or close your doors for good. Your choice." He turned to his partner and nodded to the young girls standing at his back. The officer in street clothes had already left. "Round them up and let's get out of here. I feel like I'm in the fucking *Twilight Zone.*"

Lauren locked her eyes on Officer Markey as she collected the two underage drinkers. Lauren was desperate for eye contact, for a glimpse into what she was feeling. She needed to know if one out of two cops were on their side. But the ruckus was out the door almost as quickly as it had come in. No more than seconds past before Berit stormed off to her office, Lou hot on her heels.

Dee shot Lauren a sympathetic shrug. "I want to talk to you about this, but…" she said with a thumb pointed in the direction of thirsty patrons who didn't seem to care much about the police crashing their party. "It'll be okay."

"I appreciate that, Dee. They can't serve themselves, can they?" Lauren's smile was fake as she went back to pouring drinks. The moment Dee had the line under control, she rushed to the back to find Berit.

For the second time since Lauren had started at the Dollhouse, Berit had closed the door to her office. Over the music and through the door, Lauren could still make out Berit's raised voice. She picked up the end of a conversation.

"Fired, without a doubt." Berit's voice was harsher than Lauren had ever heard, and her heart started to pound. She was about to be unemployed. Again.

"Just pay the fine. This happens to bars all the time." Lou's voice was clear, but quieter than Berit's, making it hard to hear through the door.

"Of course I'm going to pay it. What pisses me off is having this added to my reputation. I can see the headline now: *Homosexuals serving alcohol to children*. This is great!"

Lauren backed away from the door just as it swung open. Lou looked at her with wide eyes. "I was waiting to talk to Berit. I didn't want to interrupt."

"Now probably isn't a good time."

Lauren squared her shoulders. "I'm sure a good time will be just as hard to find after tonight. Excuse me," she said, stepping around Lou and entering Berit's office. "Berit?"

Berit raised her head from her desk. She pierced Lauren with her worried eyes. "I'm not in the mood for this right now."

"We have to talk, for many reasons, but most importantly because I'm the employee that just caused all of that."

"But you're not *just* my employee," Berit said as she stood and approached Lauren. "This makes everything more complicated than it has to be." She wiped her face roughly.

Lauren wanted to touch her, to ease Berit's troubled mind, but she knew better.

"What am I going to do?" Berit's rhetorical question came out low.

"I really am sorry."

"You should've known better," Berit said. Lauren bristled at her condescending tone. "You know what I went through to get this place open. I literally just told you. Did you forget? Did it slip your mind that I don't have much of a fan club around here? That was the most idiotic error a bartender could make." Fire danced in Berit's eyes. "And now I'm wondering if I'm the one who's made a mistake."

Lauren took a step back at Berit's words. She swallowed hard, trying to loosen her tight throat enough to speak. "I understand," she said shakily before exiting Berit's office. She couldn't hear any more.

The sad truth was Lauren really did understand. She and Berit weren't meant to last. Everything about them as a couple was too good to be true. She didn't deserve Berit as a friend, let alone as something more. Lauren untucked the dish towel Berit had gifted her and gave it one more glance. She fingered the corner where the small American flag was stitched on. With a small smile, she folded it once and then twice before setting it on a nearby shelf. The Dollhouse and Berit had been very good to her, but just like all good things in Lauren's life, their time had come to an end.

Lauren walked into the employee break room to collect her things and ran into Lou as she exited the bathroom. Lauren hurriedly wiped at her tears in hopes of reviving what little strength she had left.

Lou looked from Lauren's face to her purse and back again. Her brows furrowed deeply. "Where are you off to?"

"Home," Lauren stated simply.

"Why? What did Berit say to you?" Lou gripped Lauren's elbow.

Lauren stared at the caring touch and smiled sadly. "I'm fired, without a doubt," she said, repeating Berit's earlier words with a shaky voice. "It was nice working with you. All of this has been wonderful."

Lauren left with her head held high in spite of her wilting spirit. No one noticed her on the way out. It was a small detail, but it made the departure easier for her. She sighed as she opened the back door, just before she stepped out into the dark night.

Berit stormed out of her office moments later and looked around. She marched to the bar and got Dee's attention. "Go work the door and send Danny back to talk to me." She barked out her orders. "And I don't care if you've already served someone, check their ID again."

"It's too busy to be down a bartender."

Berit looked around. "Bellamy can come up from the tables and help Lou out."

"That'll leave only three waitresses with full tables."

"Where's Lauren?"

"I thought she was with you." Dee took a quick order and poured two glasses of red wine, leaving Berit to look frantically through the crowds for Lauren. "No one's seen her since she went to your office," Dee said with a shrug.

Berit replayed her last words to Lauren in her mind. She shook her head. "I guess I'll catch Danny later." She walked away from the bar without another word, her feet unsteady as her focus wavered from business to personal. "Lauren?" Berit called out as soon as she stepped through the swinging door. Lauren wasn't in the stockroom. All Berit spotted was a folded-up towel stuffed between two bottles of bourbon. She pulled the towel off the shelf and threw it across the room, narrowly missing Bellamy's face.

"Whoa. Are you okay?"

"Why wouldn't I be okay?" Berit ran her fingers through her hair, scratching roughly at her scalp in frustration. "I've got a three-thousand-dollar fine on my desk, and now Lauren's gone."

"What did you say to her?"

Berit's jaw dropped. "You're assuming this is my fault?"

Bellamy had the gall to laugh out loud. "Berit, you're a beautiful person, but we all know how you get when you're angry. Mixing that anger with something happening in your bar? Forget about it. It turns you damn near explosive. Do you remember when the delivery guy forgot two cases of liquor the day of Pride?"

"I wanted to rip that guy's head off."

"And you would've if it hadn't been for Lou."

Berit slumped against the doorway. "She served a minor, Bellamy. That's one of the few rules for bartenders."

"A rule any one of us could've broken tonight. Lauren wasn't even supposed to be working the bar, but she stepped in when she was needed. What would you have done if Dee had served that girl? Or Lou?"

"I would have fucking lost it," Berit said with a sigh. "I would have gone berserk, screamed my head off, but then apologized and asked that we all put our heads together to think of a way out of this."

Bellamy chuckled. She walked up to Berit and grabbed her hand before saying gently, "We all expect you to be an asshole when you're angry, but Lauren didn't."

Berit's head fell in shame.

"What did you say to her?"

"I—" Her words were stuck in place by embarrassment and sadness. She cleared her throat. "I told her what she did was idiotic and maybe I made a mistake."

"You didn't..." Bellamy dropped Berit's hand and took a step back. "Berit, why would you say that? Lauren's incredible, and you're going to let something like this end your relationship?"

"This is all new to me," Berit said in a near shout. "I've mixed business and pleasure before, but never business and...and—"

"Love?" Bellamy's eyebrow hitched knowingly.

"No. Yes. I don't know, maybe." Berit grew frustrated at how she stuttered and stumbled over her words. "All I know is my judgment is clouded, and this wouldn't have happened tonight if I wasn't so distracted." Berit began pacing.

"How are you so sure?" Bellamy said, stepping out of Berit's path.

"This has Mayor McCarthy written all over it. He sent those girls in here, I just know it. If I had been at the bar or walking around as I usually do, I would've seen this coming. But I got a late start to my evening routine because—" Berit stopped suddenly, redness filing her cheeks.

"The rendezvous in your office. We all heard."

Berit slapped her hands over her face.

"It's okay to be happy with someone." Bellamy pulled Berit's hands away from her face and smiled when their eyes met. "It's okay to have something else in this world monopolize your brain and heart other than the Dollhouse."

"It's hard to see the good in it now."

"Stop doing that. Don't blame your relationship for some old dickhead having it out for you. Now, go after your girl while you still can."

Berit looked at Bellamy. Her eyes and smile were full of hope, but Berit couldn't muster up that kind of positivity. "Not tonight," she said, placing her hand on Bellamy's shoulder. "I think we both need a little time to cool down."

"Don't wait too long. You'll regret it if you lose her."

Berit stood back as Bellamy returned to the bustling bar. The Dollhouse was still busy, still standing after the police had stormed in and caused a scene. She still had a business, and while the city's fine was substantial, Berit knew Bellamy was right. Her relationship with Lauren wasn't to blame for this. Lauren wasn't to blame for this. Berit knew she couldn't blame anyone but herself for the destruction of her own happily ever after.

CHAPTER TWENTY-TWO

Berit stared at her sister like she was speaking a foreign language. "I fired Lauren?"

"I know, and I'm asking you why," Lou said in a harsh whisper. They were standing just outside their parents' home, readying themselves for what was supposed to be a pleasant celebration. "You should've seen her face, Berit. She was heartbroken."

Berit's mind reeled. A hundred different thoughts and scenarios flooded her head, but she couldn't process any of them once their mother opened the door.

"My girls," Florence said as she wrapped her daughters in a robust hug. She practically pulled them in and then pushed Berit and Lou into the house. "And my grandson." Florence doted on Hugo as he circled her feet. She reached into the pocket of her apron and pulled out a treat just for him. He marched off with a bone proudly in his mouth.

The scent of slow-cooked roast beef flooded their senses, but anxiety kept Berit from finding the savory smell pleasant. Her stomach rolled. "Hey, Mom, listen, I'm not feeling very well, but I wanted to stop by for a quick hello. I really ought to go home and lie down." Berit felt her mother evaluating her well-being. Florence wasn't buying her excuse.

"Nonsense. You're tired from working too much and need a good home-cooked meal."

"She's not wrong," Lou whispered in Berit's ear as she passed.

Florence ushered them into the dining room where the whole family waited around the table. "Berit, dear, I thought you were bringing someone special. Will she be arriving soon?"

Berit looked to the extra place setting beside hers and winced. "Actually, she won't be able to make it tonight. She had a prior engagement." Out of the corner of her eye, Berit noticed Lou open her mouth to speak. She elbowed her sister to shut her up. "She sends her apologies."

"You should be the one apologizing," Lou muttered under her breath.

"That's a shame," Florence said, genuine disappointment dripping from every word.

"Hey, JJ. Where's Christen tonight?" Berit said to Jeffrey Junior, who was already filling his mouth with a dinner roll. Berit didn't actually care where her brother's second wife was. Christen was sweet but high maintenance in a way that drove her crazy. She couldn't fill her own plate or open her own bottles, and God forbid she had to drink directly from that bottle. But Christen was an upgrade from JJ's first wife, a wandering cheater.

JJ swallowed. "She got caught up at work late."

"Massage therapy is that demanding?" Berit didn't mean for her words to sound so judgmental, but Christen rarely spoke of her career at length. Berit had begun to believe she didn't actually work.

JJ sat back and stared his sister down. "She works for an upscale, very busy spa. Sometimes they get a late booking, and there's nothing she can do about it."

"Huh."

"What's that supposed to mean?" JJ's neck started to grow red, and the scalp beneath his light hair even redder, an indication that a fight was about to start.

Berit raised her hands in an early surrender. "I haven't heard much about her career, that's all. I think it's great how dedicated and professional she is. Christen doesn't talk much about her job." *Or anything, for that matter*, Berit added to herself. JJ sat back, calmer than before.

"This is for you, Dad." Berit placed an envelope with a gift card to a local electronic store on the table. She bought her father the same gift year after year.

"Thank you, Berit," Jeffrey Senior said quietly as he sliced the roast.

Bart emerged from the kitchen with Florence and placed serving dishes on the table. The family said grace. Berit never lowered her head or closed her eyes. Her family wasn't religious, but this tradition never seemed to fade away. They were thankful for the food on the table, the family surrounding them, and the roof over their heads. Berit looked at her father. Maybe it was an actual miracle her family still had all of these things.

"So what does your girlfriend do, Berit?" Bart asked before slapping a spoonful of mashed potatoes onto his plate.

"She, uh…" Berit looked to Lou for help.

"Lauren worked at the bar for a bit," Lou said evenly. "But she's a paralegal and is looking to get back to that."

Berit took a deep, steady breath and began to relax. She'd always been grateful for Lou, but at this moment Lou was her shining star. "I gave her some work to help her out while she was between jobs."

"That was kind of you," Jeffrey said.

"It was a temporary gig. I'm sure she'll be happy to get back to paralegal work."

"Are you sure her leaving the Dollhouse had nothing to do with serving underage drinkers?" Matt said. He was the youngest and the brat of the family. "I heard you fired her."

Berit's nostrils flared. "Who told you that?"

"Berit, why would you fire your girlfriend?" Florence said.

Matt smiled smugly. "You always forget I hang out with Monica's little brother. I hear about a lot of things that go on in your bar."

Bart's laughter cut through the tension. "No wonder you're always single." He pushed his long, dark curls away from his scruffy face.

"And what's your excuse, Bart the fart? Is it your name?" Lou said, coming to her sister's defense.

"I don't want a girlfriend."

"Well, I didn't either until I met Lauren." Berit pushed her full plate aside. Her appetite was gone, and a headache started to form behind her eyes.

"Then why did you fire her?" Florence asked again.

"I didn't fire my girlfriend!" Berit shouted. She fell back into her chair with a huff. She turned to Lou. "What exactly did Lauren say to you?"

Lou acted as if she was truly searching her rattled brain for Lauren's exact words. "She said she was 'fired without a doubt.'"

Bart snorted. "Harsh."

"I never said...Oh my God. She must've overheard our conversation. Right after the police left, you came into my office, and we talked about what we were going to do, about the fine and about Danny and Lauren. I said any other bar would fire those employees, without a doubt."

"Oh shit, that's right." Lou looked at her mother apologetically after letting the curse slip. "I completely dismissed it because I knew you wouldn't fire them."

"Your employees should be trained better, or at least know better," Jeffrey said slowly but loudly.

Berit turned to her father, who was eating calmly. She didn't appreciate his two cents when it came to her business.

"I understand why they'd get fired," he said. "It's common sense."

Berit scowled. "What would you know about running a successful business? Or about success at all?"

"Berit..."

She brushed Lou off. "Tell me, Dad, please. Bestow upon me this knowledge you've gained while working at the same body shop for the same old geezer and throwing not just your money but your family's money into foolish schemes. I bet having Matt follow in your footsteps feels pretty great, like maybe you didn't mess us all up."

Florence dropped her silverware loudly. "That's enough, Berit," she said in a firm tone.

Berit looked to her mother with big eyes. "If it wasn't for the extra time you spent selling Mary Kay and Tupperware, we would've never had money for food or clothes. Am I the only one who remembers this, or am I the only one who was really affected?"

"That was a long time ago," Jefffey said.

"Maybe, but your poor decisions continue to haunt me, not you. You go about your life keeping the past behind you, while I'm hitting roadblocks with my business and having the police send underage girls into my bar because of your recklessness with other people's money."

Jeffrey set his jaw. "You don't know Mayor McCarthy had anything to do with this."

"You say the same thing every time another threat comes to my bar. How many times am I going to have to dodge being closed down before you drop your denial and actually believe your daughter?"

Berit saw her own stubbornness shimmer deep in her father's eyes. He would never admit his actions had greater consequences. She stood up, and Hugo trotted over to her side.

"Forget it. I'm going to get out of here so you can enjoy the rest of your birthday." Berit looked at her sad mother. She hated this pattern they'd fallen into as a family, but she was powerless to improve it. "Good night, Mom."

Berit grabbed Hugo's leash and secured it to his harness before leaving. She made it no farther than the lawn before Lou ran after her. "Go back inside before your food gets cold," Berit said. She didn't even have to look at Lou to know she had just sounded like their mother.

"Are you okay to drive?"

"Yeah, I'm fine." Berit knew that didn't quite describe her feelings, but it'd do for the moment.

Lou continued to head to the car. "Good, because you drove us here, and I really didn't want to get in the car with a madwoman."

"You don't have to leave. You know any of the guys would've driven you home." They got in the car and buckled up. Berit started the engine just as Lou laughed.

"I know they would have. But Matt would've bitched and

moaned about it the whole time, I would've owed Bart a huge favor in return, and JJ would've talked about Christen the whole way. I'd rather ride with my volatile sister than listen to that." Lou slapped Berit's thigh. "It's important to me that you know I'm on your side."

Berit drove silently for a minute, glancing at Lou out of the corner of her eye. "I thought you wanted me to forgive Dad."

"Oh, I do, but that doesn't mean I don't understand why you still feel this way. I do have one question, though."

"This doesn't surprise me." Berit waited until she came to a full stop at a red light. "What's your question?"

"Something seems different this time. You're always short with Dad and you always let it be known when the Dollhouse hits a snag because of him, but I've never seen you like this. You didn't even mention how he was on time for once."

Berit tightened her grip on the steering wheel. "That's not a question." She stepped on the gas a little too heavily when the light turned green, and the car bucked forward.

"Are you just worried about losing the Dollhouse, or are you more scared of losing Lauren?"

Berit could feel Lou's eyes on her. She heard Hugo's whimper and wondered if he could sense the tension in the car. "I know how to handle problems with the business. I feel in control." Berit said quietly. "But the one thing I don't feel with Lauren right now is confidence and control. I'm not scared of losing her, Lou." Berit looked at Lou briefly during a stop. "I'm terrified she's already gone."

"Have you tried calling her?"

"No, and she hasn't tried to call me, either."

"And you're expecting her to? Jesus, Berit, pick up the phone and fix things." Lou's voice grew louder. She looked up at her apartment building as they pulled up to the curb. "I know you're not stupid."

Berit rolled her eyes, definitely disagreeing with Lou.

"Call her," Lou said sternly. "Clear up this misunderstanding about the job and make sure she knows how you feel about her. Make sure she knows you love her."

"I don't—" Lou shot Berit a look that stopped her words in their tracks. She sighed. "I don't know if I'm ready for her to know that."

"If you feel it, it's time for her to know it." Lou patted Berit's arm before opening the car door. "Call her."

"Bellamy said the same thing, but I don't think I can." Berit swallowed thickly. "Maybe that makes me sound like a coward, but I don't feel like I have a right to approach her, not after how I acted. What if she doesn't want to talk to me, like she's okay with things ending now? I don't know how I'd handle that."

"You'd just handle it."

"My heart would break."

"Is your heart doing any better right now?"

Berit bent forward and rested her head on the steering wheel. "People always wondered why I was okay keeping things casual. Why would anyone want this?" Berit groaned dramatically.

"Think about the smallest, most wonderful moment you shared with Lauren."

Berit thought about the last night they spent together, and the way every touch turned soft and they talked for hours.

"That," Lou said, pointing directly at Berit's face. "That's why." She got out of the car and bent into the door to pet Hugo good night. "Call her, Berit. Don't lose that ooey-gooiness you were just feeling. It looks good on you."

Berit lifted Hugo over the center console and plopped him onto the seat. She stared at her dog, who sat excitedly in the passenger seat. "Why can't loving people be as uncomplicated as loving dogs?" Hugo tilted his head. His big ears pointed straight up. "That's what I thought."

If everyone's advice was to call Lauren, then why did it feel like the wrong thing to do? Berit drove home, still determined to wait for Lauren's phone call.

Chapter Twenty-three

Lauren lay in bed, watching the blades of her fan go around and around. Late August was the worst time to turn off the air-conditioning, but they had no choice since Lauren's income had ceased again. She hadn't moved in nearly thirty minutes, which made the sheets beneath her body feel hotter, but the air around her felt cooler. She couldn't win with this extreme summer heat. She'd spent Sunday and Monday wallowing and crying over her failures—both professionally and personally—and Tuesday appeared to be following suit. Except now she was too hot to cry or move, and even the thought of wallowing made sweat trickle down the side of her brow. Lauren could hear Briana making noise out in the kitchen, and the television was louder than necessary.

Questions came to mind, a million different instances of what-if and if-only. Her decisions were always the best she could make at the time: a seemingly steady career, laying low in office politics, the right friends, and sticking with a girlfriend simply to fill a void of loneliness and feed an insecurity. If Lauren allowed herself to be honest, she hadn't made very many decisions with herself or her well-being in mind.

Berit was the first of many things for Lauren. Until Berit, Lauren had never stepped outside of a heart-shaped box when it came to love. She believed in chemistry and sensibility, and when that approach was no longer fruitful, she turned to accepting what she was given—Rebecca. Lauren believed she had learned from repeating that mistake and knew she'd have to shield her heart. That shield should've been impenetrable to Berit. But it hadn't been.

Lauren's heart ached for Berit. She felt incomplete and silly for it. In such a short time, Lauren had grown to depend on Berit for her support, her kindness, and more recently, the love she so willingly gave.

Lauren groaned at her ceiling and pulled her pillow over her face. No other person made Lauren feel the way Berit had. Their every exchange carried a unique softness and a fierce heat that burned uncontrollably within their shared passion. Their connection was remarkable—and just another thing Lauren could add to her list of losses.

A loud crash resounded from the kitchen. Lauren threw her pillow across the room and jumped out of bed. She was done being patient, kind, and considerate. If she had lost the one person in her life who treated her that way, no one else deserved to experience it either. She swung her bedroom door open and stormed into the common area. Briana was in the kitchen, harshly whispering to Jorge about too many mugs being in her way, while Rebecca was gathering her keys to head out.

"I'm done," Lauren said in a growl. Not one person acknowledged her. She looked at the pile of colorful, jagged remains scattered across the floor and felt her blood pressure rise. Amongst the ceramic shards lay lone pieces of clear glass. Lauren quickly identified it as the pint glass Berit had given to her after their flair training. She screamed, "I'm done!" Rebecca froze at the door while Jorge and Briana looked at Lauren the same way a skeptic would stare at Bigfoot.

"Should I pick up more mugs while I'm at the store?" Rebecca said, her voice barely loud enough to travel through the room.

"No." Lauren met Rebecca's worried eyes. "What I *need* is for you to find somewhere else to live."

Rebecca's jaw dropped. "But I—"

"And you," Lauren said through clenched teeth as she pinned Briana with her wicked stare. "You either need to start contributing or get the fuck out."

Jorge stepped in front of Briana. "Don't talk to her like that."

"No. I'll talk to her however I damn well please, and you will watch how you talk to me. I've dealt with this long enough. I understand how the dynamics of a friendship change when you get into a serious relationship, but we're not in college anymore. If this," Lauren said with her thumb pointed at Briana, "is what you want to spend the rest of your life with, I'm here to support you. But you will no longer disrespect me in the process. I'm done." Lauren threw her hands up and turned to make her retreat, but decided go back to Jorge and lean in to whisper, "Please stop being a pussy."

Lauren walked back to her room, collected her toiletries, and headed for the bathroom. She needed a long shower before she got out of the house for the day, and getting outside was a necessity.

She stood beneath the steady stream of warm water and felt her muscles relax one by one. She moved slowly as she scrubbed her skin clean, the image of every poor decision and rough year swirling down the drain playing behind her eyelids. But those images had little effect on the one worry in her mind: What was to come next?

She'd eventually have to face her roommates and have a mature conversation, if any of them were capable of such things. She cut the water and towel-dried her red skin. When Lauren wiped the moisture away from the mirror, she was startled to see how bloodshot her eyes were. Crying over Berit didn't solve anything, and it certainly didn't do the rest of her any good. Lauren gave her hair a quick blow-dry before pulling it back as best as she could. She threw on the first clean outfit she spotted and ran out of the house, wanting to avoid another confrontation.

Lauren sat in her car and considered where to go. She picked up her phone more than once to call Amber, but she couldn't reach out to her. Lauren felt guilty for being a shitty friend lately. Every time she sat with Amber, she'd go on another tirade about her own misfortunes and completely ignore whatever it was Amber was going through. She'd have to work through this latest debacle on her own and call Amber later to find out what had happened with her instant family.

She wanted to go to Mel's Café, but Lauren wasn't sure if it was the coffee or the chance to run into Berit, so she shut the idea down. It dawned on Lauren that she didn't have a place, a sanctuary to turn to when she needed time to herself or when her mind and heart needed calming. Berit had the overlook at the river, and the only peace Lauren had lately was Berit. Lauren imagined the most peaceful place she had been, thoughts of Berit and the sun filling her mind. Lauren did a quick search on her phone and started the car.

Lauren might have added fifteen minutes to the drive after getting lost, but eventually she had arrived at the public gardens. The space seemed different when you looked at it with a broken heart. Lauren dropped off her embarrassingly small donation at the front desk and hurried to the spot where she had watched the sunset with Berit. Families and couples now crowded the area, sucking the intimacy from it, but that didn't deter Lauren.

If she stood still and remained quiet, she could almost put herself back into the moment. Berit had looked at her with such love, she could remember the way her heart beat and tripped over itself when she realized they were falling in love with each other. No sunset or floral display could outshine love. Lauren walked away with her head down and continued to stroll through the gardens. A peacock crossed her path, and she watched, unaffected, as the bird went along its way.

She walked along a path lined with wildflowers and poppies. Just as she came to a fork in the road, her phone buzzed. She considered not checking it, but she hadn't heard from her mother in a while, and the chance Berit was reaching out to her was slim, but a possibility. She checked the phone, deflated when Rebecca's name lit up on the screen.

Are you okay? Lauren was momentarily touched by Rebecca caring enough to check on her.

She typed her response quickly. *I'm fine. Getting some fresh air to calm down.* She sent the message and looked back to the path. She noticed an older couple strolling hand in hand down one side of the split path, basking in the beautiful day together. Her phone buzzed again, and she ignored it. Lauren noticed one elderly woman wearing an easy smile while sitting on a bench. Lauren wondered if she frequented the gardens and if she was always alone. Her phone buzzed two more times in succession, but she kept her eyes on the woman on the bench. Lauren imagined she had also come here once with someone special, and that fond memory still lived in her heart. Lauren grew annoyed the next time her phone buzzed, and she checked it.

Rebecca's messages read like a paragraph. *I think we should talk, one-on-one. I can't say everything I feel in front of Briana and Jorge. I want to be alone with you. And make you feel better. If you're single again...and even if you're not.*

Lauren laughed humorlessly at the predictability of her sad life. Rebecca was there, yet again, after a breakup. Their pattern was starting over, but this time Lauren felt more confident, more sure of her resolve to say no. She didn't need Rebecca or her validation. Lauren felt an inexplicable pull to the elderly woman. She walked along and took a seat beside her. She waited to speak, listening instead to the chirping birds in the trees around them. In the distance, Lauren watched as tiger lilies swayed in the breeze.

"I started coming here for the roses, but now I think they're boring," the elderly woman said.

Her hair was white and her skin pale. She wore perfectly pressed navy trousers with a light pink button-up. Lauren smiled and said, "What do you come for now?"

The woman's sweet blue eyes were strikingly soft. "Everything else." She looked back out to the trees and the wildflowers. "Once upon a time, I'd come here and ignore anything that wasn't a rose. It's kind of funny how we can do that, not notice what we don't care enough to see." She pointed with her right hand. "Imagine all the beauty we miss in the world because we just don't care enough."

Lauren's heart ached as she thought of Berit. She felt tears well in her eyes, even after she had convinced herself she had no tears left to cry. "What if you saw that beauty, had that beauty in your life, but lost it?"

"Nonsense," the old woman said with a laugh. The joke was

lost on Lauren. "I made the choice to only see the roses, just like how I'm making the choice now to see everything but. The roses are still there, and will be if I decide to see them again."

What this woman was rambling on about had no real connection to her life or her problems, but she searched for a hidden, significant meaning anyway. She looked at her phone again and reread Rebecca's messages. Rebecca was the roses and Berit was everything else. Or maybe Rebecca was everything else and Berit was roses.

"A flower analogy isn't going to help you, dear." The woman patted Lauren's shoulder and stood gingerly. "Whatever's troubling you, just do what you think is best for you. Screw everyone else."

Lauren sat in shock and watched as her temporary companion walked in the opposite direction down the path. The phone vibrated again.

Come home. Rebecca's message was so simple, and Lauren felt consumed with clarity.

Lauren smiled gleefully as she typed. Maybe she had found a way to see the whole garden and smell the roses, too.

CHAPTER TWENTY-FOUR

Berit grabbed a stubby piece of white chalk and climbed the small ladder in front of the specials board. Maybe adding some new recipes would help keep her wandering mind in place. She had yet to hear from Lauren, and she was beginning to doubt Lauren would come to her. She'd been such an ass to Lauren and felt unworthy.

Berit crafted each letter slowly and focused not just on her handwriting but also on the dust falling from the board. She wasn't fully satisfied when she stepped down from the ladder. It wasn't whimsical, but you could at least read the words and prices.

"Seriously?" Bellamy's voice startled Berit.

"What?" Berit asked, looking at Bellamy, then scrutinizing her artwork again. "I think I did a pretty good job."

Bellamy began reading the list. "Silk Panties, Absolut Pleasure, a Cocksucking Cowboy—"

"For the guys," Berit interjected.

Bellamy looked blankly at Berit before continuing. "Bitter Crush, Broken Heart martini, and a drink called Loneliness. Do you want to talk about it?" Bellamy's voice was sarcastic and concerned.

"The drink? It actually has egg white in it."

Bellamy glared at her.

"No, I don't want to talk about it," Berit insisted.

"Okay."

"There's nothing left to talk about."

"Got it," Bellamy said as she started to walk away.

"I'm running home for a bit to check on Hugo." Berit came up with the excuse out of nowhere. "He ate something he shouldn't have and wasn't himself this morning. I'll be back before it gets busy." Hugo was fine and Berit felt awful for lying, but she needed to get away from concerned eyes and all the details of the bar that reminded her of Lauren. The only problem was *everything* seemed to remind her of Lauren.

"No need to worry," Bellamy said confidently. "It's Tuesday." Tuesdays were their slowest night.

Berit grabbed her keys and practically jogged to her Jeep. She didn't head home. Instead, she drove straight to her safe haven, the river where she and Lauren had grown much closer. When Berit stepped out of her Jeep and felt the warm breeze touch her face, she was stricken by tears. Her safe haven had memories of Lauren, but it did not feel tainted the way her bar and bed did.

The sun reflected off the water, sparkling hypnotically. She remembered the exact way Lauren looked at her that night, her soft, dark eyes caring despite their exhaustion. Berit knew Lauren was special the first moment she spotted her in her bar. She couldn't explain it.

She'd spent days trying to think of what to do next. She had Lauren's last paycheck sitting on her desk at the Dollhouse, but she wasn't sure whether Lauren would come to pick it up or if she'd prefer to have it mailed. Berit knew she should mail it, but she wanted to force Lauren to come to her again.

She sighed deeply. Lauren's home life would only get harder now that she was unemployed again. Lauren's roommates would more than likely blame Lauren and mistreat her more than they already did. Berit even wondered if Lauren would get back together with Rebecca.

Berit squinted against the sky as she tilted her head back. She filled her lungs with fresh air and the faint smell of murky water. Berit looked out across the river, watching small watercraft launch from a dock but not really seeing the details. If she loved Lauren, she had to make a decision to live with or without Lauren Daly for the rest of her life.

❖

Berit rushed back into the bar in search of Lou. She needed sisterly advice because winning a woman back was so far outside Berit's wheelhouse, it scared her. She ran into Dee in the stockroom. "Hey," she said, slightly out of breath.

"How's Hugo? Bellamy told me he wasn't feeling well."

"He's good, really. Is Lou working the bar alone?"

"I've been working it so far, but I had to run back here for a bottle of Chambord. We keep getting orders for the Broken Heart martini. It's a hit."

"Of course it is," Berit said with a wry laugh. "You'll be okay if I steal Lou for a bit?" Berit already started on her way to the bar before Dee answered.

"Yeah, go ahead. Lauren's here, too."

Berit's heart stuttered. She turned back to Dee with a million questions in her mind, but instead of asking, she rushed out to the bar to find the answers for herself. She spotted Lauren right away, standing at the end of the bar closest to the door, the same spot where she'd sat on the first night Berit met her. Lauren looked nervous, and everyone around her was invisible to Berit. All she saw was Lauren; all she wanted to see was Lauren. The anxiety of what was to come next paled in comparison to the happiness Berit felt.

"Lauren..." Berit walked forward with purpose. She stood in front of Lauren and stared in awe at how beautiful she looked, even with a hint of sadness and apprehension. Lauren wasn't fully comfortable. She tugged nervously on the hem of her red tank top, and Berit wanted to fix that. "How are you?"

Lauren stayed silent, her face unreadable until she looked at the woman beside her. Berit didn't recognize her until she smiled and spoke.

"Hey, Berit."

"Ashleigh? What are you doing here? Do you know each other?"

"Not until this afternoon," Ashleigh said. "Lauren found me

online and sent me a message. After a long introduction, she told me about the troubles you've had."

Lauren cleared her throat at Berit's curious look. "I explained we have a mutual friend." The use of the word "friend" hurt Berit. "I mentioned your name, and we got to talking a bit. I'm sorry if I've overstepped, but I had to do something. I was going crazy thinking your business was in jeopardy."

"We're fine." Berit looked at Ashleigh again. "Your dad's been giving me a bit of a hard time, but I've handled him pretty well."

"You won't have to worry about handling him at all. Why didn't you get in touch with me earlier?"

"Because," Berit said with a shrug. She lacked a real answer, so she told the best version of the truth she could come up with. "You and I had grown so far apart, and I felt like maybe I should pay for my father's mistakes. Why burden you with them?"

Ashleigh grabbed Berit's hand and smiled softly. "You've always been too kind for your own good. Just as you've dealt with your father, I've dealt with mine. My dad knew investing with your dad was a risk. Why should you be held responsible?"

Berit shrugged and held Ashleigh's hand more tightly.

"That's pretty much what I told him, too," Ashleigh said. "I also threatened to not show up for the holidays if he didn't stop."

"You do have quite the holiday celebration every year," Berit said. Out of the corner of her eye, she noticed Lauren start to move toward the door. Berit panicked and dropped Ashleigh's hand. "I'm sorry if this is rude. You just did so much for me, but I have to go after her."

"I knew this story had more to it. Go after your girl, but promise me something."

"I owe you at least a million promises."

"Promise me you'll keep in touch."

Berit smiled softly at Ashleigh. "Definitely." She looked at Lou, who'd been surprisingly quiet during the entire exchange. "Wish me luck."

"Good luck." Lou patted her shoulder and Berit was off.

Berit stopped Lauren just as she opened the door. "We need to talk."

"I should really go."

Berit swallowed hard. "Please." She started to walk backward toward her office the moment Lauren finally looked at her, more worried about Lauren bailing on her than bumping into a patron or full tray.

Lauren began to explain the moment they stepped into Berit's small office and the door shut. "I needed to do something to fix what I had done. You've helped me so much over the past couple of months, and my mistake wasn't the last impression I wanted to make around here, or the memory I wanted to leave you with." Lauren bounced from one foot to the other and picked at her nails nervously. She hid her eyes.

Berit's heart raced and broke at the finality in Lauren's voice, the resignation and sadness. "Leave me with?" She stepped forward as Lauren retreated.

"I'm sorry for everything," Lauren said, wiping a tear from her cheek. "For treating you the way I did before I really knew you, for burdening you, and for hurting your business. I hope you can forgive me?" Lauren smiled sadly, her cheeks now wet with unleashed, heavy tears. "You've brought such happiness and ease to my life..." Her voice crackled, making it hard to speak.

Berit closed the distance between herself and Lauren. She held Lauren's face in her hands gently and waited a beat. She needed to know Lauren wanted this as much as she did. She leaned in slowly, tilting her head and bringing her lips to Lauren's. Berit kissed Lauren deeply, nearly crying when Lauren gripped the bottom of her shirt and pulled her closer.

Lauren broke away and buried her face in Berit's neck. Berit held Lauren and they swayed slightly, the rocking motion comforting.

"I'm sorry," Berit whispered into Lauren's ear.

Lauren pulled back and tilted her head. "For what?"

"For acting the way I did and saying what I said." Berit ran her fingertips over Lauren's cheeks and down to her lips, needing to feel Lauren's physical presence.

"You were upset, and you warned me that you're awful when you're mad."

"I was and I did, but you didn't deserve that. I should've never questioned us over something happening at work." Berit grabbed Lauren's hand and held it to her chest. "I'm going to work on how I act when I'm angry, because I don't want that kind of behavior to be what you expect or accept from me."

Lauren nodded. "I guess we both have a few things to work on now that we're back together," she said with a smile.

Berit dropped Lauren's hand and frowned deeply.

"Oh. I—I thought…" Lauren started to retreat again. "I guess I assumed because of the kissing…"

Berit grabbed the belt loops on Lauren's jeans and held her in place. "Your assumption isn't wrong. I just didn't know that at any point we weren't together."

"But I messed with the bar, and you thought we had made a mistake."

"I blew up and I wanted to apologize, but I'm too stubborn and was waiting for you to come to me first."

Lauren looked stunned. "What?"

"It's the truth. I was ashamed of how I acted and unsure of what to say. I didn't think I should be the one to call first. I figured it'd be easier if I waited until you were ready to talk. And then today, I knew I had to fix things as soon as possible because I'm going crazy without you. I couldn't take it anymore. I need you back in my life every day. I love you, Lauren Daly."

"I'm scared," Lauren said, her voice so quiet it barely reached Berit's ears.

"Why?"

"Because I love you, too, in a way I've never felt before."

"I think that's a good thing. If you've never felt this before, it means we have something new. Something that'll be great as long as we stop assuming and stop being stubborn idiots," Berit said with a thumb pointed toward herself. "I think we're in for a wonderful future together."

Lauren wrapped her arms around Berit's neck and kissed her fiercely. The taste of Lauren's love was divine enough to wash away every ounce of pain.

Lauren pulled back breathlessly, her eyes now shining with happy tears. "What did I do to deserve you?"

Berit tucked a strand of Lauren's chestnut hair behind her ear and took a moment to admire the soft skin there. "You told me no." She held Lauren tighter as she laughed loudly. "You were yourself from the moment I met you, and that's rare. *You* are rare." Berit kissed Lauren chastely before asking, "What did *I* do to deserve *you*?"

Lauren ran her hands over the bristly hair on the back of Berit's head and pulled her face close. "You wouldn't take no for an answer."

They kissed, and Berit lifted her up and spun her in a circle. The small office was filled with laughter and the gleeful sounds made by two women in love. Lauren's feet touched the ground as Berit's heart soared toward the sky. Her future, her forever had been put back into place. But for now, for this very moment, Berit knew what had to happen.

She grabbed Lauren's hand and said, "It's time to get back to work."

EPILOGUE

L auren checked over the list in her hand again because so many options had already been crossed off. Thankfully, her favorite remained. "I still think we should go with the raspberry one." She ran the tip of her index finger around the rim of her empty highball glass and eyed Berit, who stood with her hip cocked against the bar. Lauren felt her heart speed up.

Over the past two and a half years Lauren couldn't believe the way her life had changed. She still worked nights at the Dollhouse so she could spend them with Berit, but she'd also secured a paralegal position in a female-owned and operated firm. The firm dealt mostly with women who couldn't afford legal help or were uncomfortable with male representation. Lauren felt like her career was making a difference, and that happiness bled into every other aspect of her life.

"I'm afraid it'll be too sweet." Berit tasted her drink again. Lauren watched the way Berit sealed her lips around the cool glass, and marveled at how beautiful she was. She had cut her hair shorter, styling it into a more controlled coif each day, and Lauren found the change striking and mature. "It's one thing for a sweet drink to be a dessert beverage or served during cocktail hour, but it shouldn't be available throughout the night."

Someone from the long table cleared his throat. Lauren's brother, Jack, raised his hand. "I don't think the cucumber one is a winner."

Lauren crossed it off the list. "Okay, so we're left with the raspberry mojito, the mandarin gin and tonic, and your strange spin on a Manhattan."

"It's a great spin," Berit said with a smirk.

"Not everyone likes curry."

"Then those people can order a different drink."

Lauren shot Berit an unamused look.

"Fine," Berit said. "What about the gin and tonic?"

Lauren scrunched up her nose and shook her head. "Not everyone likes gin."

Berit looked at Lauren with a soft expression and head tilt. "You've wanted the raspberry mojito this whole time, haven't you?"

She nodded emphatically.

"I just don't know if it's sophisticated enough. I feel like this drink should be a show-stopper."

"Berit, I'm going to give you a little piece of advice, even though I know you haven't exactly trusted your old man over the years." Berit's father clapped his hand onto his daughter's shoulder. "When your woman wants something you can give her so easily, don't fight it. Let her have whatever she wants. Especially for her wedding."

"But it's my wedding, too," Berit said with a playful pout.

Lauren's heart warmed at their exchange now that the bond between Berit and her father had been repaired. "He has been married for a while, Berit. You may want to listen to him."

"Jeffrey is a lucky man and a smart one, too. He knows when to listen to me." Florence took another sip of her mojito.

Berit and Lauren wanted a special cocktail they picked out or concocted together to be served at their wedding reception, and they'd decided to use their families as taste testers.

"I agree with Lauren," Florence said. "The raspberry mojito will be perfect. The mandarin was a little acidic for my taste."

"And gin makes Simon angry," Olivia Daly said, adding her two cents into the conversation. Her English accent was much more pronounced than Lauren's ever was, and it added a whimsical quality to her every word. "Giving that man gin is a recipe for disaster."

Simon Daly stood at the back of the bar, chatting with Berit's youngest brother, Matt. Lauren never thought she'd get her family on the same continent again, never mind combining them with the Matthews clan. "I guess that settles—"

"Doesn't your maid of honor get a say?" Those who didn't know Amber would think she was truly angry from the scowl on her face. Amber looked between Berit and Lauren before taking a deep breath and holding it dramatically. "I'm on Lauren's side here."

"Shocker," Berit said under her breath, adding an eye roll for good measure.

"Yes," Lauren cheered, pumping her fist in celebration. She wrapped her arms around Berit's waist and gave her a squeeze. She stood slightly on her toes to whisper in Berit's ear. "I win."

"Since you picked our wedding drink, I get to name it."

"It better be PG rated and not mention anything about panties."

"Well, there go my first two ideas. How about Kiss Me Daly?"

"Don't mind if I do." Lauren pulled Berit forward and placed a smoldering kiss on her lips.

Berit's eyes were dazed when she pulled back. "And hopefully that happens every time I order one."

"Huh?"

"Kiss Me Daly; that's what I'd like to name the drink," Berit said with a smug smile. Lauren felt her heart flutter, much like it had every day since she and Berit declared their love to one another.

"Aww," Amber said, her voice deep and mocking as she started to walk away from the sugary-sweet couple. "I can't believe I'm paying a snobby babysitter way too much money just to watch you two be gross."

"We had to sit through your wedding," Lauren said, sticking her tongue out at Amber only to have Amber stick hers out in return. She turned back to her fiancée with a big smile. "I love it, and the drink, and you." Lauren gave Berit a quick peck.

She looked around the room at their family and close friends. The entire staff of the Dollhouse was there, including new hires and veterans like Dee, Monica, and Bellamy—who stood with her girlfriend of almost two years, Rosa. They were the most shocking couple to come out of the Dollhouse yet. "Are you ready for tomorrow?" Lauren smoothed her fingertip over the crisp collar of Berit's black dress shirt.

"I'm ready to dance and party with everyone I love, and I'm definitely ready to start my forever with you."

Lauren fell into Berit, who cradled her softly. "How is it that you're still so sweet?" Lauren could hear Berit's smile and closed her eyes when she placed a gentle kiss to her temple.

JJ walked into the bar with his cell phone in hand and a disgruntled look on his boyish face. "Bart the fart is still stuck at work and sends his apologies but assures me everyone in the office knows he's off-limits for the next four days."

"Why four days?" Lauren asked Berit.

"He'll need the time to recuperate, trust me."

Jeffrey tapped a fork against his glass to get everyone's attention, and he asked them to take their seats. Lauren noticed her brother, Jack, switched places so he could sit beside Lou.

"I'm so happy you all could be here this evening. Rehearsal dinners are nothing new to the Matthews family," Jeffrey said, looking directly at JJ, who'd just married his third wife the previous winter. JJ shrugged and wrapped his arm around his wife. Everyone had teased him, but all they truly cared about was his happiness. "But when Berit announced she was engaged to someone as lovely as Lauren, I couldn't wait to celebrate the love my oldest daughter had found."

Lauren linked her arm with Berit's and rested her head on her shoulder. She felt warm in spite of her sleeveless black dress.

Jeffrey cleared his throat. "I don't have an easy history with my daughter, and we spent a long time butting heads, but all I ever wanted was for her to find the kind of love I was fortunate enough to find early in life." Jeffrey nodded to Florence, who was blushing profusely. He raised his glass. "Berit and Lauren, I wish you more happiness than I've ever known, more love than you ever thought possible, and more success in every venture you face together."

The room erupted in cheers and clinking glasses. Lauren kissed

Berit's shoulder. "I see where you get your sweetness from." She giggled when Berit shushed her.

The catering company Berit and Lauren had hired for this rehearsal dinner began serving, but before either woman could dive into their full plates, Lou spoke up from across the table. "What are you both looking forward to the most about being married?"

"Getting to wear the ring," Berit said. Everyone within earshot laughed. "Seriously, I already have the greatest perks. I get to wake up to her gorgeous face every morning, even when the hour is ungodly and I'm only awake to watch her get ready for work. We share our highs and lows, and she's been my best friend for years. Now I get a nice piece of jewelry as proof." Berit popped a piece of roasted potato into her mouth.

"Okay then," Lou said with a shake of her head before looking to Lauren. "What about you?"

"I already have a nice ring." Lauren held up her hand and showed off her solitaire. Berit chuckled next to her. "I do agree with Berit. We act like a married couple. We have the house we just bought together and the dog who's constantly fighting with the cat I insisted we adopt, but signing our names to the marriage certificate makes all of those good things more permanent to me. I'm looking forward to that security."

Berit leaned into Lauren's ear and whispered, "I love you."

"I'm a little disappointed neither of you said anything about experiencing sex after marriage." Lauren gawked at Amber, who looked entirely too self-satisfied. "What? It's really good." Amber's wife, Annalise, smacked her forearm gently.

Everyone remained awkwardly quiet, save for a few squeaks of barely contained laughter from Lou. Finally, Simon commented on the food and everyone continued enjoying their meal. Conversation throughout dinner was light and friendly. Berit and Lauren kept going over small details of the ceremony and reception. The evening wrapped up around ten o'clock and everyone went their separate ways, including the soon-to-be brides.

"We don't have to spend the night apart," Berit said. "Hugo is going to miss you, and Ramsey is going to wonder why his one and only protector isn't there to save him."

Lauren ran her hands up Berit's chest and warded off a chill, both from desire and the early spring breeze. "Ramsey is a big furball that can handle himself. Seriously, I think that cat is a better protector than Hugo and me combined."

Berit opened her mouth and closed it twice before letting out a long sigh. "You're right. There's no way I can convince you to come home?"

"Nope," Lauren said, letting her lips pop loudly. "I like this old-fashioned tradition."

"Fine. I guess I'll survive." Berit sulked for a moment before she kneaded Lauren's backside. Lauren shuddered. "But we don't have to say goodbye just yet." Berit's grin was wicked.

Lauren's heart started to beat harder and she couldn't imagine being happier than she was in that moment. Lauren owed it all to the Dollhouse and its delicious drinks and even more delectable bartender. Life and love happened when she had least expected it to.

She opened the back door to Berit's car and said, "Better make it quick."

Berit wore the same lopsided grin she had when she'd first approached Lauren, the same smile that turned from warning bells to welcome home. "No promises," she said. Lauren knew what Berit meant, but she also felt the unspoken sentiment.

Berit was promising forever—a perfectly balanced, shaken, flavorful, dirty, and strong forever together.

Kiss Me Daly

8 fresh mint leaves
6 fresh raspberries
1 lime, juiced
2 ounces white rum
2 ounces simple syrup
1 cup ice
1/2 cup soda water

In a tall, sturdy glass:

Muddle mint, raspberries, lime juice, rum, and simple syrup.

Add ice and top with soda water.

Garnish with mint or raspberries.

Kiss a loved one and enjoy!

About the Author

M. Ullrich has always called New Jersey home and currently resides by the beach with her wife and boisterous feline children. After many years of regarding her writing as just a hobby, the gentle yet persistent words of encouragement from her wife pushed M. Ullrich to take a leap into the world of publishing. Much to her delight and amazement, that world embraced her back.

Although M. Ullrich may work full-time in the optical field, her favorite hours are the ones she spends writing and eating ridiculously large portions of breakfast foods for every meal. When her pen isn't furiously trying to capture her imagination (a rare occasion), she enjoys being a complete entertainer. Whether she's telling an elaborate story or a joke, or getting up in front of a crowd to sing and dance her way through her latest karaoke selection, M. Ullrich will do just about anything to make others smile. She also happens to be fluent in three languages: English, sarcasm, and TV/movie quotes.

Books Available From Bold Strokes Books

Exposed by MJ Williamz. The closet is no place to live if you want to find true love. (978-1-62639-989-1)

Force of Fire: Toujours a Vous by Ali Vali. Immortals Kendal and Piper welcome their new child and celebrate the defeat of an old enemy, but another ancient evil is about to awaken deep in the jungles of Costa Rica. (978-1-63555-047-4)

Landing Zone by Erin Dutton. Can a career veteran finally discover a love stronger than even her pride? (978-1-63555-199-0)

Love at Last Call by M. Ullrich. Is balancing business, friendship, and love more than any willing woman can handle? (978-1-63555-197-6)

Pleasure Cruise by Yolanda Wallace. Spencer Collins and Amy Donovan have few things in common, but a Caribbean cruise offers both women an unexpected chance to face one of their greatest fears: falling in love. (978-1-63555-219-5)

Running Off Radar by MB Austin. Maji's plans to win Rose back are interrupted when work intrudes, and duty calls her to help a SEAL team stop a Russian mobster from harvesting gold from the bottom of Sitka Sound. (978-1-63555-152-5)

Shadow of the Phoenix by Rebecca Harwell. In the final battle for the fate of Storm's Quarry, even Nadya's and Shay's powers may not be enough. (978-1-63555-181-5)

Take a Chance by D. Jackson Leigh. There's hardly a woman within fifty miles of Pine Cone that veterinarian Trip Beaumont can't charm, except for the irritating new cop, Jamie Grant, who keeps leaving parking tickets on her truck. (978-1-63555-118-1)

The Outcasts by Alexa Black. Spacebus driver Sue Jones is running from her past. When she crash-lands on a faraway world, the Outcast Kara might be her chance for redemption. (978-1-63555-242-3)

Alias by Cari Hunter. A car crash leaves a woman with no memory and no identity. Together with Detective Bronwen Pryce, she fights to uncover a truth that might just kill them both. (978-1-63555-221-8)

Death in Time by Robyn Nyx. Working in the past is hell on your future. (978-1-63555-053-5)

Hers to Protect by Nicole Disney. Ex–high school sweethearts Kaia and Adrienne will have to see past their differences and survive the vengeance of a brutal gang if they want to be together. (978-1-63555-229-4)

Perfect Little Worlds by Clifford Mae Henderson. Lucy can't hold the secret any longer. Twenty-six years ago, her sister did the unthinkable. (978-1-63555-164-8)

Room Service by Fiona Riley. Interior designer Olivia likes stability, but when work brings footloose Savannah into her world and into a new city every month, Olivia must decide if what makes her comfortable is what makes her happy. (978-1-63555-120-4)

Sparks Like Ours by Melissa Brayden. Professional surfers Gia Malone and Elle Britton can't deny their chemistry on and off the beach. But only one can win... (978-1-63555-016-0)

Take My Hand by Missouri Vaun. River Hemsworth arrives in Georgia intent on escaping quickly, but when she crashes her Mercedes into the Clip 'n Curl, sexy Clay Cahill ends up rescuing more than her car. (978-1-63555-104-4)

The Last Time I Saw Her by Kathleen Knowles. Lane Hudson only has twelve days to win back Alison's heart. That is, if she can gather the courage to try. (978-1-63555-067-2)

Wayworn Lovers by Gun Brooke. Will agoraphobic composer Giselle Bonnaire and Tierney Edwards, a wandering soul who can't remain in one place for long, trust in the passionate love destiny hands them? (978-1-62639-995-2)